The Summer We Ran

PRAISE FOR
The Summer We Ran

"A perfectly nostalgic story of love, loss, and secrets that refuse to stay buried. It's exactly what I hope for in a summer read."

—ANNABEL MONAGHAN, author of *Same Time Next Summer*

"Rising political star Tess Murphy grapples with memories of a youthful, bittersweet summer romance with a man who is now her fierce professional rival. Perfect for fans of Emily Giffin and Taylor Jenkins Reid."

—JAMIE BRENNER, author of *A Novel Summer*

"At once a tender portrait of first love and a captivating tale of long-buried secrets, *The Summer We Ran* . . . explores how we never quite let go of the people we love when we're young."

—BROOKE LEA FOSTER, author of *All the Summers in Between*

"First loves turn political rivals in this glorious exploration of nostalgia, ambition, and the complexities of the human heart. Book clubs will devour it!"

—EMMA GREY, author of *Pictures of You*

"A mesmerizing buffet of mystery, lost love, beautifully realized settings, and intriguing characters. Ingram weaves a story between past and present that you will not be able to put down."

—ETHAN JOELLA, author of *The Same Bright Stars*

"Perfectly captures the societal, political, and moral complications that can both bring people together and tear them apart. I am forever an Audrey Ingram fan!"

—NEELY TUBATI ALEXANDER, author of *Love Buzz*

Also by Audrey Ingram

The River Runs South
The Group Trip

The Summer We Ran

a novel

Audrey Ingram

Zibby Publishing
New York

The Summer We Ran: A Novel

Copyright © 2025 by Audrey Ingram

All rights reserved. No part of this book may be used, reproduced, distributed, or transmitted in any form or by any means without the prior written permission of the publisher, except as permitted by U.S. copyright law. Published in the United States by Zibby Publishing, New York.

ZIBBY, Zibby Publishing, colophon, and associated logos are trademarks and/or registered trademarks of Zibby Media LLC.

This book is a work of fiction. Names, characters, places, historical events, and incidents are the product of the author's imagination or are used fictitiously. Any resemblance to actual persons, living or dead, events, or locales is entirely coincidental.

Library of Congress Control Number: 2024943191
Paperback ISBN: 979-8-9899230-6-9
eBook ISBN: 979-8-9899230-7-6

Book design by Neuwirth and Associates
Cover design by Nicolette Seeback Ruggiero
Cover art © Valery Rybakow / Shutterstock

www.zibbymedia.com

Printed in the United States of America

10 9 8 7 6 5 4 3 2 1

For my husband, Jeff

PART I

Tess

Prologue

JANUARY 1997

I was never a good liar. My heart raced and my stomach churned like a washing machine. My mother asked how I was feeling and I said, "Fine," but it was obvious that wasn't true.

Fine was the answer you gave when other words were inadequate. Devastated. Angry. Heartbroken. None of them felt like enough.

"You should go to work," I said. "You can't cancel more shifts or you'll get fired."

I rolled over in the adjustable bed, careful of the IV in my arm and the sensors on my chest. My mother looked at the monitors, as if she could interpret the jagged line that pulsed across the screen or the repetitive beeps that made sleep impossible.

"Why don't I bring you some of my squash soup," my mother suggested. She lifted the cover off the hospital tray and frowned at the soggy turkey sandwich.

I shook my head. I had lost my appetite along with the most important parts of myself. That summer, I learned that no one disappoints you as deeply as you disappoint yourself.

My mother tucked her short brown hair behind her ear and joined me on the hospital bed. When her leg brushed up against mine, I scooted to the side, but she stopped me. Her hands cupped my face as she said, "Tess, I know you're not fine. Talk to me."

She made it seem like a simple task. But how could I cobble together an explanation when nothing made sense anymore. I was seventeen; discussing my emotions with my mother seemed like a pointless exercise. How could she know what it's like to love someone so deeply, so fully, and have them ripped away?

I closed my eyes, trying to imagine the slope of the mountains, the way the blue hills melted into a green meadow. I wanted to rewind time, back to the beginning of the summer and all the things I would have done differently. But I couldn't. My eyes fluttered open, as I was confronted with reality. A hospital room. My mother's hand clutching mine when I would have given anything to weave my fingers into his.

"He's really gone." I didn't hide the crack in my voice, or the tears that fell down my cheeks.

My mother nodded.

No one ever expects to have their heart broken, but I suppose I was better prepared than most. Windows, car engines, eggshells in our kitchen sink. My life was full of broken stuff. My mother used to say that cracks showed character, but none of her advice prepared me for that moment. I stared at the freshly sewn stitches on my skin. I didn't want to be the broken one.

"He's part of me," I whispered. Even after everything, I wanted him back and felt powerless as he slipped away.

"I know." My mom squeezed my hand.

It was only a few months. He shouldn't have meant so much. He shouldn't have changed my whole life. But he did. And somehow, I had to keep living in a world where we'd never be together.

Maybe that's why I hid him into the darkest corner of my heart. I thought I could get away with keeping him a secret. And I almost did.

One

JUNE 2021

There's a familiar thud against my front door and I know our paper has been delivered. I can't open the door in just the tank top I slept in so I reach for Dean's jacket and zip it up, my obscenely tall husband's clothes swallowing me like a child. If a photo is going to be snapped of me, I'd rather look sloppy than indecent, although my campaign staff would tell me both are unacceptable. I shouldn't be worried about photographers wandering the streets of Charlottesville at five in the morning, but lately I've been surprised by things I never thought possible.

I hang up Dean's jacket and walk into the kitchen, slipping the flimsy wrapper off the paper. I'm anxious to see the front page, although I already know what to expect. The photo doesn't look like me, this polished woman with lipstick too red and hair curled too tightly. My smile is genuine and my eyes are hopeful. That's why I agreed to this picture for the campaign, even though everything about it feels unnatural.

Audrey Ingram

I sit at my kitchen table, my long dark hair braided down my back, my face free from makeup, my outfit revealing the fact that I have both breasts and an ass. I study the two photos on the front page of the paper with the words "Tess Murphy vs. Grant Alexander" written underneath. Our faces are pointing toward each other, our eyes looking off into the distance, as if neither one of us can be bothered to look at anyone else.

My hand stops beside Grant's photo, and I let my finger trace the outline of his jaw. When I hear footsteps behind me, I quickly shove my hand under my thigh.

Dean walks into the kitchen and wraps his arms around my shoulders, the familiar scent of his pine aftershave swirling in the air.

"Eyeing the competition?" Dean innocently asks as he nuzzles my neck.

"Something like that," I say, flipping over the paper, then getting up and walking toward the coffee pot. I pour a scoop of grounds into the filter. "What are you doing up so early?"

My husband usually spends the first week of summer break sleeping in, savoring his hard-earned vacation. I've often thought summer is a necessary tool in teacher retention. But Dean isn't going to have a restful summer this year, and that's my fault. He's already dressed in his standard uniform of a plaid shirt neatly tucked into jeans, looking like a comfortable lumberjack on his way to a job interview.

I stand and hook my finger into his belt loop, pulling him closer as his arms wrap around my hips. Dean's hands slowly rise upward, sliding beneath my tank top, his fingers dancing along my skin. I inhale sharply and bite my lip unconsciously. In one fluid motion, he sweeps me up and my legs wrap around his waist as he sets me on the kitchen counter. My hands weave into his thick, curly hair as he kisses my collarbone, my neck, my cheek, eventually diving into my mouth. I'm filled with heat even though I'm barely dressed.

Dean raises his eyebrows as he says, "If I slept in, I'd miss making out with you in the kitchen. You turn into Candidate Tess too early these days."

He's right. Candidate Tess doesn't sit on the kitchen counter in her underwear, daydreaming about dragging her husband back to bed. Candidate Tess discusses poll numbers and fundraising dinners. Both of us tolerate her because we think Governor Tess is important. I'm lucky Dean loves me, even the parts I don't like.

"Besides, the work of the First Gentleman never stops," Dean says. "I have scones to bake, luncheons to attend, china patterns to review."

Dean optimistically jokes about his life next year, after I've won the election and we move to the Virginia governor's mansion. His imaginative scenarios vacillate between policy wonk and man of leisure.

"You hate scones. You're a doughnut man," I reply.

He smirks. "You know me so well."

I slide off the counter and reach for two mugs. "What's going on this morning?" I ask, Candidate Tess making her appearance.

"I have media training for the spouse interviews before the first debate."

"Right. I forgot." I nod, trying to focus on the never-ending campaign checklist instead of on my panicked spirals about tonight.

Dean sips his coffee, his eyes dancing over the mug's rim. "We can't all have armies of young interns reminding us of our schedules."

"I only have the armies because they constantly change my schedule," I say defensively, reaching for my cup.

"You forgot your schedule before the campaign too. I know your secrets, Tess."

I recoil momentarily, my pulse quickening and the air sweeping out of my lungs. Dean has known me for twenty years. Of course he thinks he knows every part of me.

Dean walks to the kitchen table as I try to slow my breath and act normal instead of panicked about a person from my past. He flips over the paper, scanning the story about the campaign, and reads aloud bits of the article, chuckling at the descriptions of Grant, "the hedge fund manager and proven businessman with a *fresh approach* to running the state." Dean's finger jabs the paper as he reads Grant's statement: "Tess Murphy is a career politician. I'm not looking at the governor's mansion as a pit stop in my political career. Virginia is my home and my priority."

"What a load of shit." Dean pushes the paper aside as he sips his coffee.

I can't help wincing at Grant's description of me. It's a narrative I have fought my entire career, from city council to the Charlottesville mayor's office. The fact that I don't have children adds to the fallacy that I'm too ambitious to be trusted.

I've been misunderstood before but rarely by those who know me. I wonder what else Grant will say to win this election.

Sometimes this dream of becoming governor feels too big. I'm afraid everyone will realize I don't deserve this honor. They'll see the girl who grew up in her grandmother's trailer and finally decide I've climbed too high and push me back down to where I belong.

Dean stares at me, seemingly puzzled by my silence. "Are you ready for tonight? You aren't nervous to go up against this guy, are you?"

I can't speak, all of my fears from the last two decades wrapped around that question.

Up until now, my life could be spun as a few strategic omissions. I've often wondered, if I told Dean everything, would he understand? After all, that's what love is, right? Filling in the craters of someone's character with your love of the whole landscape. But I'm afraid some holes are too deep, too dark, to be overlooked.

"I can handle Grant Alexander," I say with faux confidence.

Dean stands and kisses the top of my head, unable to see my cheek twitch. "Of course you can."

Tonight I'll stand across from Grant Alexander—the man who changed my whole life—and pretend we've never met. Assuming my heart doesn't betray me.

Two

JUNE 1996

I was bored the summer I met Grant. Bored, annoyed, and forbidden from expressing even an eye roll of teen angst for fear of ruining our future.

Most of the two-hour car ride with my mother was spent staring out the window as I counted houses. The longer we drove, the farther apart they became. My mother's car had no air-conditioning. We rigged the roof with thumb tacks so that the felt ceiling didn't drop on our heads. Luckily, it wasn't too hot that day, but by next month, the car would be unbearable.

My mother barely spoke the entire drive, the whites of her knuckles visible from the persistent grip on the steering wheel. Pulling into this imposing place, with its stone entrance and driveway so long the house was hidden from the road, only increased her nerves.

We both gasped when the house where we would spend the summer finally came into view. Houses, more accurately. There was the main house, with white columns and multiple chimneys looking more like a museum than a place anyone actually lived. Some distance away, there was a barn, and the more we looked, our eyes adjusting to the size and wealth of this place, the more we saw. There were cottages throughout the property.

"Which one is ours?" I asked.

"Whichever one they tell us to sleep in," my mom quickly replied.

She parked in front of the main house, flipping down the visor as she slid the mirror open. I wasn't sure what she was hoping to see. She looked the exact same every day. Dark hair pulled into a ponytail, no makeup because the kitchen's heat melted it away. She seemed satisfied by her reflection and looked over at me, nodding as if I passed whatever standard she imagined was required of this summer.

"Ready?" she asked as we got out of the car.

I looked around. There wasn't a single stray leaf on the driveway. The flower beds were perfectly symmetrical, the paint smooth on the front door. I was used to chipped surfaces and weeds in gravel. My mother's ancient gray sedan parked in front of this house did not belong.

"Do we go in the front door?" I asked warily. "Isn't there some servants' entrance or something?"

"I'm following the instructions," my mother said before adding, "and I'm not a servant. I'm an employee."

I tilted my head sideways. "Somebody here is going to call you a servant this summer."

"Tess. I need you to be on your best behavior. This is our opportunity for a new life. Do not mess it up with your smart mouth."

I kicked the gravel, feeling simultaneously frustrated and

defeated. Everything I said was wrong these days. My mother and I existed in a perpetual state of heightened criticism, each of us disappointed that we couldn't be what the other needed.

"What am I supposed to do all summer?" I mumbled.

"Read those books you packed and stay out of trouble. We're lucky they let me bring you."

"I still don't know why I had to come."

"Because I'm not leaving a seventeen-year-old alone for three months."

Alone. I was never alone before, but after my grandmother died, I felt alone all the time. My mother worked long hours as a line cook, caterer, baker, any job she could scrounge up. We lived with my grandparents, in their small trailer nestled in the woods of southwestern Virginia. When my grandfather died, it was just the three of us. My grandmother was home when I got back from school, read to me at bedtime when my mother was at the restaurant, and whispered dreams in my ear about the things she knew I could accomplish. She died a year ago, but every day I missed her more, especially when it felt like my mother didn't understand me at all.

She constantly scrutinized. My mother wanted better for me, "a future with possibility," she'd often say. If I studied for an hour, I should have studied for two because one bad grade erased any chance of a scholarship. If I met friends at the gas station after school, she warned me not to get caught up with a bad crowd, as if Slurpees and Cheetos were a gateway to prison. I wore a tube top and she told me to change because it brought *the wrong kind of attention*. I wanted her trust, but all I got was her criticism.

"Explain to me again how working at some fancy house is going to change our lives?" I asked.

The Summer We Ran

"Madeline Milton offered me this job on a trial basis. She has a very busy life in Washington, D.C. This is her weekend home and she needs someone to manage the property and prepare meals when she's visiting. It's the kind of job I've dreamed of my entire life. I wouldn't have to fight over shifts or try to pick up side jobs to cover our bills. If she likes me—likes us—this could turn into a permanent position, with a steady paycheck, housing, and good schools. Wouldn't you want to live here instead of in Grandma's trailer?"

I considered this for a moment, not sure whether a place like this would ever feel like home but also knowing my grandmother's trailer wouldn't either. Not anymore.

When I didn't respond quickly enough, my mother huffed. "Don't you understand what's at stake?"

I appeased my mother with a small nod rather than any verbal assurances. Because what I wanted to shout was *Of course I know what's at stake.* When your mother constantly reminds you of every tiny consequence to your actions, that's something no one can ignore. But I didn't want to fight with her, especially here, in front of this imposing estate, so instead I asked, "Why does she have a house this big if she doesn't even live here all the time?"

My mom swiped her cheek. "It's a different world, Tess."

"How can she afford this place?"

"I don't know. I didn't ask for her résumé. She was born or married into money, most likely." She said this like it was some unspoken law I ignored. My mother placed a hand on my shoulder as she added, "You lost out on the first opportunity, but there's still hope you'll find the second."

My mother defined herself by her place in life, her job, her bank account, or lack thereof. I hated her narrow view of the world. She believed there were impenetrable gatekeepers to success. No matter how hard she worked, she was born poor, didn't have a rich husband, and would never amount to much. But once in a while, it seemed like she had higher hopes for me.

My mother knocked and we waited. After a minute, she knocked again, this time more forcefully, the brass fixture shaped like a fox clanking against the massive oak door.

We could hear a faint shout and then the door was flung open by a woman in a peach silk robe, clutching the opening with a hand dripping in gold jewelry and an emerald ring bigger than a pecan. I immediately looked down at my nubby, dirty fingernails and felt inadequate by comparison.

My mother's voice cracked slightly as she said, "Hello, Ms. Milton. I'm Genie Murphy, the new summer house manager."

The woman looked from my mother to me, making me swallow nervously with the intensity of her stares.

"This is my daughter, Tess. She can help out. Or not. Whatever you want. She's very quiet and very smart."

Only one of those things was true, but I didn't speak, not wanting to ruin my mother's introduction.

For a moment, I wondered if we were in the right place or whether my mother had completely misinterpreted this job offer. But then the woman lunged forward and pulled my mother into an uncomfortably tight hug. "I'm thrilled you're here. This place is a disaster. Come in."

We followed Ms. Milton inside a home that absolutely no one else would describe as a disaster. It was a grand space, with gleaming hardwood floors and a double staircase that swept upward.

"Come into the sitting room," Ms. Milton instructed.

The Summer We Ran

The room smelled like lemon polish and was filled with ornately upholstered furniture and draperies that looked as if they weighed more than I did. In the center of the room was a round table with a sterling tea set surrounded by stacks of cups and saucers.

"I completely forgot you were arriving today, but the timing is perfect," Ms. Milton said. "My meeting in D.C. ran late last night and I couldn't get out here until this morning. I'm running behind and my guests arrive in an hour."

"You're hosting a party?" my mother asked. "In an hour?" The pitch of her voice rose with each question, hardly masking her panic.

"Yes. I do it every year. It's casual. Only twenty or so people. A little fundraiser for the local historic society. My neighbor is the chair."

"Should I check in with the caterers?" my mother asked.

"Well, if they'd bothered to show up, you could. That's why I'm so frantic. I have no food. Nothing set up. My neighbor, Kay, was supposed to be here an hour ago and she's nowhere to be found. And I'm not even dressed."

My mother nodded. "I can pull together food in the next hour. Tess will set the tables. You take your time getting ready. We have this under control."

Ms. Milton sighed, hugged my mother again, and seemed to float upstairs.

"Do we have this under control?" I asked in a whisper once Ms. Milton was out of sight.

My mother's eyes widened. "Not at all. This *is* a disaster. I'm going to move my car around to the back and try to pull together a menu. Do your best setting up the cups and plates."

My mother went outside, and I picked up the linen cloth lying next to the teacups.

My hand shook. The cups were so delicate, the china so thin I was surprised they weren't transparent. This was probably a bad assignment for me given my general clumsiness and the fact that each of these cups likely cost more than my mother would make that summer. But something about the intensity of my mother's instructions told me I should zip it, wipe the cups, and pretend I knew how to set up a tea party.

I was almost done with the first stack of teacups when I heard footsteps.

I turned around and saw the fanciest woman I'd ever encountered. She was wearing a cream silk sheath dress, a long strand of pearls, and strappy heels that would make me trip. Her hair was short, a blond cap that set off her bright blue eyes and bold red lips.

She was beautiful and glowing, and looked years younger than my mother, though they were probably the same age. That summer, I quickly learned rich people hide their age, their weaknesses, their personalities, behind cloaks of cash. And this woman was the richest I'd ever seen.

"Sorry. I didn't hear you knock," I stuttered.

"I've been coming to this house my entire life and never once knocked."

She walked into the room and surveyed the space. She picked up a cup from the set I was wiping and immediately flipped it over. "Madeline's making you wipe down her mother's Wedgwood? She's really putting on airs today." She walked toward me and asked, "Who are you?"

Under normal circumstances, I had no problem speaking my mind, but from the first moment I met this woman, I was intimidated.

I'm sure my eyes turned into saucers. "I'm the cup wiper," I stammered.

"What's your name, child?" She stared directly at me. "If you are going to define yourself by your occupation, please let it be something more noble than cup wiping."

I quickly replied, "But I've always dreamed of being a cup wiper, ma'am."

A flash of panic shot through my mind as I realized, not even an hour into this summer adventure, I had already broken my mother's number one rule of not revealing my true personality by speaking to anyone in this house.

But I was immediately relieved when a booming laugh erupted from the bold red lips in front of me. She extended her hand. "I'm Kay Alexander and I may have met my match."

I wiped my sweaty palm on my shorts before shaking her hand. "I'm Tess and I'm certain no one would put us anywhere near the same category." I returned to the cup wiping. "My mom is working here this summer. Ms. Milton asked us to help set up for the party while she's getting dressed."

"I suppose that's because I'm late. Madeline panics about her parties. She views every event as a client networking opportunity and always tries to impress."

I nodded, as if I knew about the spectrum of parties.

"Although, I suppose that opportunistic nature has served her well. If you think this place is impressive, you should see her townhome in Georgetown."

I had no idea why this woman was talking to me as if I was deserving of any information, but I took the opportunity to satisfy my curiosity. "Does Ms. Milton work in D.C.?"

"Some might call it work. Some might call it calculated socializing. She's a lobbyist." Mrs. Alexander walked across the room to retrieve crystal water glasses and brought them back to the table. "Madeline never married, much to her parents' disappointment. She always did exactly what she wanted, unburdened by the expectations that seem to limit the rest of us. She used her father's money and connections to get started, but she's created her own empire through sheer determination."

"It's impressive," I said. I had no idea what lobbyists did, but somehow it afforded two grand homes and a life I could only dream about.

"Yes, but we grew up together. Our parents were neighbors and raised us in these homes. We got in trouble for climbing trees by the river and sneaking frogs into the kitchen. It's hard for me to see Madeline as impressive."

Mrs. Alexander walked over to the mantel and picked up a vase of peonies. "Especially when she doesn't even take care of her flowers."

It was a pale pink arrangement and the petals had begun to droop. I crossed toward her and asked, "Want me to freshen those up?"

"And how would you do that?" she asked, eyebrow cocked.

"A teaspoon of sugar in the water usually does the trick. I'll snip the stems under fresh water too. They're not too far gone. I can get them perked up in a few minutes."

"Where did you learn that?"

I shrugged. "I know flower stuff. Do you want me to take them to the kitchen?"

Mrs. Alexander nodded. "Yes. I'll finish up setting the table."

I cradled the vase of peonies and shuffled out of the room.

When I walked into the kitchen, my mother was pulling a sheet of something sweet and warm out of the oven as her head whipped around, eyeing me and the vase of flowers. "What are you doing?"

"Changing the water in these flowers. Mrs. Alexander asked me to."

"Who is Mrs. Alexander?" my mother scream-whispered.

"The neighbor who was supposed to be here an hour ago to help. She walked in and we chatted a bit."

My mother sighed. "Please don't chat with guests. We're working. Don't mess this up, Tess."

I nodded and removed the flowers and placed them beside the kitchen sink, dumping the old water and trying to ignore my mother's criticism. "Where's the sugar?" I asked.

"In the baking pantry," my mother said, her eyes wide and full of glee.

She pointed toward a small room off the kitchen lined with shelves of flours, sugars, and baking tools I didn't even know existed. No wonder my mother was so excited. I quickly scooped a spoonful of sugar into the vase and returned to the sink, filling it with fresh water and snipping each stem before returning them to the vase.

"When you're done with that, help me get this ready," my mother said as she moved her signature scones from the baking sheet to a serving platter.

How she threw those together in twenty minutes, I had no idea. "You baked already?"

"Of course. That's my job." She inspected each scone, lifting the spatula before arranging them in a circle around a bowl of whipped cream. "These are not my best, but they'll do. I didn't get to chill the dough, and I had to make them smaller than usual, but I'm not messing up on my first day. I came here to impress Ms. Milton, and that's exactly what I'm going to do."

I gave my mother a high five with her free hand as she drizzled lemon glaze on the scones.

She nodded at the vase by the sink. "Those are already perking up."

"We're basically domestic superheroes, rescuing flowers and baked goods from peril. What else is on the menu?"

"It's bare pickings in the fridge. I'll need to shop. But I scrounged together enough for some goat cheese puffs and cucumber sandwiches. Let's take the scones out and check on your table settings and then you can help me finish the menu."

"Sounds like a plan."

We walked into the sitting room to find Mrs. Alexander sprawled across the chaise lounge, her heels kicked off.

"Hello, Tess Cup Wiper," she said.

My mother looked at me sideways and I whispered, "Just a little joke. Don't worry."

"Hello, Mrs. Alexander. This is my mother, Genie Murphy. We'll drop off these flowers and scones and then get out of your way."

"Those smell heavenly. What are they?"

"Lemon vanilla scones, ma'am." My mother placed a scone on a plate and handed it to Mrs. Alexander, who took a bite, closed her eyes, and moaned.

"Thank God none of these women eat, so I can devour that platter myself."

"None of the women eat?" my mother asked, alarmed.

"Oh no," Mrs. Alexander said, sighing. "Madeline Milton and every other woman we know survive solely on those dehydrated packets of Nutrisystem. Occasionally a SlimFast shake. They like having food around for decoration purposes only."

I saw the color drain from my mother's face. Her food was amazing but not exactly low-calorie.

Mrs. Alexander walked toward me, inspecting the vase of flowers. "You did a nice job with these. Do you like flowers?"

I nodded, my mother's scrutiny making the room feel ten degrees warmer.

"What's your favorite flower?" Mrs. Alexander asked.

I shrugged, looking nervously over at my mother. I didn't want to say the wrong thing, so I figured saying nothing was better. This approach did not work.

Mrs. Alexander took a step closer to me. "Let me give you some advice. If you look around the room for permission to speak no one will care what you have to say. Speak your mind; speak it clearly, especially when you are asked. Now, what is your favorite flower?"

"Goldenrod," I said quickly.

"That's a weed."

I shrugged. "Depends on who's looking, I guess. I like it. So do the bees and butterflies. It is great for cutting, easy to grow."

"You'd put goldenrod in a vase?"

"Yes, ma'am. You could mix in some hydrangeas, purple coneflowers. It makes a nice arrangement. A little more informal than this, I suppose." I placed the peonies on the mantel and turned to leave.

"Have you spent much time around gardens?" Mrs. Alexander asked, stopping my retreat.

"My whole life. My grandmother liked it. We spent a lot of time growing things together."

"Such as?"

"Food, mostly. My grandmother grew almost everything we ate. But she loved flowers, especially roses. They're too much work, in my opinion, but they brought her a lot of joy."

Mrs. Alexander pointed to an arrangement in the center of the table, tightly bloomed roses in varying shades of pink. "Can you identify those?"

I peered at the arrangement. I couldn't figure out this woman, but I excelled at tests. Before my mother could stop me, I started rattling off the names of the roses. "The dark pinks are Gallicas and these brighter ones are centifolias. They're easy to spot because of their petals—cabbage roses. The lightest ones are probably noisettes." I pulled a leaf off one stem. "There are some spots here. I'd spray for aphids soon, before they take over the plant."

Mrs. Alexander walked toward the arrangement and examined the leaf I removed. "You're right."

I knew I was right, about the aphids and about her weird test on rose varieties, but it was still nice to hear. I felt like my grandmother was smiling down at me, unlike my mother, who hadn't taken a breath since this conversation began.

"And you're working here this summer?" Mrs. Alexander asked.

My mother finally interjected. "I'm Ms. Milton's summer house manager and cook. This is my daughter."

"I see."

"The other guests will be arriving soon. We better finish up the cooking," my mother said as she turned and left the room.

I faced Mrs. Alexander and curtsied, which was one of the more ridiculous things I had ever done, but that room was getting to me.

Mrs. Alexander laughed. "You'll get used to this place. It's not as fancy as it looks."

I walked toward the kitchen, but Mrs. Alexander followed me into the hallway.

"Tess?"

"Yes," I said, nerves bubbling inside.

"What are you doing this summer? While your mother is working here?" Mrs. Alexander asked.

I shrugged. "Helping out, I guess. I don't think my mom and Ms. Milton have talked that over yet."

She cocked her head slightly. "Would you like to work with me this summer? I could use some help with my gardens."

I wasn't sure how to answer. It didn't seem like a question I had the authority to answer. "Do you think that would be okay with Ms. Milton?"

"Oh, I'll handle Madeline. Would it be okay with your mother?"

I nodded. "She'd be happy to have me occupied." I hesitated and then asked the question that every teenage girl needed to know: "Is this a paying job?"

Mrs. Alexander's face remained somber as she said, "Yes, I would compensate you for your time."

"Okay."

"Would you like to negotiate your rate?"

I made four dollars an hour babysitting for the twin toddlers that lived next door to my grandmother. This job sounded easier, but this woman looked like she could afford more. "Five dollars an hour?" I asked tentatively.

"All right. Come by at seven tomorrow morning. Is that too early?"

"No, that's fine. I'm used to waking up early with my mom." I turned, excitement bubbling inside. I had a summer job.

Mrs. Alexander's voice stopped me. "Tess, I would have paid seven dollars an hour. Negotiate better next time."

I smiled as I said, "I would have done it for free."

Mrs. Alexander laughed, her eyes twinkling as she took another bite of the scone.

The next day, I woke up at five in the morning to help my mother. Despite the early hour, I hopped out of bed, wanting to confirm the reality of this situation because it still felt like a dream. My mother seemed equally giddy, smoothing the sheets longingly as she made her bed. We were both on a high after the success of the afternoon tea party. My mom's food was a hit, even among the diet-conscious crew, and Ms. Milton kept thanking us both for *saving the day*.

"I still can't believe we're living here," I said.

The cottage we were assigned was an old stable that had been remodeled into a guesthouse. It was without question the nicest place I had ever slept. Wooden beams lined the ceiling. Crisp white plaster on the walls contrasted with the giant stone fireplace in the middle of the room. I immediately claimed the upstairs loft with its bed tucked under the eaves and a porthole window view of the Blue Ridge Mountains. The furniture was old but not in a thrift-store way. It was furniture that had been loved for decades, the wooden farm table with more history than my mother and a four-poster bed that looked like it was built when women had dowries. I found myself sitting up straighter and walking more carefully in this space.

Part of my mother's job was making breakfast for the seasonal workers required to run the farm. Madeline Milton was an avid horseback rider, and the care and training of her animals was a significant operation, especially in the busy spring and summer months. We made big pots of grits, bowls of scrambled eggs, and platters of biscuits. Everyone seemed thrilled that there was finally a cook on the property, greeting my mother with smiles and sly requests for seconds. She was in her element, basking in the praise of her cooking. As out of place as we felt at the tea yesterday, it was a relief to feel immediately accepted by Ms. Milton's other employees.

I understood why my mother was nervous about this job and eager to make the best impression. Most of Ms. Milton's employees had been working there for years. They liked it. They had health insurance. They lived in real houses and didn't worry about a leaky roof during a rainstorm. This job felt like a precious opportunity, a winning lotto ticket threatening to blow away in the wind. I wanted to help my mother hold on.

After breakfast service, I shoveled a plate of food into my mouth and left for my first day of work. It was just next door, which should have meant walking a few steps. But here, there was close to a half-mile between properties, and I had to cut through the back field.

I walked past the barn with the same bubbling nerves as the first day of school. I wanted this job to work out, but if it was anything like school, I shouldn't get my hopes up.

I groaned at the thought of one last year of high school. Potentially at a new school, if Madeline Milton hired my mother full-time. It felt overwhelming, the idea of starting over at the beginning of my senior year, although there was a part of me that welcomed a fresh start. I hadn't exactly been the most popular girl at my last high school, especially not with the opposite sex.

Up until then, I had kissed three boys. One was a mortifying game of truth or dare. No one's first kiss should be in front of an audience where half the room is cheering and half the room is saying "yuck." The second was my friend Emily's cousin. I'm pretty sure she paid him to kiss me. The third and final kiss was the culmination of a painful junior prom where my date drank three beers and burped into my mouth.

All terrible kisses. My track record was an embarrassment. I had faint hopes that my luck would change this summer in a new place. I suppose I had a reputation for being hard. I had little patience for the antics of boys my age, and I couldn't make myself giggle at their jokes like the girls who got kissed properly could. I also had an unfortunate habit of reciting facts whenever I got nervous, and boys made me nervous. But maybe it would be different here where I was unknown. Maybe I would be different.

By the time I made it to Mrs. Alexander's property, the walk had calmed my nerves. I surveyed her house. It was smaller and older than Madeline Milton's house but no less grand. It was made entirely of stone, thick mortar making it seem unbreakable, ivy-covered walls making it seem ancient. I started walking to the front door but heard a voice calling me.

"Tess, I'm out back. Come around."

I walked to the back of the house and my breath hitched. I'd never seen gardens like these in my life, not in any of the books I pored over at the library, memorizing the names of plant varieties my grandmother and I daydreamed about growing. We'd tear out pages of magazines with beautiful gardens and my grandmother would circle what she liked, teaching me the importance of color and texture and scale in a way that she seemed to innately understand. I'd go to the library and research the plants, studying famous British gardens and grand American estates. I'd draw up plans and my grandmother would smile as she'd say, "Someday, Tess, you'll live in a place like that."

Here, I found myself standing in a place far better than I could have dreamed. Mrs. Alexander's gardens extended into the countryside, stone terraces melting into the rolling hills with wild grasses. There were raised beds with more flower varieties than I could count and an entire expanse dedicated to tea roses. Lines of lavender and lightly mowed paths led into a wild explosion of color, purples and pinks and reds melting into the rising sun. There was a formality to the garden that matched the home, plenty of sculpted boxwoods and neatly maintained pathways with pea gravel, but the patches of colorful chaos were my favorite.

I was so mesmerized that I didn't even notice Mrs. Alexander standing next to me.

"What do you think?"

"They are the most beautiful gardens I have ever seen," I said and sighed.

I turned to Mrs. Alexander and was surprised by the difference. Gone was her slinky silk dress and boldly applied makeup. She was barefaced, her short blond hair hiding behind a baseball cap. She wore an oversized T-shirt and knee-length biking shorts. Somehow, she looked younger in this stripped-down version of herself. The bold persona seemed to have disappeared with the bold clothing. Her voice was quiet as she said, "Let's get to work."

"Should I check in with your gardening staff about where to start?" I asked.

"This isn't Madeline's house. You're looking at the staff."

I looked around at the expanse of manicured gardens, shock settling over my face. "You take care of this yourself?"

She nodded slightly. "Yes. It is something to fill my days, as my husband would say."

"Wow." It was the only reaction I could muster.

"This is my space. I don't let others touch my flowers."

"But you're going to let me touch your flowers?"

"Yes," Mrs. Alexander said. "You surprised me."

"With my flower knowledge?"

She nodded.

"I'm weird. I don't know why I can't be like other teenagers."

She shook a finger in my direction. "Different isn't weird. Don't dismiss the things that make you special."

I felt my shoulders straightening like they did only when I was around my grandmother.

"Let's get to work," she said, handing me a pair of gardening gloves and a cultivator. "I don't like to use chemicals. I hope you are prepared to hand-weed for most of the summer."

I nodded enthusiastically. "That's how I was taught. Thank you for this job, Mrs. Alexander."

"I've never met anyone else as excited to weed as me," she said. "You can call me Kay."

We worked in silence for most of the morning. I was focused, careful with my work in this beautiful space. Weeding was a fairly simple task, but it was still early summer and some of the perennials were emerging. There were a million questions I wanted to ask Kay about living here, and the gardens, and how she could be a woman in a silk dress one day and covered in dirt the next. But I kept my mouth shut, my mother's advice echoing in my ears. *Do a good job, Tess. Be quiet, focus on the work, and stay out of trouble.*

My stomach began to grumble and I glanced at my watch, surprised that it was after eleven. It always amazed me how time evaporated with focused tasks, hours seeming like minutes.

Kay seemed to feel the same because she stood up from the garden bed, her hand on the small of her back as she stretched. "Let's take a break. I'll make us some sandwiches. You can clean up in the mudroom through that door."

I watched as she shed her boots, hat, and gloves, scrubbing her hands before entering the kitchen. I did the same, surprised by the silence between us. There was a solemnity to Kay that seemed to extend beyond taking her gardens seriously.

I walked into the kitchen, finding Kay staring at a mug of coffee on the white countertops. She lifted the mug, a ring of brown liquid staining the counter. Suddenly, she raised the mug slightly before throwing it against the floor, shards of porcelain scattering.

She inhaled deeply, her eyes closed, her body vibrating with anger. I heard her exhale, the hiss of air filling the room. I wished I could disappear, but instead I stood absolutely still.

"I apologize," Kay said.

I smiled nervously and shrugged, for once unable to find any words that seemed appropriate in response to an unexplained mug-flinging outburst.

"My husband knows that these counters stain. And yet he sneaks away this morning, without a word, this mug on the counter telling me everything I need to know."

"I guess he's in for it tonight, huh?" I sheepishly replied.

"No," she said through tightly pulled lips. "He won't be coming home tonight. His job is very demanding. He is rarely home, either staying at our town house in Washington, D.C., or traveling for business."

"I guess that's the trade-off," I said tentatively, slowly walking toward the kitchen sink and reaching into the cabinet underneath, fortuitously locating the dustpan. I started to sweep up the pieces of porcelain, hoping if I removed the evidence, we could forget this ever happened.

"What do you mean, the trade-off?" Kay asked.

"I guess he has to work really hard to pay for a house this beautiful." I swallowed, regretting that I brought up this topic.

"My husband did not buy this house. This was my parents' house," she said sharply as she swept her hands over the counters. "My mother picked out this marble. I love this marble."

"Got it. That's the other way."

"The other way?"

I bit my lip, suddenly very aware that my mouth navigated me into a minefield that I needed to immediately escape if I was going to keep my summer job. "Never mind," I said, dumping the swept-up pieces of mug into the trash.

"Tess, I believe I told you yesterday, if someone asks your opinion, you should seize those opportunities and speak."

I shook my head. "I didn't mean anything. I say stupid things all the time. My mother is constantly telling me to be quiet."

Kay leaned against the counter as she said, "That may be true, but I want to hear what you have to say. What did you mean by 'the other way'?"

"I've never been around places like this, houses this big, furniture this fancy. I asked my mother how someone affords this life and she basically said either you're born rich or you marry rich."

Kay's face was tight. She didn't speak, so I filled the silence with babbling. "I'm sorry. That was rude. Things pop into my head and I should keep them there. Please don't fire me."

"I'm not going to fire you," Kay said. "I suppose there's some unfortunate truth in your mother's statement. At least for me, those were the two most likely opportunities. I inherited this house from my parents and my husband's career pays for its upkeep. We married young, and had a baby, and I supported his career. But then I blinked and now I'm standing in this kitchen with you. I'm not like Madeline, with a job of my own and the freedom that buys."

Two days in and I didn't understand the rules of this world and why this woman seemed to view her place in life just as rigidly as my mother did.

The Summer We Ran

Kay looked off, staring into the cavern of her large home. "Maybe someday you'll live in a grand home that you earn yourself. Life would certainly be better with less entanglements. At least, there would be fewer broken coffee cups."

She walked toward the refrigerator. "Sandwiches," she said on an exhale. "I suppose I should make something for my son too, assuming he eventually wakes. His father would be furious knowing he slept in like this." She seemed nervous as she rambled on. "My husband brought him here last night. My son will be spending the summer with me."

"Your son doesn't live with you?" I asked.

"Not usually, no." She seemed embarrassed as she quickly added, "He's in boarding school most of the year, at his father's insistence. How old are you?"

"Seventeen."

"He's a year older. You'll probably see him around. His name is Grant."

Almost as if he could hear his name, we heard footsteps clomping down the stairs, the sound of a sleep-filled boy who was still learning to navigate a body that grew nightly.

He rounded the corner and I saw him. I'd never been a romantic, notions of love at first sight lost on my practical nature. But the moment I saw Grant walking into the kitchen, wiping the sleep away from his eyes, his hair sticking up in a million directions, our eyes meeting for the first time—that moment was pure electricity.

Three

JUNE 2021

I'll be back in fifteen minutes," my campaign manager, Mara, says. "Take some deep breaths and review the financial stimulus talking points. You flubbed those earlier." Mara closes the door, her sensible loafers echoing down the hallway.

I'm sitting in the hotel conference room, waiting to be called to the stage for the first debate. The national party representatives have left. Mara has cleared the room, giving me a few minutes of quiet.

Mara can do anything: motivate volunteers, mount a successful grassroots campaign, strategize with representatives across the state. She can do anything but smile. She is the most serious person I have ever met. Dean thinks she's good for me. I never would have made it this far without her. My two major goals are to win this campaign and to make Mara laugh. Winning the campaign is the easier task.

One of her strengths is that she can sense my moods. She

knows my nerves are rising but doesn't probe too deeply into the reasons.

The ground floor of the Homestead Resort is a cavernous maze. I'm hoping Mara gets a little lost and I'll have twenty minutes to myself. I need every precious moment to quell this mixing bowl of anxiety.

The Homestead has traditionally hosted the first debate. It's one of the oldest resorts in the country with a storied history of visiting presidents and social scandals. It is also the place my mother worked throughout my childhood. She spent time in every kitchen of the massive property, washing dishes, chopping, and prepping. Eventually, her muffins and scones earned her a place in the market making baked goods for resort guests to purchase before their afternoons of tennis and golf.

One of those guests was Madeline Milton, and after biting into one of my mother's treats, she offered her a job on the spot. It was the first domino that kicked off the summer that changed everything.

I take three deep breaths, still trying to calm my nerves. This debate is a big deal. My first major appearance, standing on the stage of a resort where my mother used to scrub dirty dinner plates. There's so much pressure to do well at this full-circle life moment. But that's not why my heart is skipping irregularly, my forehead beaded with slick, queasy sweat.

The reason I feel like sprinting to the bathroom is because of him. I look at the posters for tonight's event, Grant's face unsettling me more than I expected. It has been twenty-five years since I've stood across from that face, never imagining that Grant and I would meet again on a stage in front of hundreds of voters.

A month after I announced my campaign, Grant's name

surfaced as a potential opposition candidate. I ignored the sinking feeling in my gut because the Republicans had a crowded field; the likelihood that Grant would emerge as the top contender was slim. But as the months passed, Grant's campaign gained momentum. I could have dropped out. And maybe I should have. Grant always had a way of making me second-guess my decisions. When it became clear that he was going to be the Republican nominee for governor, I should have told my campaign manager that I met Grant when I was seventeen. I should have told my husband—everything. But I didn't say a word. I kept quiet and stayed in the race because I promised my mother I wouldn't let my past control my future. I wanted to be stronger as an adult than I ever was as a teenager.

I know that Grant is going to alter my life again. No matter how hard I try, I can't escape him and our secrets. I tell myself it's only one lie, but when you unwind it, I realize that most of my life is tied up in that lie.

Suddenly, I'm running across the room. There's a back door with quick access to the bathrooms by the video game arcade. My years of exploring the hallways while my mother worked have their benefits. The preparations for the debate are on the opposite end of the expansive property. No one will be near this bathroom to hear the first female candidate for governor vomit her nerves away.

I narrowly make it in time, wondering if the voters of Virginia care about a candidate's ability to puke in a ladylike way. Afterward, I walk to the sink to clean myself up, relieved there is no trace of this embarrassment on my carefully selected blue sheath dress. I blot the corners of my eyes, the rest of my makeup having sufficiently survived.

My hands are braced on either side of the sink, my eyes shaking with worry at my reflection, when there's a knock.

I turn into Candidate Tess immediately, straightening my posture, smoothing hairs that can't possibly be out of place given the amount of hairspray used.

Someone clears their throat on the other side of the door. It's deep and unquestionably male.

It must be Dean coming to check on me. But I remember that can't be the case. Dean is sitting with his parents in the auditorium, handling a slew of pre-debate interviews to bolster my family values polling. A childless woman in her forties seems to skew negative on those issues.

This mystery man tentatively whispers, "Tess, are you in there?"

"Who's there?" I ask.

The door opens slowly, and it takes a few seconds for my eyes to focus. Because this should be a visual hallucination. Grant Alexander, standing in front of me, in the basement bathroom of the Homestead. But it isn't.

Grant sheepishly walks inside the bathroom, looking over his shoulder, before he turns and locks the door to the outside.

My heart cracks. I've seen pictures of him through the years, but this is the first time I'm staring into his eyes since that fateful summer.

His hair is shorter. It used to be a sandy blond, falling across his forehead. I can't count how many times I swept hair out of his eyes while his arms wrapped around me. But it's short now, so there is no need for that anymore. It's gray at the temples, which somehow makes his eyes greener. There are faint lines around his mouth from countless smiles that I had nothing to do with.

"Grant, what are you doing here?" My voice is steady despite the blood rushing out of my beating heart. "This is the women's bathroom."

"We need to talk," he whispers.

"Here?"

"You have a better idea? We are constantly surrounded by our teams, our spouses. We need to have a private discussion."

The sterile room suddenly feels too small for us to share. My fleeting nostalgia is replaced with simmering anger. "This is so typical of you. Thinking you can corner me in the bathroom and get exactly what you want." I stalk toward the door, my hand reaching for the lock, when Grant steps in front of me, blocking the exit.

"I don't want anything from you, Tess. I never have."

"Yes. I know. You made that clear," I spit back.

Grant slowly shakes his head as he says, "You're unbelievable. I'm here to do us both a favor and you're ready to dig up fights that should be long buried."

"No, Grant. You no longer have the right to make any judgments about what I do or don't say. Move out of the way."

"Five minutes, Tess. That's all I'm asking."

"You always ask too much."

Grant's face pulls and he looks at the bathroom floor. He kicks at the black-and-white tile and I wonder what he's thinking. I never knew what Grant was thinking, even when our bodies were wrapped together. "Pretty sure I didn't ask enough," he says.

My eyes begin to water. Why is it that the words we need to hear come too late? If I let myself think about what Grant has just said, I'll never make it on that stage tonight.

My voice stumbles as I try to find a new subject. "How did you find me in here?"

"I was playing Pac-Man and saw you run in."

"You were playing Pac-Man the hour before our first debate?"

"Yeah. I was. It was helping with the nerves," Grant admits.

I find myself softening. Of course Grant Alexander was playing a game of Pac-Man before he took the stage as the Republican candidate. He's full of surprises. It used to be one of my favorite things about him. But then I remember everything else, and my eyes turn frosty.

"Grant, let me leave. There's nothing for us to say to each other."

"I'm not interested in rehashing old fights. We need to discuss the present, this situation we've gotten ourselves into. We need to discuss how to handle it."

"Handle what?"

"The truth," he says, wincing.

"And what exactly is that, Grant? What truth are you so worried about?" I'm not sure why I'm pushing him. I don't want to think about what happened and I certainly don't want to hear Grant's version of the events. But I'm angry that he's been able to ignore it for half of our lives.

"Tess, someone from your team is going to come in any minute now. Do you really want to explain the two of us together or do you want to end this discussion as soon as possible?"

I sigh, knowing I need to reserve my fight for the stage. "Fine. What did you have in mind?"

"Nothing. We say nothing about our past."

I look away. Days ago, I would have quickly agreed, but I've been lying awake at night, wondering whether we can get away with this—wondering whether I'm capable of keeping this up. "I'm not sure I can do that. I can't keep lying." I stare at Grant, desperate hope seeping into my voice. "What if we admit we met as teenagers? We can laugh about it, and then move on?"

"That's a mistake," Grant says definitively. "How do you think those follow-up questions are going to play out? Don't you know how many journalists would salivate over our past, eager to uncover every dirty piece? I don't want that. I'm pretty sure you don't either. There are things that happened . . ." Grant trails off, unable to find words to describe that summer.

There's a part of me that knows he's right, but a bigger part of me that refuses to admit it. "I know you are used to getting away with things, Grant, but I live in the real world. We will be found out."

"How? It was just you and me that summer. No one else knew about us."

I shake my head. "There were other people. Other people knew, not everything, but they saw us together."

"Is your mother going to say something?"

"No," I say softly. My voice hitches as I explain. "My mother died."

He looks up, shock across his face. "When?"

"It's been a long time, Grant. She died of cancer when I was in college." I say it with the same emotion as if I were describing my dinner. I can't let my feelings surface in front of Grant, even though that year was one of the hardest of my life.

He reaches for my hand and I know why. I know that despite the way things ended, Grant understands how difficult it was for me to lose my last relative. "I'm sorry you were alone, Tess."

"I wasn't alone. I had Dean."

I see him flinch, and I suddenly realize that my comment may have hurt him in a way neither of us knew was still possible.

"What about Madeline Milton?" I ask about the woman who brought us together simply by hiring my mother. I think for a moment, about that world I temporarily inhabited. The elaborate parties at country estates. Grant's mother and her best friend, Madeline, laughing and plotting their social calendars. I was mostly in the background except when I was with Grant.

I take a deep breath. I'm not seventeen anymore. I'm no longer in Grant's world, a place where I spent one summer trying to belong and then decades trying to forget.

"The last I heard, Madeline was in assisted living," Grant says. "Alzheimer's."

Even if Madeline's memories were intact, she probably wouldn't remember me or my mother. We were just the staff, dismissible and disposable, as she proved to us that summer.

Grant continues. "Besides, my mother kept our relationship a secret."

I shrug. "Or she was embarrassed of me."

Grant swallows, his voice deep as he says, "My mother was never embarrassed of you. She loved you; you know that."

I nod, small nods, afraid of the emotions bubbling up. "I loved her too, Grant."

Grant's mouth pulls tightly as he says, "Everyone who knew about us is gone."

I feel a moment of sympathy for him, knowing that he is thinking about his mother's death and questioning whether everything would have been different if she'd lived. I look at Grant, my own grief tangling in the air with his, and I think maybe I was wrong. Maybe I should have handled it all differently. But then I remember Grant's words from that summer and I force my doubts away.

I bring up the topic both of us have been avoiding. "What about your father?"

I watch as Grant's face turns to stone. I know this reaction, anytime his father is mentioned. There was a time when Grant talked to me. Sometimes I wondered if I was the only person he ever talked to about the cruel things his father said and the pain he felt as a boy. I see that as a man, Grant's pain has been replaced with anger.

"My father won't say anything." There's a coldness to Grant's tone that stops me from asking more.

"You really think we can pretend we've never met. And get away with it?"

"Yes," Grant says. "I hope so. The alternative would destroy everything. Our careers, our—"

I cut him off. "You could drop out of the race," I say. "This matters to me, Grant. I don't know why you're even running. To punish me? To prove your father wrong? Those aren't good reasons."

"I'm not dropping out, Tess." Grant's arms are folded across his chest. I want to reach for his shoulders, to shake him, to shove some sense into him, but I keep the distance between us.

"Fine. We'll try your approach. We say nothing." I'm doubtful it will work, but I can't think of a better alternative. If anyone can get away with something like this, it's a golden boy like Grant. For a long time, I thought that kind of good fortune rubbed off on everyone in his orbit. I hope I'm not wrong twice.

"It's worked for twenty-five years. What's a few more months?" Grant says, smirking. It infuriates me that he still feels like it's a game. That our lives, our pain, can be so easily dismissed. "Here's my private cell," he says, passing me a slip of paper. "Just in case we need to speak."

"Let's be clear, Grant. I have zero interest in joking with you or having any type of discussion. You were removed from my life decades ago, and having you back is an unnecessary distraction at a critical time in my career. I'm not your friend. I'm your opponent."

He looks like I've slapped him. It's the same expression that was on his face the last time we spoke. "Understood, Tess. We always did what you wanted, anyway. Isn't that right?"

I look away, unable to meet his eyes.

"We'll stand on that stage and pretend we're strangers," Grant says.

My voice hitches. "But we are strangers, Grant. At least we are now."

Grant looks into my eyes, his face somber as he slowly nods once. "Good luck," he says, before flashing a quick smile. I watch him open the door and walk out, and then stare at myself in the bathroom mirror.

I feel the flood of a million conflicting emotions, because the teenager inside me could never resist Grant's smile and the woman I am now is so goddamn resentful of everything about him.

I don't have the luxury of dwelling on any of these feelings because it's almost time for the debate. I take a deep breath and go find Mara.

There's a flurry of last-minute instructions and makeup application and spritzes of hair spray as my heart races in the wings of the auditorium.

Mara nods, I reciprocate, and I push my shoulders back and walk on stage, waving confidently. I approach Grant and shake his hand. Zero emotion. It is a handshake of formality, as if I've accepted my high school diploma. I don't let my body react the way it used to when Grant's skin was pressed up against mine. I turn toward the crowd, and the spotlights heat my face and blind my eyes. It's impossible to see anyone in the audience, but I know Dean is in the front row, sitting next to his parents.

The moderator is a female national news correspondent who has clear aspirations for the presidential debate in three years. It was the subject of heated negotiations with Grant's team. Mara pushed hard for a female moderator, sure that it would bolster the significance of the first female candidate and assure a friendly debate. I wasn't so sure. It could cut both ways.

The moderator starts with easy, somewhat neutral topics, from education to infrastructure. The first hour is smooth. Grant and I both deliver a handful of zingers and it feels pretty even. But it certainly isn't natural. I keep having flashes from the past. It's hard to see Grant now and reconcile him with the boy I knew. I find myself smirking when he says something so overtly adult that it's unsettling. I still expect him to be a teenager. I hope that no one notices and I focus even harder on keeping my face indifferent.

When the moderator moves to juvenile justice, I'm ready. It's a central issue of my platform and I'm grateful for the easy question she's asked that allows me free rein to present my ideas.

"We need a comprehensive overhaul of our juvenile justice system," I begin. "Kids should be allowed to be kids, to make stupid mistakes without derailing their futures. I guarantee if you poll the audience here, there isn't a single person who didn't make a bad decision when they were a teenager. The difference is, when you're caught making those bad decisions and you enter our state's justice system, the consequences are dire, even more so for offenders of color. In our state, young people of color are 43 percent of the intake population and 70 percent of the commitments to the system. For every year spent in youth prison, a person's probability of being arrested for another crime increases by a third. The reconviction rate in Virginia for juvenile offenders is almost 75 percent."

Grant blinks in an exaggerated manner. "Wow. My eyes glazed over. That was a lot of statistics, Ms. Murphy. Numbers may sound impressive, but when you break down what's behind that information, the facts are clear. Criminals repeat offenses. The only time they stop repeating these crimes is when they are behind bars. I strongly believe that the youth of Virginia need clear consequences. Otherwise, we're creating a pipeline of crime in our state. I am and will always be tough on crime, no matter the offender."

I look in his eyes, unable to believe the blind privilege underlying his position. Before I can stop myself, I say, "You seem to have a clean record, Mr. Alexander. Are you telling us that you never made any stupid mistakes as a teenager? A mistake you were lucky enough to get away with so that you could be standing on this stage tonight?"

Grant hesitates for a moment, unsettled by my question. It's a delay that most won't notice; only those that know him best will see. I'm not naive to think that I'm alone on that list. Does his wife know his face better than I do? Of course, she does.

Grant retorts, "There's a difference between stupid mistakes and breaking the law, Ms. Murphy. There is a difference between typical teenagers and juvenile offenders. I doubt the people of Virginia want to hear us trading stories of teenage antics. I want to focus on the future and how we can create a state with the most opportunity for our good, law-abiding citizens."

The moderator moves to another topic, but not before I see Grant staring at the side of my face, and I wonder if he gets it. If he ever understood how lucky he was.

The next day, our exchange on juvenile justice fills the papers and begins to divide the state. It is the same cracks Grant and I felt decades ago. But we were only kids then, our eyes filled with stars and haze, able to overlook differences. Those differences could have bound us together, but instead we split apart.

He edges ahead in the polls. I'm not surprised. He's a new candidate, and for most people in the state, this debate was their first impression of Grant Alexander. I know all too well that he makes excellent first impressions. But maybe the voters will see the other side of Grant. The man who makes promises he never plans to keep.

Four

JUNE 1996

He cleared his throat, a deep rumble reverberating in the room. As he walked toward his mother, his eyes never left mine. I smiled, then felt a blush creep across my cheeks. I averted my eyes and stared at the floor to preserve some dignity. I'd always been one of those girls who blushed immediately, making it impossible to ever play it cool around any boy who was even slightly attractive. And this boy, with his shaggy blond hair and green eyes that examined me with intensity while twinkling with mischief, made my cheeks burn hotter than ever before.

Grant bent down and kissed his mother's cheek as he said, "Good morning."

Kay slammed the fridge. "Grant, it's nearly lunchtime. No one would consider this morning. I'll give you a pass today, but you're not going to spend the summer—"

He cut her off and said, "Mom, aren't you going to introduce us?" I looked up to find his eyes still focused in my direction.

"Tess, this is my son, Grant." Kay placed turkey and cheese on the counter. "Tess is helping me with my gardens this summer."

"Cool," he said.

"Yeah, it's cool," I said, flipping my hair over my shoulder. I tried to make the gesture natural, but it wasn't. My fingers got tangled in my hair. As I extracted my fingers, I turned toward the window to see my reflection. I was a disaster. I'd spent the morning in the gardens and my hair was full of dirt and mulch. My face was streaked with mud.

The phone rang and Grant's mother said, "That's Madeline. She always needs to chat after her party. You two fix your sandwiches while I take this upstairs."

She left the room and my stomach did somersaults. I was alone, in a very fancy kitchen, with a very cute boy, and had no idea how to function. I folded my hands on the counter and then immediately removed them. No amount of scrubbing would have removed the dirt under my fingernails. I tried to occupy myself with making a sandwich, but my eyes kept darting around the room while Grant continued to stare at me.

"Hi," Grant said, grabbing a plate and reaching for slices of bread.

"Hi," I said, disappointed with my inability to find a more creative response. I swallowed. "Did you know sandwiches were traditionally viewed as meals for ladies' lunches? It wasn't until the club sandwich was invented in the late 1800s that it became an acceptable lunch for men." My nervous recitation of sandwich trivia spewed out so quickly that I wanted to bury myself in a deep pit of embarrassment.

"I did *not* know that," Grant said, assembling his own sandwich. He moved close enough that I could smell the scent of soap on his skin.

"Well, now you too possess that useless piece of knowledge."

I closed my eyes briefly before saying, "I'm sorry, I recite stupid facts when I'm nervous."

"That's not a stupid fact. I'm going to use that the next time I'm eating a sandwich with a stranger," Grant said, sitting at the kitchen table.

I pulled out a chair, joining him.

Grant lifted his sandwich, about to take a bite, when he asked, "Why are you nervous?"

I nibbled slightly on my lip. Grant's eyes darted briefly down to my mouth before he quickly looked away. He shifted in his seat, setting down his sandwich and rubbing his palms on his thighs, his eyes focused on the table. It seemed impossible, but maybe Grant was nervous too.

I took a small bite of my sandwich, chewing carefully before I started talking. "I'm nervous for about a million reasons. I'm in a new place, my mother started a job that she cares a whole lot about, and, to be perfectly honest, I have a habit of saying things that get me in trouble. And now I'm starving and covered in dirt in the fanciest kitchen I have ever seen, trying to talk to you without food in my mouth. Nervous is an understatement."

Grant smiled. "Do you always say whatever is on your mind?"

"Yes," I replied, sighing. "Unfortunately."

"Well, I almost got expelled from boarding school on my last day of classes for sneaking a couple of goats into the gymnasium. I couldn't even walk in graduation. My father banished me to the country for the summer so I don't get in any more trouble. There is no reason why you should be nervous around me. I am a 'walking disaster,' as my father would say."

"Wait, how did you get the goats?" I asked. "Did you put

them in your car? Did you carry them? Sorry, I have a million questions."

"Thank you. Finally, someone that appreciates the effort that went into this prank."

We settled in over our lunch as Grant explained the details of his goat adventure. He was a good storyteller. I found myself hanging on to the details of how Grant and his friend Stuart carried the goats into the gymnasium, laughing at the part when they discovered that a goat had chewed the upholstery of a borrowed car.

"So why didn't they kick you out?" I asked. "You did destroy the gym floor."

Grant's face fell. "My dad. I guess he worked that out. He's used to getting what he wants. My best guess, he wrote a giant check."

"Oh," I said, wondering what it would be like to live in a world where you were allowed to make mistakes, knowing you had the money to fix them.

"Why are you spending the summer here?" I asked. I looked around the room. "This place doesn't seem like much of a punishment to me."

"Yeah, well, things aren't always what they seem," Grant said. "My friends are in D.C. for the summer. This house is my dad's version of solitary confinement."

As we finished our lunch, I leaned in closer and asked, "Did your dad really say you are a 'walking disaster'?"

Grant nodded. "That's definitely not the worst thing he's called me." Grant shrugged like it didn't matter, but the way his eye twitched suggested different.

"I'm really sorry," I said. "My mom can be hard on me too, but she's never said anything like that."

"She's never called you the 'greatest disappointment of my life'?" Grant acted like it was a joke, but I saw through that.

"Your dad said that to you?" I asked softly.

"I overheard him saying it to my mother last night. It was not a good night in the Alexander house. They fight a lot."

"About you?"

He shook his head. "I'm probably the lowest item on their battle list. They can't seem to agree on anything these days."

"I don't really see how one prank equates to life's greatest disappointment."

"That's because you haven't met Richard Alexander." Grant sat taller as he said his father's name, his face pulling into a stoic expression as he mimicked his father's voice. "*It is an honor to carry on the Alexander family name. Represent it with dignity, not disgrace, son* . . . What a load of shit."

"Well, I guess I'm lucky there are no expectations associated with the Murphy family name," I said.

"You have no idea how lucky. Even though he thinks he's punishing me by sending me out here this summer, I'm secretly relieved. His world is always intense. I get why my mother escapes it so often."

"Are your parents divorced?" I asked, and then quickly added, "You don't have to answer if you don't want to."

"If they were divorced, our life would make some sense. I don't know why they're still married, but they seem to have come up with some type of arrangement. My mother comes into D.C. for certain parties, mostly to make an appearance, and they act like they tolerate each other. Then she comes back here as fast as she can."

"Don't you miss her?"

"Sometimes. But she's . . ." Grant seemed to search for a

word to describe his mother. "She's in her own world a lot of the time. If I lived with her, I'm not sure I'd miss her any less." Grant shrugged as he said, "My family is weird."

I placed a hand over my heart as I said, "I am in no place to judge anyone as weird."

"Most people judge."

"Well, that sucks."

"Yeah, it kind of does."

I finished my lunch and walked to the sink. As I washed the plate, I felt Grant walk toward my side. He reached over my hands, squirting out too much soap and scrubbing with clumsy motions that made it pretty clear dish-washing was not part of his usual routine.

His arm brushed mine as he reached for a dish towel, my entire body pulsing at the near connection. I took a sharp breath inward as our bodies pressed closer together.

"Are you going to the bonfire tonight?" he asked. "The staff at the Milton farm always do a big summer kickoff the first Friday of June."

I had heard rumbles about the bonfire at breakfast, but the idea of standing in the woods with a bunch of strangers seemed miserable. I looked over to Grant. There was a shaky pitch to his voice as he asked me about the bonfire and it made me react reversely, oddly calmed by the fact that he seemed just as affected by me as I was by him. Suddenly, the idea of standing in the woods with Grant sounded like the only thing I wanted to do.

"I was thinking about going," I said, pretending it was totally normal for a boy to ask me out. "So, I'll see you there?"

His face erupted into a smile before he caught himself. He shrugged and said, "I guess. Not much else to do around here."

Kay walked into the kitchen, grabbing an apple as she said, "Back to work, Tess. I want to finish up the pruning before the sun gets too high."

Grant and I jumped apart, the space between us widening immediately.

"You got it, Mrs. Alexander—I mean, Kay," I quickly said.

I followed her toward the door before turning back and saying, "See you around, Grant. Try to stay away from the goats."

"Listen to this smart girl," Kay said, shouting over her shoulder.

Standing at the door, Grant watched us walk toward his mother's garden. I waved, thinking that this summer job just got so much better.

I expected some heavy negotiation, but my mother dismissively agreed when I asked if I could go out that night. I suspected that exhaustion was her primary motivator. My mother had just finished a sixteen-hour day and she had to be up again at four in the morning to prepare the breads Ms. Milton wanted to serve at dinner. She had two instructions: "Be home by midnight and do not get in trouble."

When I got to the bonfire, there was a group of kids milling around the field. The fire was roaring, a big pile of debris off to the side that someone kept feeding into the flames. Kids were reaching into a cooler of beers, and cans were being passed around. I didn't know anyone there, but no one seemed to mind an extra body around the fire.

I scanned the crowd, trying to find Grant without looking like I was trying to find Grant. Someone brought out a boombox, hooking it up to giant speakers in the back of a truck. Music filled the air, the sounds of Pearl Jam quickly replaced by Brooks & Dunn as a group of boys started chanting song lyrics in between commands to chug.

Three boys grabbed a long tree limb, hoisting it over their heads and throwing it into the fire. Sparks flew, a broken log bouncing outside the stone circle. A group of girls shrieked, jumping backward.

I paused, feeling uncomfortable and unsure. It was clear this party was only getting started and it already seemed to be teetering out of control. I decided to head toward the edge of the group, but as I turned, I ran into a solid chest. I looked up and found Grant's bright smile.

"Quite the party, huh?" Grant commented.

I looked over my shoulder at the growing bonfire. "Someone is going to get burned."

"Agreed," Grant said. "Let's head over there," he said, pointing toward a circle of pickup trucks at the edge of the woods.

"This is the type of situation that Darwin would find essential to the survival of society," I said, my eyes narrowing at the group of kids around the bonfire. "Tonight, some stupid boys are going to find out that they aren't quite as fit as they think."

"So, we're here for scientific observation, then?" Grant said, hopping onto a tailgate and moving to the side to make room for me.

"I'm certainly not here to join that," I said, pointing to the group taking swigs of some brown liquid before tossing the bottle into the fire. "But please, go ahead and show me how strong you are by throwing around heavy objects and tossing flammable liquids into a poorly controlled fire." I stopped myself from saying more, my nervous, judgmental rambling making it abundantly clear why I was never the most popular girl in school.

My eyes darted toward Grant, hoping he wanted to stay with me but realizing that most kids wanted to be a part of the party instead of sitting on the sidelines.

"Nope, I'm good here," he said, to my relief. He gestured to a cooler that was in the back of the truck and asked, "Want a beer?"

"No," I quickly replied. "Bad prom-night memories," I added.

Grant reached for a beer and took a sip. I looked up at the night sky and then turned back toward him. He was discreetly pouring out most of his beer off the side of the truck.

"What's that about?" I asked.

"Oh, nothing," he said.

I sat quietly, waiting for him to answer.

Grant finally said, "I don't drink. But it's easier at these parties if you have one in your hand. That way you aren't getting questions all night about why you aren't drinking."

"Why aren't you drinking?" I asked.

He held up his beer. "Oh, but I am."

I shook my head. "You already showed me your secret party trick. I want the truth. Not the fake answer you tell everybody else."

"How do you know I give everyone else a fake answer?"

"Because you are fake drinking. There's a cover-up."

I noticed the foot or so of space between us, my mind debating whether there was a way to close that space without it seeming too obvious.

Grant must have read my mind because he slid closer as he said, "Things between my parents are messy. They get messier when they drink. Just the smell of it makes me anxious."

"I get it," I said.

"Is it the same with your parents?" he asked.

I shook my head. "No. I think I've seen my mother sip a Coors Light once or twice." I started pulling on the threads of my cutoff shorts as I continued. "I understand wanting to be different from your parents. I don't want to make the same mistakes as my mother."

I didn't say anything about my father and Grant didn't ask. It's a question I couldn't answer anyway. All my mother ever said was that he was *someone who passed through*. She didn't even know his name.

Grant looked at me and we smiled. Then we both nervously looked away, staring back at the crowd. There were small groups of kids swaying to the music, laughing easily at jokes we couldn't hear. I knew the loneliness that came from watching other people enjoy themselves, yearning to be on that side of the viewfinder. I wondered if Grant ever felt that way.

"Can I be perfectly honest?" I asked.

"I've known you less than twenty-four hours, but I'd expect nothing less."

"I'm not exactly a bonfire person. Or a high school party person. I don't usually get invited to these things, which used to bother me, but now I'm realizing I wasn't missing out on much."

"Overrated for sure," Grant agreed. "Although, I find it hard to believe that you don't get invited to parties."

"Well, I don't. Or I didn't." I looked upward before quietly commenting, "You probably get invited to all the parties."

Grant shrugged. "Boarding school is a weird place. I'm happy to have all this high school shit behind me." He looked over in my direction, nudging my shoulder. "You only have one more year, right? It's just about survival, at this point."

"True," I said.

"If you aren't a party person, what's your favorite way to spend a Friday night?" Grant asked.

I shook my head. "No way I'm answering that question. I just met you. I'm trying to keep my freak flag at half-mast."

"Too late, sandwich girl." Grant elbowed my side and I felt my cheeks flame.

"Fine. Since I already exposed my inner nerd," I said. "Brace yourself."

"Lots of buildup for a simple Friday-night description," Grant teased.

"There's a 7-Eleven in our town. My typical Friday night is spent with a jumbo-size Slurpee, mix of every flavor, obviously, that I sneak into the library and drink in the stacks. Our library stays open until ten p.m. on Fridays. It's a wild place."

"I had no idea I was sitting next to such a rule-breaker."

"Well, my mom wants me to study and stay out of trouble. She never complains when I tell her I'm going to the library. How about you? What's your wild Friday?" I asked shyly.

"Mostly stupid dorm parties. Sneaking off campus when we can." Grant hesitated before he continued. "My favorite place to escape is the gym roof. The stairway is supposed to be locked, but it's easy to force open."

My eyes locked with Grant's and his slow smile immediately put me at ease. "What can you see from up there?" I didn't ask Grant what he needed to escape. I understood how messy life could feel, even when we're supposed to be at its beginning.

"The monuments all lit up at night. Life makes more sense when I'm up there. Seeing those lights makes me realize there's more than the people and paths my dad tells me to follow."

"Your boarding school is in D.C.? But doesn't your dad live in D.C.?" I couldn't mask the confusion in my voice.

Grant swallowed, hesitating before answering. "He's never around. And he said the structure of boarding was good for me. I stopped asking questions because it's easier to go along with his commands."

"Do you think everything will be better when you're in college?" I asked.

"I hope so. It's the best days of your life, right?" His tone was genuine, as if his life was sheltered enough to believe in this kind of possibility.

"That's what they say."

"Princeton is two hundred miles away from my father. It has to be better," Grant said.

I nodded in agreement. "Definitely."

Grant leaned back in the truck bed and I joined. We stared at the night sky, the endless stars making everything except the two of us feel far away. "What about you? Dream school?" he asked. "If you could get in anywhere, what college would you pick?"

I was quiet for a moment because in Grant's world, the biggest obstacle was getting accepted. Even if I got a full scholarship, there were still expenses that would be a stretch. My mother insisted we'd figure it out, but my part-time jobs didn't earn much. I wasn't even sure how we were going to afford the college application and testing fees. Being smart wasn't enough. The more time I spent adding up costs, the clearer it became that college was unlikely.

"I don't dream like that," I said. "I can't let myself." I didn't want to explain any of this to Grant, so I asked, "Is Princeton your dream school?"

He hesitated, the silence consuming the space around us. I expected him to answer immediately, but the way he seemed to think about my question made me wonder if it was something he had ever thought about. Eventually Grant said, "Yeah, definitely. I've always wanted to go to Princeton."

I looked away, not believing his answer but knowing it wasn't my place to ask more.

Grant inched closer as he said, "Tess, you should let yourself dream."

"College is expensive," I said, gnawing on the inside of my cheek as I repeated the phrase my mother had said countless times.

He nudged my side. "I think the whole point of dreams is that you forget about the practical stuff. What's your dream school, Tess?"

A part of me was so jealous that Grant lived in a world where he could easily dismiss practicality. He asked a simple question and I think he expected a simple answer. He didn't know about all the meetings I'd had with my guidance counselor where she explained that I needed more than a 4.0 average and a near perfect SAT to even be in contention for a full academic scholarship. Or my mother's concerns about the price of textbooks and her constant nagging about my grades. When there wasn't room for the tiniest mistake, dreams felt impossible. But in that moment, I wanted to imagine that I could approach life with Grant's ease, so I answered his question.

"I want to go to University of Virginia," I said. I didn't tell him that my UVA brochure was frayed at the edges from how many times I read through it, imagining my face mixed in with the smiling photos of students lounging on the campus green. Or that I'd already studied the class offerings, highlighting the ones I wanted to take.

"Great school. I'm sure you'll get in." He nodded assuredly.

I wished it was as easy as Grant thought. I could have been annoyed by his lack of awareness, but instead I was comforted by his confidence. It was a mistake, letting myself believe, even for a moment, that the rules of Grant's world could apply to me.

I watched as his hand slowly inched closer to mine, wondering what it would feel like when our fingers met. I could sense the warmth of his body next to mine and the anticipation was killing me. Just as his fingers reached out, a loud pop rang in the air.

Grant and I sat up quickly and both instinctively moved closer to each other. I looked over at the kids who were chugging beers. They had apparently decided that they needed more excitement than throwing large objects into the fire. They were firing shotguns into the sky.

I looked at Grant nervously. "Is this what usually happens at parties?"

"Discharge of firearms? Umm, no. At least, not any parties I've ever attended."

Another round of shots rang in our ears. I flinched and Grant wrapped his arm around me. I wasn't sure whether it was the guns or Grant's body making me more nervous. But feeling him pressed up against my back felt like the best development of the night.

I heard a kid suggest stacking up a pyramid of beer cans for target practice. I looked at Grant and he said, "I think we should leave."

"Yeah," I said, nodding vigorously. "I'm definitely ready to go."

Grant hopped down from the truck bed and turned to help me, placing his hands on either side of my waist and lowering me slowly.

His hands lingered on my hips longer than necessary and I leaned into his chest, my body sliding against his.

"I walked," I whispered, our mouths inches apart. I gestured across the field, Ms. Milton's massive home no longer visible due to the darkened sky.

"Then I'll walk you home," Grant said.

"It's out of your way," I murmured obligingly.

"That doesn't matter. You could get lost in the dark." Grant swept a strand of hair out of my eyes as he said, "I'll keep you safe, Tess. I promise."

I believed him.

"Let me grab my sweatshirt," Grant said. "I left it by the bonfire."

We split up, Grant in search of his sweatshirt and me in search of a safe distance away from the fire and the increasingly large crowd of teenagers. I had a giant smile across my face, thinking that this night was going even better than I'd hoped. I thought this was going to be the most boring summer of my life and now it was looking like the opposite.

I scanned the crowd, finding Grant walking around to the other side of the fire. I waved subtly in his direction and he smiled. A big, bright smile, his eyes crinkling and my heart thumping. Then I heard the sirens.

All of a sudden it was chaos. Police lights tore through the field, a spotlight pointed at the gathering and officers shouting, "Everyone stop!"

No one followed those orders. Kids scattered in different directions, running toward the tree line for cover.

I turned to follow the mass of people but hesitated. I didn't know where I was going and the woods all looked the same, especially at night. If I didn't go in the direction of Grant's house, I could get lost. Ms. Milton's closest neighbor on the other side was over a mile away. My mother would lose her mind if I was a second late for curfew. I searched for Grant but couldn't find him in the mass of people.

Then the spotlight blinded my eyes. I couldn't see anything but heard the sounds of police officers shouting and arrests already starting. It seemed like anyone within reach of the police was being handcuffed.

"Tess!" I heard my name and turned to see Grant running up to my side.

A police officer was a few feet away and he looked in our direction, shouting, "You two. Do not move. Stay exactly where you are!"

Grant grabbed my hand, lacing his fingers between mine like it was something we had done a million times.

We locked eyes and he said, "Run."

That's exactly what we did, the officer chasing after us but giving up after a hundred yards. We made it to the tree line before I looked back. A dozen or so teenagers were standing in handcuffs. The music was being shut off, the shotguns in the hands of the police officers.

Everyone else dispersed. It was eerily quiet, save for an occasional laugh and then refrains of shushing echoing through the woods. Grant said he had a pretty good idea of where we were, but my heart pounded too loudly to concentrate.

He was at my side, his hand still woven together with mine. I looked up at him, his green eyes dancing. "What do we do now?" I asked.

"This," he said, pulling me into his chest, bending his face down toward mine and lightly kissing my lips. He wrapped his arms around my waist, pulling me closer. I melted into his body, my lips slowly parting as a tiny moan escaped my mouth.

I knew we had just outrun a police raid. I knew there was a

The Summer We Ran

crew of local cops just beyond the tree line. But when Grant's lips met mine, all logic went away. It was impossible for me to pull away from a place I wanted to spend my life exploring.

He kissed me gently, his lips firm against mine, and I reciprocated with an unfamiliar urgency. Up to this point, my life was full of plans and checklists. Grant erased all of that with a single meeting of our lips. Once I had a taste, I only wanted more, foreign feelings of reckless desire overtaking my body.

He lowered his forehead as our lips slowly inched apart and he said, "We have to keep moving."

"I know," I said, even though I didn't. He made me forget everything.

His hands cupped my face and he whispered into my ear, "I am very, very glad I came here tonight."

I laughed as I said, "You're crazy. We almost got arrested and you're glad you came to the world's worst bonfire?"

He held my hand, leading me through the woods as he said, "Yes."

We walked the long way around the property, both of us trying to be as quiet as possible. When we got to the back gate of Ms. Milton's property, I kissed his cheek and said, "See you around."

Grant grabbed my hand and said, "I will definitely see you around, Tess Murphy."

I wanted to ask when and where and find out exactly how long I was going to have to wait before his lips would be on mine again, but instead I said, "Cool."

When I got home, my mother was asleep. I tiptoed carefully up the loft stairs, but I must have woken her up.

"Good night?" she asked sleepily.

"Best night of my life," I said.

It was true. That summer, Grant was all of my bests. Best night. Best kiss. Best person.

My mother rolled over, the shadow of her small body bouncing against the cottage wall. "And just think, your life is only getting started, baby. Everything is going to change this summer," my mother said.

She was right. Although not all change was good.

Five

JULY 2021

As I open the front door, I hear the sound of a woman's voice coming from my kitchen. "Slower. A little to the left. That's perfect. Hold that position."

My bag falls to the floor and I cautiously peer around the corner. I'm home earlier than expected, exhaustion finally taking its toll. Mara gave me the night off and I want to take a shower, shove food into my mouth, and collapse onto my bed. I'm too tired to deal with whatever is happening in my kitchen, though this doesn't seem good. Dean's car is parked in the driveway and he didn't mention any plans tonight. Especially not plans involving additional women in my house.

When I walk into the kitchen, I see Dean is standing next to the stove, the sleeves of his button-down shirt rolled midway up his forearms. He's holding a wooden spoon, stirring what I assume is batter. There's an entire crew of people making microscopic adjustments to his hair, the flower arrangement on our countertops, the lighting. And there is one commanding female photographer suggesting that my husband "grip the spoon tighter."

"What is happening?" I ask, unable to erase the humor from my question.

The manufactured smile on Dean's face immediately disappears. "Ask Mara," Dean mumbles.

Mara mentioned that Dean agreed to some interview she'd been pushing for, but I had no idea that was happening today, or that it involved a photo shoot.

I walk over and kiss Dean on the cheek and quietly ask, "How long has this been going on?"

"Hours," he says.

A makeup artist quickly swoops in and applies powder to Dean's cheek where my lips smudged her smooth canvas.

"What have you been doing that whole time?" I whisper.

"Cooking and talking. My two favorite things," he says, his sarcasm oblivious to everyone in the room except me.

I hate cooking. Dean knows this. It's not his favorite pastime either, but he's mastered a few recipes. A survival tactic, most likely. A couple can live on only so much takeout.

I move back toward the hallway, but not before the photographer asks, "Can we get a few shots of you next to Dean? He could hold out the spoon while the candidate licks it?"

"Absolutely not," Dean and I say at the same time.

"I haven't had hair and makeup," I explain. I also don't think licking things is the way I want to win an election. I have no idea where Mara found this photographer, but I'm questioning her judgment.

"We could pop you in the chair," the photographer quickly replies. "The glam squad we used for Dean is still here."

I look over at Dean and mouth "glam squad."

He rolls his eyes and mumbles, "I don't want to talk about it."

I turn toward the crew, using my most professional campaign voice, and say, "It's been a very long day. Any chance we can wrap this up? If you have other questions for Dean, please send them to Mara and she'll make sure you get whatever you need." I add on a giant smile and the message is conveyed. The crew starts packing up and I watch as Dean finally relaxes.

Once everyone is out of our house, I deadbolt the door and slump against the wall.

"I need a shower," I say, as I slowly walk upstairs.

"I'm joining you." He holds on to my hips and follows me into the bathroom. "I need to scrub this stuff off." He runs his hand through his over-gelled hair and it stands straight up.

"I cannot believe you agreed to this."

He shrugs and explains, "Mara is very scary when you say no."

I nod in agreement.

Our shower is quick, both of us too spent for any extracurricular activities beyond washing. I want to be the woman who comes home from a long day and has sex with her husband in the shower. But I also want comfy clothes and Netflix on my one night off in the last three weeks.

My campaign schedule has been brutal, as we've tried to cover more ground than Grant's camp. I have attended every county fair, eating my weight in funnel cake and placing ribbons on prized pigs. I've started the day at local diners, visited all the major agricultural processing plants that dot the southern tip of the state, and listened to teachers explain how budget cuts impact their classrooms. Nights are spent at town halls or dinners with donors.

We'll see if it works, because it isn't the typical Democratic strategy. Since I grew up in southwest Virginia, I'm hoping that the voters there will connect with me more than a hedge fund manager who spent most of his life in Washington, D.C. It's impossible to predict the changing tides, the tiny connections that can domino into voter surges. But I'm going to squeeze every drop of my energy into trying.

For one night, I get to sit inside my house instead of churning through another meeting. There is no place I feel more myself than inside the home Dean and I made together. That's why Mara sent me here instead of to the roadside motel where I was supposed to spend the night.

As students at the University of Virginia, Dean and I would wander the Belmont neighborhood of Charlottesville, eyeing our favorite houses, commenting on the best porch swings and arched doorways. We would invent stories about the families living inside. "A yard this neat makes me nervous. I bet they alphabetize their pantry," Dean would joke. "Maybe they're foreign spies trying to blend in. The level of perfection is concerning," I agreed. Our stories became more and more elaborate, making it difficult to remember that we'd made it all up. When we eventually bought a bungalow in the neighborhood, we were disappointed by the mundanity of our neighbors. The truth is rarely as exciting as lies.

I step out of the shower and throw on my worn UVA sweatshirt. Sometimes I like to pretend I'm still that girl, the college student who fell for Dean. Two history majors debating whether Napoleon Bonaparte would defeat Julius Caesar. We'd spend hours after class nursing our beers and our mutual crushes, discussing hypothetical battles between world leaders. Dean continues to have these discussions with the high-schoolers he teaches each year. I wonder what my life would be like if I had followed a similar path, teaching kids about history instead of trying to make it.

Dean wraps a towel around his waist, finally looking like himself again, the makeup and gel rinsed down the drain. He tells me that there are leftovers from the photo shoot and we both head downstairs to eat.

"I do not deserve you," I say to Dean.

"I know," he replies, smirking. "At some point, when you aren't so tired that you look ready to keel over, you will find a way to make it up to me." Dean's eyebrows shoot up.

"Did you have something particular in mind?" I ask.

"Since I had to sit in a makeup chair, I think it's only fair you have to wear that costume I want."

"Absolutely not," I say, shaking my head back and forth.

"Oh, yes," he says, drawing out each word.

"Dean, I'm not dressing up as Martha Washington for your AP history class."

"Yes, you are. I spent four hours with that crew answering all kinds of bullshit questions about what a First Gentleman would cook for the governor. You can wear a wig for one afternoon."

"Fine. But now we are both furious with Mara."

"Yes, we are," Dean says, pulling out two plates from the cabinet.

"Thank you for participating in the most humiliating and sexist interview of all time." I hold his face between my hands and stand on my tiptoes as I kiss his lips. "Which is saying a lot, coming from a female candidate."

"You are welcome," Dean says, deepening our kiss. He pulls me into a tight hug. "You are going to eat and then you are going to sleep. Sit," he orders.

I comply because I cannot think of anything better than eating dinner with my husband. He places a plate in front of me and I moan. Biscuits dripping in butter and drizzled with honey, a salty, pink slice of ham, and green beans flecked with bacon.

"Who made this?" I ask.

"I did. That was the whole point of this interview. Apparently, Cecilia Alexander made a quinoa salad with beets."

"You win."

"You're damn right I win. I'm a one-trick pony. But it's a good trick," Dean says.

I take a bite of the meal Dean prepared, my favorite meal. It's so familiar and comforting that it almost makes me forget the mention of Grant's wife. Dean is too good for me.

When my mother was sick, she gave Dean a stack of handwritten recipes. "All of Tess's favorites," she had said. "My daughter will never sit still long enough to cook. But food is the way I've taken care of her my whole life. It's your turn now." My mother died before Dean and I got married, but when she gave him her prized recipes, that was more monumental than any giving away at the end of an aisle.

Dean sits beside me and we dig in. The room is mostly silent, except for the sounds of enjoyment escaping from my mouth.

I've made a significant dent in the plate when Dean says, "I don't know where it all goes."

"What?" I ask between bites.

"The food. I've watched you eat two breakfasts every morning this week so that you can meet with double the voters and I could still pick you up with one arm."

I shrug. "It's genetics. My mother was scrappy. So am I."

"You're like a mini garbage disposal," he says.

I grab a bite of biscuit off his plate and say, "Yep."

I lean back, looking around our kitchen and thinking about the comfortable life we've created. It's all about to change if I win, when I win, and Dean has never once faltered. His support is the one constant in my life. I wrap my arms around his neck as I say, "Thank you for taking care of me, Dean."

"It's the first husband's duty," he says, feigning somberness. He grabs our plates and walks them over to the sink as he asks, "Are you okay? This schedule has been intense, even by your scrappy standards."

"I'm okay. It's important. The more people I meet, the better our chances."

"I don't know much about campaign strategy, but I wholeheartedly agree with that one. Everyone who meets you loves you."

"Not everyone," I say with a sideways smirk.

Dean laughs, knowing I'm referring to my failed speaking engagement at his high school. Half the audience was asleep. The only question I was asked was whether the lunch schedule was different because of the mandatory assembly.

"Teenagers are a tough crowd," he says. "The career day speaker last year was a retired football player. You're no pro athlete, Tess."

"Obviously."

Dean sits back at the table and pulls me onto his lap. "What's bothering you?"

I look up, worry creasing my face. It has been weeks of packed schedules and lurking fears, and, if I'm honest, I don't know if I'm pushing so hard to help the campaign or to occupy my mind. I needed this night off, but without the distraction of being Candidate Tess, my anxiety is boiling over.

"I'm afraid I'll ruin everything," I finally say.

His arms tighten around my waist. "Like what? Name one thing."

"Us. What if this election ruins us?" I whisper, still unable to meet Dean's eyes.

He shakes his head. "It's not possible," he says gently. "You're already doing things you don't want to do. Like stupid interviews. This is just the beginning, Dean. Everything is going to change. And we have a good life."

"You're right," he says. "We have a good life. But you are destined for greatness, Tess. I'd stand in front of a hundred stoves if it meant helping you get there. Besides, we're stronger than this election."

I swallow because Dean would do anything for me. And I can't even tell him the truth. He doesn't know about the girl I was that summer; he believes in the woman I pretend to be now.

"I don't know if I can do this," I confess.

"We've been through tough spots before." Dean's voice softens, and I can tell he doesn't want to revisit the fights that almost tore us apart. "If we got through that, we can get through anything."

The problem with getting married young is that you assume too much and discuss too little. For us, it was the topic of children. Dean and I rehashed the same argument for years, often ending with one of us sleeping on the couch, the other becoming a silent-treatment expert. He wanted a family; kids weren't part of my plan. He assumed I'd change my mind. We went around in circles, and eventually, Dean gave up. Maybe when I started approaching forty, he didn't think it was a battle worth fighting anymore. Or maybe he loved me more than he desired a child. But I don't want to think about the worst moments of my marriage as proof of its strength.

Dean's trying to comfort me, but instead I'm even more unsettled. I nod and say, "You're right," trying to erase the tremble in my voice.

"Don't let this guy rattle you."

"What do you mean?" My eyes dart across the room.

"I can tell you're worried about Grant Alexander."

"You can?"

"When you first walked onstage at the debate. You almost seemed scared to shake his hand," Dean says.

"Pre-debate jitters," I lie.

"No. I've seen you before at a debate. This was different. He rattles you. I don't know why. You're smarter, more qualified, and—"

I cut Dean off. I can't listen to him tell me I'm a good person when I know the opposite.

"It's not him. It's not Grant who rattles me. It's the office. Governor is a big deal."

"You are a big deal, Tess. You are the most impressive person I have ever met. You deserve this."

I know I should tell Dean everything now. This is the time for me to come clean. But that's the problem with lies. Their inertia pulls too strongly, and it becomes easier to continue down the same thorny path. In my experience, the truth often means losing love, not keeping it. And I can't afford to lose Dean. I know it's a mistake, but I do it anyway. I keep quiet.

Besides, the lie that Grant wasn't a part of my life is almost impossible to unweave. If I'm honest and tell the real story, from the day I first met Grant until now, Dean will know how much of myself I hid away. Because when I first met Dean, I was too fragile to accept the truth of how my relationship with Grant altered everything about me.

"You need some rest," Dean says. "You'll feel better in the morning."

I nod and stand up. As I walk toward the stairs, I turn back. Dean is still sitting. "Aren't you coming up?"

He shakes his head. "I have some stuff to do in the garage."

"Manly stuff?" I ask. "Something to compensate for all the makeup-wearing this afternoon?"

"You're hilarious," he deadpans. "The magazine wants to run some of your mother's recipes alongside the article. I know her old cookbook is in a box out there somewhere. I'm going to dig through your hoarder's paradise for the world's worst magazine article."

"I'm so sorry," I say. "I'll come help."

"No. You need to sleep. Plus, if you come, we'll be there all night while you sift through the elementary school report cards your mother insisted on keeping. I'll find the recipe for your mother's Brunswick stew."

"You're sure you don't need help?" I ask.

He nods and walks toward the garage.

"Thank you, Dean. I love you."

"I know," he says over his shoulder. "You're one lucky woman."

"The luckiest," I whisper to myself, wondering how long that will last.

Six

JULY 1996

"You need a hat, Tess. Your cheeks are pink."

I looked up at the sun, already high and hot even though it was still morning. "I ran out this morning without it. I'll be okay."

"Nonsense," Kay said. "I've got plenty inside. Besides, I could use a break. Come." She stood up and I followed, knowing it was easier to go along with Kay Alexander than try to fight her on something.

It had been a few weeks since I started working for Kay. There was a rhythm to our days that I came to enjoy, and despite the perpetual dirt covering my body, my mother was relieved I was occupied.

I was surprised by how happy we both were in this place that was so different than anything we'd ever known, surrounded by a culture of wealth that made us seem like foreigners in our simplicity.

My mother worked for rich people before, especially at the Homestead. Whenever she came home from those shifts, she'd mumble complaints about being invisible. She refused to even let me consider applying for a job at the hotel. "It's not a world where you belong," she'd say. We didn't belong in Ms. Milton's world either, but at least we felt welcome.

I loved my early mornings, helping my mother with breakfast preparations, and then walking to the Alexander house, where I got to watch the summer come alive. The heather bloomed tiny purple flowers, the yellow black-eyed Susans scattered across the fields. It took about thirty minutes to trek across the properties. My mother offered her car, but I knew she needed it for grocery runs. Besides, I liked to walk alongside the sunrise.

I kept my head down, focusing on my job. Kay seemed to trust my abilities more and more. At least I thought that was the case, because she spent less time in the gardens and more time occupying herself upstairs.

But this morning, we worked together for a few hours, pruning the new growth on the forsythia bushes that created an explosion of yellow in the spring and a green fence in the summer. Sweat beaded down our foreheads as the sun's heat intensified. We left the pile of debris and headed inside in search of a hat.

I followed Kay upstairs, tiptoeing since Grant would still be asleep. Kay stomped. "Don't cater to his lazy schedule," she said. "He needs to wake up."

We entered her bedroom and I gasped as Kay turned on the light to her walk-in closet. My old bedroom would fit in the space where she stored her shoes. I stared at rows of beaded evening gowns and shelves of handbags. Diamond tennis bracelets and chandelier earrings hung in a jewelry cabinet. I couldn't imagine why one person would ever need so much stuff. I glanced over at her, a woman dressed simply in worn linen and a straw hat, knowing that she would look equally comfortable draped in jewels and a silk gown. I tugged the hem of my cutoff shorts and knew that would never be me. I wasn't sure if I was disappointed or relieved.

Kay pointed to a wall where various hats hung on pegs. There were beautiful woven hats with ribbons around the brim. They looked like something I saw women wear to the Kentucky Derby. "Pick one," Kay said.

I shook my head. "Oh no, I couldn't." One minute in a hat like that and it would blow off my head and be ruined. "I'll just take a ball cap."

"Suit yourself," she said, opening a bottom drawer filled with caps in every color. I searched for the most worn and picked it up.

"That was Grant's Little League team," Kay said, smiling longingly.

I slipped my ponytail through the back of the hat. "It fits," I said.

Kay pulled the brim of the cap downward as she said, "Good. Now that beautiful face of yours will be protected."

I stared at the floor as I said, "Thank you."

"You are beautiful, Tess. Get used to hearing it. Accept a compliment with grace. It will serve you well in the future."

I looked up and forced myself to smile as I said, "Yes, ma'am." I wanted to believe Kay. I wanted to feel beautiful, but standing next to her, I just felt silly.

"Follow me," she said, walking into her bathroom. She led me over to a vanity with bright lightbulbs and every possible item of makeup. "Sit," she ordered.

I sat on her stool, the silk upholstery smooth against my thighs as the blazing lights illuminated every millimeter of my skin.

Kay spun me around, removed my hat, and got to work. She pulled out brushes and began painting my face with her jewel box of cosmetics. I followed each of her commands as she told me to "close my eyes" and "look up" and "stop squirming."

Midway through this makeover, Kay laughed. "This isn't torture, Tess. It's supposed to be fun."

"I have no idea how to act right now," I said, my body finally relaxing.

"You've never had your makeup done?" Kay asked.

"Not unless you count sharing Lip Smackers in the girls' bathroom."

Kay's face pulled tightly. "You are almost an adult. Your makeup should not be flavored like bubblegum." Kay began applying mascara on my lashes, and although she said it wasn't torture, trying to hold still while she pointed a wand at my eyeball felt a little bit like it.

"Your mother never taught you about makeup?" Kay asked.

I shook my head. "She doesn't wear it. Never has."

"You remind me so much of myself at this age."

I snorted because it was impossible that this polished, glamorous woman saw even a sliver of herself in me.

She turned my chin to swipe powder on my cheeks and stared into my eyes. "It's true. I grew up here, and unlike Madeline, I wasn't shuttled back and forth to D.C. I'm a country girl just like you. The makeup and jewels and gowns came when Richard entered my life. I learned how to adapt to what was expected." She didn't say this proudly. There was an unexplained sadness in her voice.

I didn't outright disagree, because it was flattering that a woman like Kay thought we were similar. But I doubted she ever clipped coupons or had the lights shut off in this grand home that happened to be located in the countryside.

I tilted my head and said, "Our *country girl* definitions are different."

I saw the realization on her face as she nodded. "Yes. I'm sure there are some differences. Substantial differences in the ways we grew up. All I'm saying is that I know what it feels like to be thrust into a different world."

I nodded. That's exactly how my mom was feeling that summer too. One week, she had to let a six-course meal go to waste because Madeline took off on a last-minute business trip to California. And then the next, she was helping her pack for a quick getaway to St. Barts, which we had to look up on a map to see where in the world Madeline was.

And yet, Kay's house made me feel comfortable even though I was there only because she hired me for a job. I was sitting in her bathroom, and she spoke to me as if, someday, I'd belong instead of just being employed in this world.

She swept one last brush of powder across my forehead. "Well, another day, I'll give you a lesson, but for today, look at the results." Kay spun me around and I faced the mirror.

I smiled, and this time it was completely genuine. I looked like myself, only better. The gold flecks in my brown eyes seemed to shine. My lips looked fuller and there was a smoothness to my skin that I thought existed only on magazine covers. I turned my head from side to side, examining every angle of this new version of my face.

"The most important thing to remember is that it's your face. You choose to cover it in makeup or let your skin shine in the sun. You do it for yourself. Not to impress someone.

Certainly never to impress a man. We have only one life, Tess. Don't make decisions based on some false belief that anyone else's opinion matters more than your own."

I tried to hear what Kay was saying, but mostly, I couldn't stop staring at my face and thinking how much I liked the way it looked and wondering whether Grant would like it too.

"I might call it a day, Tess. The sun is getting to me. Do you mind hauling away the rest of the debris? It needs to go into the burn pile."

"Of course not," I said, standing.

Kay had a wistful look on her face. I realized how fleeting her smiles had been the last week. Grant mentioned that his father stopped by. I never saw Richard Alexander, but his presence was obvious. For days after he left, Kay was on edge and Grant was grumpy.

"I'll take a long bath," Kay said. "Maybe even go into town for lunch today. I'll call Madeline and see if she can join. She's been working so much, I've hardly seen her this summer. She's worse than Richard these days."

Spending this morning with Kay, I realized that it was nice to see her back to herself, or at least back to the person I first met. We spent so much time gardening together that I felt like I knew her, but I supposed I didn't really know Kay Alexander at all.

We both heard a door creak open and a familiar clomping down the stairs.

"Good. He's waking up," she said. "Do not let him touch my roses."

"I know, I know," I said, eager to get downstairs.

Grant was not allowed to touch Kay's flowers. She referred to it as the Rose Massacre of '85. Apparently, a seven-year-old

Grant had butchered her prize roses when he thought it was a good idea to use the petals to create a jumping pit. Despite Grant's promises that he could be trusted, Kay refused to let him near her flowers. I didn't blame her. Kay's roses were some of the most beautiful I'd ever seen. Grant had laughed it off, explaining that only his mother would think it was punishment to prohibit working in the garden.

I glanced at myself once more in the mirror before leaving Kay's bedroom and heading downstairs. Grant would be waiting.

Most mornings, he hung out while I worked. We discussed books, and our friends, and sometimes our parents. But mostly he lay in the grass beside me, a comfortable silence between us, until he broke it with a joke that made me laugh so hard, I had to stop pruning the flowers.

Grant spent afternoons at the ice-cream shop in town, scooping treats for desperate children and starving mothers. He hated every second of it, but it was part of his summer punishment, getting some type of employment. Grant would come home in the early evening with the best stories of town gossip and ice-cream meltdowns. Kay spent late afternoons walking barefoot among her flowers, snipping blooms for her table. She'd set the flowers in the outdoor dining area, and I'd find plates of cheese and crackers, ripe olives, and nuts, and always a bottle of wine. Kay frequently invited me to stay, which made me uncomfortable at first, but after a few days, I started giddily accepting, trying cheeses I'd never heard of, watching the sky turn to purple. The three of us would sit, snacking and chatting, and it seemed like a place where I was meant to be, which was a dangerous feeling. I'd leave before Kay finished the bottle of wine, but I'd see it empty the next morning, along with the dishes on the table. It was the first thing I'd do when I arrived at the Alexander house. I cleaned up any evidence of the night before. Messes led to regrets, and I didn't want Kay to regret my presence in her life.

"Good morning," Grant said. He had pillow lines on his face and clothes still settling on his body. He liked to pretend he had been awake for hours, but I could tell that he'd just pulled himself out of bed. For me.

"It's almost noon, Grant."

"You sound like my mother," Grant said. "Although maybe you're both right. I'm starving."

Grant's eyebrows shot up and he looked over his shoulder before grabbing my hands and pulling me against his solid body. He bent down and kissed me, slowly at first and then with more urgency.

For the last few weeks, I'd woken up to the memory of Grant's kisses; I'd gone to sleep dreaming about more of them. It turned out that my unlucky streak ended. After three horrible kisses, my fourth, and fifth, and all of the dozen after that had been perfect. It was hard to keep track of how many times we kissed when every stolen moment was spent plotting how we could get our lips together.

We broke apart at the sound of footsteps about to enter the room. I'd hoped Kay would stay upstairs a little longer. I loved talking to her, but I loved being alone with Grant even more.

As soon as Kay walked into the kitchen, a nervous energy filled the room.

"I just got off the phone with Madeline. She is beside herself," Kay said.

Grant rolled his eyes behind his mother. But I politely asked, "What happened?"

I hoped I hadn't done something wrong. I hoped my mother hadn't done something wrong. I didn't want this summer to end any sooner than it had to.

Kay scurried around the kitchen, placing items in her purse—a container of Tic Tacs, a hair scrunchie, sunglasses, and her large bifold wallet. "It turns out that a few of the stable boys she hired were arrested. They had taken shotguns from Madeline's property. The sheriff returned the guns today. The barn manager never mentioned missing guns. He only told Madeline that they needed to hire more staff since some of the boys stopped showing up for work. Her employees were in jail and she had no idea. I'm going to head over to Madeline's to see if I can calm her down."

My eyes whipped toward Grant, but he was staring at the floor.

"Did you know anything about this, Tess?" Kay asked.

I swallowed, unsure how much to say. Grant finally looked up, his body behind his mother's as he shook his head slowly, mouthing, "No."

I answered as honestly as I could. "I had no idea anyone took guns from Ms. Milton. What's she going to do?"

Kay shrugged. "Right now, she wants to fire everyone. I'll admit, someone wasn't doing their job if a bunch of teenagers got access to guns that should be locked away. My guess is that she'll be looking for a new barn manager."

I felt a wave of panic. I didn't know what kind of responsibilities my mother had as the house manager, but could she be fired too?

Kay continued, "Madeline is lucky that the police arrested those boys before they hurt her. She really should do better background checks on the people she hires."

I found this to be an incredibly ironic statement, given that

Kay hired me without knowing anything other than the fact that I could identify a few flowers. But I decided that this was not the time to speak up.

Kay walked toward the back door, looking out at the garden as she said, "I'm heading over to Madeline's now. Do you want a ride home?" Kay asked.

I shook my head. "I haven't finished hauling the debris."

Grant quickly added, "I can give you a ride home on my way in to work." Before his mother could say anything, Grant added, "I won't touch any flowers. I promise."

Kay nodded and waved goodbye, preoccupied with the agenda of soothing Madeline.

Grant and I waited in silence until we heard Kay's car driving over gravel. The space between us evaporated. He pulled me in for a kiss, starting with my lips and then trailing down my neck. "Finally," he whispered.

Despite the thrill of Grant's body next to mine, the sandpaper of his stubble rubbing against my cheek, my mind was elsewhere. I couldn't stop thinking about Kay's news. Grant sensed this and pulled back.

"You okay?" he asked.

"I feel horrible. All those kids are in jail and the manager could lose his job."

Grant ran his hand through his hair, leaving it standing up before it flopped back to the side. "I know. It's intense, right?"

I looked at him suspiciously. "The SATs are intense. This is life-changing. For the rest of their lives, this will be something that follows them. It's terrifying."

I'd seen the kids in handcuffs, but I didn't think anyone would be charged. Or maybe I was too focused on Grant's lips to consider the consequences of that night.

Grant chewed on the inside of his cheek. I learned he did

this when he was nervous to tell me something. Like when he said staring into my eyes made him forget what he was going to say. I didn't understand why Grant would be nervous.

But then he said, "They deserve it."

"Deserve what?" I asked, unaware of the weight of this simple question.

"They deserve to get fired. They deserve to be in jail."

"Grant, we were at that party too. Should we have been arrested?"

"We weren't chugging beers and shooting weapons."

"The police arrested more than just the kids with the guns," I said, my eyes darting across the room with its china dishes and marble counters. I didn't know what made me feel less like I belonged: this house or his words. "It could have been me."

Grant joked, "Well, I know, you froze like a rabbit. It is a good thing I was there to grab you." He meant to comfort me, but it did the opposite. I sat on the edge of so many different emotions with a person I was just getting to know.

I looked at Grant and asked, "And if you weren't there, and I was sitting in a jail cell right now? How would you feel? Would you think I deserved it? Or if you ran slower and they arrested both of us? What then?"

Grant tossed his hair back with little effort. "But none of that happened," he said. I began to realize that Grant's whole life required little effort. "Why are you worrying about this?" he asked.

"Why aren't you? You're eighteen, Grant. Forget goats in a gym. Do you think Princeton would let you come this fall if you were arrested at a bonfire?"

Grant shrugged. "But I wasn't arrested, so I guess I don't have to worry about that."

His nonchalance frustrated me, but I recognized that he never knew any different. I tried to explain. "Sometimes it feels like life is so fragile. One mistake can change the whole trajectory of our future. I guess I feel like my place in this world is a lot more precarious than yours."

"Tess, that was not one mistake. Those kids made a series of mistakes that you had nothing to do with. If you were unlucky enough to be arrested, you would have been released right away. You weren't drinking. You didn't have a gun."

"No, if I'd been arrested, I'd still be sitting in a cell. I have no doubt you would have been released. Your family can afford to hire a lawyer. Your mother probably knows the sheriff. A few phone calls and you'd be back in your own bed. But my life is nothing like that."

"Tess, let's not fight about hypotheticals. The bad guys got arrested. And I made lunch," he said. He gestured to a picnic basket sitting on the counter that I hadn't noticed before and reached for my hand. "Can you stop worrying so that I can take you someplace special?"

I looked at him, with his genuine smile and sparkling eyes. I wanted to stop worrying. But I knew how close I had been to wrecking my future just by attending the bonfire, and that was hard to shake.

Instead of letting it ruin my day, I pushed those fears away. Because I was seventeen, and there was a boy who packed me a picnic, whose kisses made it hard to focus on anything but the feeling of our heartbeats synching.

"Come on, I want to take you down to the river," Grant said. "You up for a walk?"

"Yes," I agreed, trying to let the conversation about the arrests drift away.

I motioned toward the giant fruit basket in front of Grant and said, "Give me an apple. I need some fuel for the walk. One of us did a lot of work this morning."

"I'm going to let that subtle dig slide," Grant said, handing me the apple. "Because even though I left the manual labor to you, I did prepare a feast. So I'm not completely useless."

"When did you prepare this feast?"

"Last night. I planned ahead," Grant said, wiggling his eyebrows.

Grant and I walked outside, his fingers laced with mine. We hiked to the river, along a path cut into the tall swaths of grass. The sun was high. Gone were the gentle June days. The temperature had settled comfortably in the high nineties, leaving my clothes clinging to my body. Grant kept grinning, nudging my side, and I wondered what exactly he had in this basket, because teenage boys weren't this excited about lunch.

By the time we got to the river, I was a mess of dirt and sweat. Grant unpacked a blanket, spreading it on the soft bank. I was starving, but the running water was too tempting. As Grant set up the picnic, I kicked off my socks and shoes and waded into the icy water.

The spot was perfect. There were giant oak trees dotting the riverbank, a slight bend with the stream rushing over rocks. A rope hung from one of the branches and I wondered how many days Grant spent here, swinging into the river. The mountains in the distance stretched out beyond the reaches of my vision and I thought if I grew up here, I'd never leave this place. I wanted to make a little house in that spot and wake up every morning to that view, bathing in that river.

I turned to climb up the bank and join Grant on the blanket, but he was already easing himself into the water, a mischievous grin on his face. He was too quick for me and before I knew it, he scooped me up, twirling me around and then lowering me dangerously close to the water.

"Grant, do not drop me. I cannot go back to my mother in wet clothes."

"Then maybe we should take our clothes off. For the sake of decency," he said, laughing as my body hovered precariously over the rushing river.

"Threats are not the way to get a girl naked, Grant."

"Oh really. What's a better strategy?"

"Well, I can't speak for those big-city girls, but I expect some romance," I said with false confidence.

Grant lowered me down, my body sliding against his. The river water was so cold that I should have been shivering. But my skin against his left me burning.

Grant kissed my cheek and then whispered in my ear, "That's what the picnic is for."

I looked over at the riverbank, where Grant had a spread of food prepared. There were sandwiches and bags of chips and a big plate of cookies that I hoped he bought somewhere because I didn't trust Grant's ability to follow a recipe. He even managed to gather some flowers.

It was just lunch, but it was also so much more. It was the first time someone other than my family had done something for me, not out of obligation but out of want.

All of our physical interactions had been under scrutiny or the threat of scrutiny. Quick kisses before his mother emerged from the house, fingers brushed under the table, sideways hugs that allowed us to touch without garnering suspicion.

But now we were alone. It felt exhilarating and terrifying.

Grant led me to the blanket and pulled me down beside

him. We were kissing and his hands were moving over my body. I was on sensory overload, keenly aware of the location of every one of our body parts. We were lying side by side and his left leg swung over mine. His hand rested on the small of my back and then slipped under my shirt, moving toward my bra.

I felt the breeze prickle my skin as he moved on top of me, my entire body electrifying. I could kiss Grant for hours. I no longer needed food. My air intake requirements were minimal. All I wanted was the sensation of Grant's lips pressed against mine, the feel of his warm mouth trailing across my neck, my collarbone, and finally back to my swollen lips.

Grant leaned back and pulled off his shirt, grabbing it from the nape of his neck and removing it in one fluid motion. It was probably something he'd done a thousand times, but it left me speechless. I'd obviously seen a boy without a shirt, but I'd never seen a boy without a shirt while he was straddling my body. His body was harder and more muscular than I'd imagined. Suddenly, he didn't seem like the teenage boy swinging me around the river. He seemed so mature. And I felt very self-aware of how inexperienced I was in all of this. With someone who clearly wasn't.

He leaned down and kissed me gently, cupping my face and drawing me toward him. "You are so beautiful, Tess."

He moved to pull up my shirt and I inadvertently tensed, instinctively pushing my shirt back down. I wanted to stay tangled in that moment of intensity, but my nerves wouldn't let me. The air seemed to shift, all the heat between us evaporating. Grant rolled off me, not away from me but clearly inserting space between our bodies.

I sighed, wanting to reverse time but knowing I couldn't. Up until this moment, I'd only dreamed of having a hot, smart guy lying on top of me. Clearly into me. But, of course, my swirling mind of logistics and insecurity messed up my dreams.

"Grant, I'm not . . ." I stuttered, embarrassed to admit what I was about to say. "I'm new to all of this. I haven't . . ."

I saw a momentary flash across his face, surprise, maybe embarrassment. I was still memorizing his expressions and this wasn't one I'd seen before.

"Shit. I had no idea." Grant looked away, running his hand through his hair and leaving it sticking up in a million different directions.

For a moment, I worried that my virginity and my mouth full of confessions and lack of action had ruined whatever was developing between us. But Grant fixed it for me. Above all else that summer, I remembered believing that Grant could fix any of our problems.

He turned to me, reaching for my hand and kissing the back of it as he said, "I'd never rush you, Tess. We're on your timeline. Let's eat lunch. All we have to do is eat."

"We don't have to just eat," I said, my eyebrows raising. We kissed again, slowly at first and then with more urgency. I could feel his hands moving across my body, tingling warmth spreading from every brush of his fingers. I grabbed the hem of my shirt and started to pull it upward, but Grant's hand stopped me.

He groaned as he said, "You're making a hard situation even harder."

My eyebrows shot up and I smirked, feeling him press against me. He kissed my lips softly and then my cheek as he said, "We should take this slow, Tess. It's a big deal." He disentangled our bodies, creating unwanted space between us. "As much as it is killing me, we should stop. Your first time should be special."

A part of me was relieved, but another part of me didn't want to stop. I thought that maybe a picnic by the river was as special as it got. Especially with someone like Grant. I leaned toward him, hoping my actions changed his mind, but he shook his head.

"Tess, I care too much about you to rush this. When you're ready, and there is a bed instead of a questionably dirty blanket, and I don't have to leave you to serve ice cream to whiny kids, then we will do it."

"I didn't know the blanket was dirty," I said, smiling.

"I'm an eighteen-year-old boy. Do you think any of my blankets are clean?"

"Eww, Grant. I can't believe I almost had sex with you. Dodged that bullet," I joked.

He reached over and pulled me onto his lap, tickling me until I could barely breathe. When I begged him to stop, he finally relented and said, "Let's eat. You must be starving."

"I am," I said, reaching for a sandwich. The tension and excitement frizzling between us had now transferred to my appetite. We both dove into our lunches. He even remembered to put pickles and mustard on my ham sandwich.

"I love it here," I said between bites. "It would have been such a great place to lose my virginity. Too bad."

Grant shook his head, "Tess, I am using every ounce of my restraint."

"So, you're saying you want to have sex with me, just not right now, because you are trying to be a good guy?"

Grant nodded slowly.

"Okay, just clearing things up. Did you have a particular date in mind when you think you will want to have sex?"

Grant shifted uncomfortably between bites. "I will want to

have sex with you every minute of every day. But I'm not going to have sex with you until you are 100 percent ready."

I nodded and stopped joking, because he was right. I wasn't ready. And the fact that he could see that left a lump of gratitude in my throat.

"Do you come here a lot?" I asked.

"I used to. I used to come here every day when I was a kid. But it's been a while. I miss the days when I could come here whenever I wanted."

"I'd be here every chance I got."

"*Well, a young man should be cultivating his future, not wasting it away in the woods,*" Grant said, imitating his father, a voice I wasn't sure I ever wanted to hear in person.

"And what exactly does '*cultivating one's future*' entail?" I asked.

"Mostly being around the right people, as far as I can tell." Grant took a bite. I wasn't sure if he was done talking or just thinking about what he wanted to tell me.

After a minute or so, he continued. "My father stopped coming out to Virginia when I was in seventh grade. We used to spend almost every weekend, the summers, and all the holidays here. I don't know what happened between my parents, but something changed. My dad was traveling all the time. My mom never wanted to stay in D.C. They couldn't be in the same room anymore without screaming. It's not like either of them were ever going to win some parenting award, but it became clear that I was an inconvenience to the life they both wanted."

Grant poured us cups of lemonade and continued. "They hired a few nannies to keep track of me in D.C., but I was in middle school and the last thing I wanted was to have a babysitter. I'd spend a few weeks out here during school vacations and the beginning of summer. Then my dad started shipping me off to these 'young leader' retreats that I didn't even apply for, surrounded by kids who were dying to be there and have mock debates. Then there were the private coaches for lacrosse. It was miserable. Every August it was a different camp—Maine, Vermont, Connecticut. If it's full of rich white boys, I've been there."

"Same. I surround myself with rich white boys too," I said, nodding.

He laughed and I was glad because sometimes you need a break from the heaviness of life. Whenever Grant mentioned his father, his heaviness seemed inescapable.

"I guess I never made the connections my father was hoping I'd make," Grant said. "I'm a terrible lacrosse player, and as my father likes to say, I seem to seek out the losers. Each year, he'd sit me down and outline the *'new plan for success,'* including specific friendships I was supposed to make, the grades he expected, the internships I would land."

When Grant repeated his father's instructions and criticisms, his body would tighten. A rigidity came over him and the playfulness in his eyes disappeared.

"Every aspect of his life is calculated with detailed goals, and he forced that same plotting on me," Grant continued. "Nothing like turning fifteen and being handed a bar graph charting your personal failures along with expectations for *'significant improvement in the next fiscal quarter.'* I think he's only moderately less interested in me than in one of the companies he takes over. Don't most fathers high-five and say 'good job'?"

"I have no idea," I said, and it was true. Because I'd never known my father, I had no idea what typical father behavior was. A part of me felt jealous for an instant, for the opportunities that Grant had that I would never in my wildest dreams experience. But it was also very clear that those opportunities came with a high emotional cost, at least for Grant.

"What about your mother?" I asked, still confused as to how she could sit silently while her son was clearly miserable.

"When she moved out here full-time, she just kind of checked out. I'd hear from her once in a while, if my dad was traveling. I'd see her when she came in for parties, but that wasn't really her. That was the woman she pretended to be when my father summoned her. She'd come into D.C., barely speak to my father. They'd go to whatever embassy party or client dinner he needed her to attend, and she'd be gone before I woke up the next morning. Like I said, I don't try to understand their marriage anymore."

"I can't imagine your mother barely speaking. She's the most outspoken person I've met."

"Besides you." Grant elbowed my side.

"Fair point."

"I know," Grant said, "I feel like this summer I'm getting to know a whole new person. I'm still shocked my dad has left me here this long. It's supposed to be a punishment, but it doesn't feel like that."

Grant kissed my neck and I felt my whole body smile. "I'm pretty sure I wouldn't make it on your father's list of the right people," I said.

"You're on my list, Tess. That's all that matters."

I stared at Grant, unsure how to communicate how much his words meant. I spent most of my life feeling invisible. When Grant wrapped me into his world, it made me feel like my life could go in all kinds of unimaginable directions.

"Grant, I'm done eating," I said, wrapping up the remainder of my sandwich.

"Ready for a swim?" he asked. "We can wear our underwear. I can even keep my back to you the entire time?"

"Nope," I said.

"Oh, are you ready to head back? I still have an hour before I have to go to town."

"Nope," I said. "I'm ready."

"Ready for what, Tess?"

"Ready, ready." I raised my eyebrows and shifted onto Grant's lap, wrapping my arms around his neck.

Maybe it was because I couldn't say the word *sex*, or maybe it was because he saw the truth in my body that I was trying to push away. Because I wanted to have sex with Grant, but I was also nowhere near ready.

Grant did the thing that no typical eighteen-year-old boy was capable of doing. He turned me down as gently as possible.

"Tess, this is a big deal. I can't sleep with you."

I looked away, rejection stinging in my eyes. I was afraid I'd ruined the moment. Grant shared feelings about his parents that I suspected he didn't tell many others. It made me want to feel even closer to him. But why would he want to sleep with a virgin when he could sleep with anyone he wanted. I was embarrassed I'd misread the situation.

"That's fine. I get it. No big deal," I said unconvincingly.

I grabbed my shoes and threw them on quickly, careful not to run away but moving fast enough so that he couldn't see the glisten in my eyes.

But Grant was too quick. He grabbed my arm and spun me around.

"Tess, I cannot wait to have sex with you. I just want it to be special. I want to make it special for you."

"Why?" I asked, before I could stop myself.

"Because you say exactly what you are thinking. And the way you listen to me makes me feel like what I have to say matters. For the first time in my life. Because you make me laugh with your quirky facts. Because I've never seen anyone so sexy with mud streaked across her face. Because you are so special to me, Tess," he said, and I felt my heart rise into my throat.

Grant wrapped his arms around my waist as he asked, "Think you can wait for me?"

"I can wait for you, Grant." We fell back on the blanket, kissing with all our clothes on while my body felt like it was going to explode in a million directions.

"I love you," he whispered. We didn't stop kissing. Maybe we both realized that it was too soon, yet nothing could slow the tidal wave of our emotions.

In that moment, I knew I'd do anything he wanted. And that summer I did. Until he asked too much and it destroyed us both.

Seven

JULY 2021

"You're dropping in the polls," Mara says. "You're down five points."

I lean back in the stiff chair of my campaign headquarters office. It's one of those badly upholstered chairs in a jarring shade of orange that looks like it belongs in a roadside motel lobby, which is probably where it was before Mara purchased it to furnish our office. I'd rather be sitting in one of those office chairs that spin, because then I could twirl and pretend to ignore the lecture Mara is about to deliver.

Instead, I reply, "That's to be expected. We knew there would be some dips coming into the fall."

"Not five points." Mara shakes her head. "What's going on with Dean? He hasn't done many events lately. It's an issue."

"You tell me, Mara." I cock my head. "I wasn't the one who forced him to do that interview."

Mara shrugs. "The article wasn't what I thought it would be.

I'll do a better job vetting the profiles in the future." It's a rehearsed statement, lacking genuine remorse. Mara's priorities rarely reflect the emotions of others.

"Dean isn't running for office. His presence shouldn't impact polling," I complain.

"Everything impacts polling. You wear pink lipstick, there's a poll. Toughen up," Mara says with zero sympathy.

I take a deep breath. "I'll talk to Dean about the events."

The problem is that he doesn't want to attend the luncheons and ribbon-cutting ceremonies that Mara schedules. There's a public-facing expectation for the candidate's spouse that she's trying to navigate, but I'm not sure following the standard playbook is going to work anymore.

Ever since the night I found Dean in the kitchen for the photo shoot, things have been different. He's been peppering me with questions about the election, showing me articles about Grant's events, and asking for my reactions to Grant's statements like some reporter in training. Dean wants to dissect my campaign strategy and how I think Grant will respond. There's an uncharacteristic intensity to Dean and it's clear he wants to be seen as valuable to the campaign beyond kitchen photo shoots.

I should have spent more time answering his questions, but after long days and countless strategy discussions with Mara, the last thing I want to do is continue those conversations with my husband. I don't even want to answer the simple question he repeats each night: "What do you think of Grant Alexander?" The more Dean pursues some variation of this topic, the more I withdraw.

I told Dean he should reach out to Mara with his ideas, but that was apparently the wrong response. Because when I try to chat about any topic other than the campaign—the weather, the new coffee shop in town, the latest gossip among the high school teachers—he shuts down those conversations, mumbling, "That's not important."

Dean has never clung to antiquated gender notions, but the interview must have pushed him too far. I never asked him to put his career behind mine, but I know that's been the expectation lately. Maybe he wants a more significant role after hearing one too many "First Gentleman" jokes and recipe requests.

But I crave a break in the intensity of politics and I search for it every night when I come home. Our needs are misaligned, which leads to sparse conversations replacing intimacy with formality. He asks about the campaign and I tell him things are good. He tells me I looked natural holding a baby at a meet and greet and I tell him I rarely feel natural these days. He tells me that he's here to listen whenever I want to talk. I nod, but the reality is that at the end of the day when I have done nothing but talk to hundreds of strangers, sometimes I want silence when I get home to him. Which isn't fair.

Mara seems to sense a shift in my mood. "The expectations on female candidates are unreasonable. After the election, we can take shots for every misogynistic moment of the campaign, but right now, we need to focus on the big picture."

I shake my head. "You're overestimating my tolerance. If we take that many shots, you'll have to wheel me out of the bar."

Mara shrugs. "I'll be too busy dancing on the tables."

My eyes bulge. "Mara, you dance?"

"I have a whole personality you will see only after we win this election. Business now. Tequila and patriarchy-bashing later."

Mara smirks because she knows she's given me even more motivation to win this election. I can't wait to peel back her Ann Taylor pantsuit layers and reveal this inner wild child.

"What's on my calendar for tomorrow?" I ask, smiling.

"A lunch with the service workers' union."

"Maybe Dean can join. Will that help?"

"Yes," Mara says. "But will he be holding your hand or standing on the opposite side of the room?"

"I'll handle it." I look out the window. "Let's discuss the campaign budget." It's a topic Mara can't resist, and I hope it changes the direction of the conversation.

Mara begins rattling off fundraising numbers. I know this is a critical time in the campaign, a lull in public appearances before the fall push. This is when I need to raise as much money as possible. Especially with an opponent like Grant who has seemingly bottomless pockets.

It's a feeling I'm used to—not having as much as the people around me have—even when the differences are as stark as the career public servant versus the hedge fund magnate. I let those differences bother me once and promised myself never again.

"Wasn't there some donor dinner in D.C. tonight?" I ask.

"No. There was a dinner with potential donors, but I declined their invitation," Mara says dismissively.

"Why?"

"It is a bunch of law firm partners in D.C. that are interested in funding key off-cycle elections," Mara explains. "They pulled together money for a race in Texas and another in Georgia. I thought maybe they'd be interested in spending their money a little closer to home, but I was wrong."

"They're not interested in this race?"

"No, they are, but I talked to the Texas campaign manager.

It ended up being way too much effort for way too little money." Mara's face may not express much emotion, but her hands gesticulate wildly enough to reflect her annoyance. "These guys are focused on hearing themselves talk and feeling important. And they demand a lot of candidate time to achieve those goals."

"Mara, I don't think we should be turning down any potential avenues at this stage."

"I agree. But your time is better spent prepping for the union meeting. There's no point driving into D.C. and attending a jerk circle when you have no dick."

I smirk and open my mouth to comment on Mara's metaphor when she says, "I know. I'm going to end up with an HR complaint. Once we're in the governor's mansion—"

I cut her off. "You'll act exactly the same. Don't make promises you can't keep."

Mara rolls her eyes as she reaches for her laptop. "I want to show you the revised talking points for the union lunch." As soon as Mara's computer is turned on, she groans and mumbles, "More of these emails come in every day."

"What emails?" I ask. Mara is quiet as her eyes continue scanning the screen, and I know she's not answering my question for a reason. "What emails?" I ask again, dragging out each word in a bossy tone that I reserve for only my most frustrating interactions with Mara.

"Photos, mostly. At first it was innocent enough. Supporters would send pictures from campaign events."

I watch as Mara scrolls, brows furrowed.

"What kind of pictures are you getting now?" I ask.

Mara hesitates before finally turning her computer around to show me the screen. There's an email from an anonymous account and the attachment includes dozens of pictures, some of them zoomed in on my legs or shoulders, some taken from far away, but a few that seem disturbingly close.

"How long have you been getting these pictures?" I ask.

Mara winces. "Since the campaign started."

"And they're all from the same account?" I hate feeling blindsided, especially by my own campaign.

"No. The accounts are all anonymous, but they're different. You've got quite the fan club." Mara tries to joke, but she must see the concern on my face, because she stands up and walks to my side.

"I don't like this," I say, understating my feelings.

"Me either. I'll reach out to the state troopers again. We'll make sure your events have added security." There's uncharacteristic compassion in Mara's voice.

"Okay. Thank you." I quickly add, "Don't mention this to Dean."

Mara returns to her chair, shifting uncomfortably as she says, "He knows."

"What do you mean he knows?"

"He asked to be included in your security briefings. He's your husband. I agreed."

"Mara, I have so many problems with that statement. But first, I want to know why I'm not included in my security briefings."

"Because it would freak you out," Mara says quickly. "You need to focus on meeting people, not being scared of them."

Despite being angry and uncomfortable about the whole situation, a part of me understands this logic. "I want to be included going forward." My eyes lock on Mara's. This is not a request.

"Fine."

"Does that mean, fine, you will include me, or fine, you hope I will forget?"

Mara scrunches her nose and that's my answer. I'll be lucky if I get a bullet-point version of meeting notes weeks after they happen.

"I'm your buffer. That's my job," Mara says. "If you are looking at creepy pictures, you're not meeting voters. It works out better if I know everything and you know only what is essential."

"Fine," I echo, knowing it's a waste of time to fight with her.

"Although this picture is good," Mara says, smiling. "Maybe we should update the website?"

Mara spins her computer around, showing me a picture where I'm bending over a reception line to shake a child's hand. It's zoomed in on my chest.

I reach for the laptop, staring at my image on the screen. "Mara, you can see down my shirt."

Mara shrugs. "It's a good thing you've got nice tits, then." Mara must see the panic on my face because she quickly adds, "This is common, especially for female candidates. But we are taking this seriously. You will have additional security. Do not worry."

No matter what Mara says, I'm going to worry. This is the part of the job that I hate. The constant watching that comes along with it, the judgment of even the tiniest choice, and the feeling that my entire being is up for public consumption and debate. Sometimes I wonder if the cost of my dream is too high.

"Are you finished with the talking points for tomorrow? I'd like to get some work done today," I say, trying to mask fear with annoyance.

Mara's fingers tap on the keyboard, her eyes darting around

the screen as an uncomfortable silence fills the office. Then Mara's entire body changes, tense anger sweeping across her face. Mara's eyes dart up to mine, a dagger of judgment, before she returns her focus to the computer screen.

"What now? A naked picture?" I joke. "I swear I've kept my clothes on since this election started."

Mara doesn't laugh. Not even a fraction of a smile cracks on her face. Mara's eyes narrow on the screen.

"You look pissed, Mara. What is it?"

Mara doesn't say a word. She stands and walks to the door, reaching for the handle and shutting it firmly to give us privacy in my small, cramped office. I watch as Mara's fingers tremble on the door handle before she turns around.

Mara stalks toward me and spins the computer screen in my direction. Her whispered voice harshly spits, "Start explaining. Right now."

I look up and my heart drops to the floor.

I should have known something like this would happen. I did know. But Grant convinced me otherwise.

On Mara's computer screen is the girl I used to be, tanned from a summer spent soaking in every drop of sunshine. My face is bare but flushed pink—my long, black hair swept back in a sloppy ponytail. Grant is standing at my side, his arm draped casually around my shoulders. His face is in profile because he has just kissed my cheek—his lips inches from the side of my face, a wide grin spreading from his mouth into the crinkle of his eyes. My face is angled toward his, mid-laugh at whatever joke Grant has just made about how he will never be able to stop kissing me. And our eyes, our eyes are locked on each other, unaware that there is anyone or anything else around.

I remember that day. I remember every single moment we

spent absorbed in each other, consumed with the microscopic movements of our bodies together and yet unaware that we were two small people in a giant, fragile world. Especially unaware that someone held on to this picture, waiting until now to establish its existence.

I'm staring at this picture of myself, unable to remain in the present. Because that's always been the danger of Grant, his ability to make me forget myself as I'm pulled into his orbit. It's been too many seconds of silence, and Mara's face hardens with every moment that I'm caught in the past.

I'm disappointed with the quiver in my voice as I ask, "Where did you get this?"

"There is a photo of you and the opposing candidate, as teenagers. A past you have never once mentioned to me. And you're worried about how your campaign manager got a copy? Because that is Grant Alexander, isn't it?" Mara snaps.

I don't answer, because it's pointless. Even though years have passed, our faces are immediately recognizable. I have no idea where to start, or even what to say.

Mara points at the computer. "This picture came in one of those anonymous emails. Someone knows more about my candidate than I do. Which means we're both in serious trouble unless you tell me everything right now, so I can figure out whether this disaster can be fixed."

"I worked for Grant's mother one summer," I stammer.

Mara's eyes narrow. "And?"

She jams her fists into her pockets as she waits for me to continue. But what more can I say? There's no explanation that could fix the disaster Mara foresees. I hesitate for a moment before deciding that maybe this campaign has taken too many pieces of me already. Maybe my only solution is to keep this one thing private.

"There's nothing more. I met him one summer decades ago." I shrug, forcing my body to act as casual as my statement.

"That's not enough information. I can think of about a dozen follow-up questions and I'm not even a reporter. Start talking." Mara's words run together.

"It will go away," I say, trying to convince myself as much as Mara.

"No, it won't!" Mara shouts. "These types of pictures do not go away. The full story will come out. You must tell me that story first."

I shake my head. I'm the candidate. I can control this situation. "Mara, you're being dramatic. Having a chance meeting with my opponent twenty-five years ago doesn't destroy a campaign."

"You're right. But photographs aren't leaked about chance meetings. You're not being smart about this, Tess. You have to tell me everything. Now."

I hear Mara's commands, but I don't comply. Instead, I sit in silence, refusing to give away any more of myself.

"We don't want this to be your last campaign." The frustration builds across her face. "The DNC called. If you win, you're on the short list for opening speakers at the next convention. You know what that means, right? This is the path to the presidency. But one scandal destroys everything."

"Enough, Mara. Drop it." My voice is clear and firm. "I'm not telling you anything else. It's up to you if you still want to work for my campaign." She may not return, and I make myself numb to that consequence.

Mara stands. "You're not thinking rationally. And I am too pissed to be in the same room with you."

Before she leaves, she asks, "Who else knows?"

"What do you mean?"

"Who else knows what happened between you and Grant Alexander?" Mara's voice is barely above a whisper.

I swallow slowly before answering. "Only Grant."

I watch as Mara absorbs what this means. Not only have I kept secrets from her, but I've kept them from my husband as well.

"I have to call him," I say.

Mara nods. "Dean should hear it from you. We don't know the source. This photo could leak to the papers at any time."

I shake my head. "No. I have to call Grant."

Mara's eyes widen. "If you wanted my opinion, I'd tell you that is a mistake. But I know my advice is pointless." She leaves my office, slamming the door so forcefully that I doubt she'll be back.

I sit at my desk. My hand trembling as I dial his number. He picks it up on the first ring, too quickly to give me any time to figure out what to say other than the one thing that terrifies us both.

"Grant, someone knows about us."

Eight

JULY 1996

"Shit," I mumbled to myself. I had cut the roses back too far. It would have been a problem if Kay were around. But ever since Grant's father arrived, her schedule had been erratic. Most days she was still asleep when I arrived, and she rarely left her side of the house.

My focus was elsewhere too. It turned out that kissing made you a terrible gardener. One minute, my hands were holding shears, pruning the roses, and the next, my mind transported me into Grant's arms, the sensation of his body pressed next to mine so real that I was unable to concentrate.

Since that day by the river, we'd snuck away every chance possible. Grant was so confident and self-assured, but when we were together, lying side by side, I felt like I got to see a version of him that existed only for me. His eyes centered on me. He touched me as if I was a precious gift that he got to unwrap. And he always stopped himself, even if my body got ahead of my mind. Because he knew I wasn't quite ready yet.

We'd lie next to each other and he'd tell me things I knew he shared only with me. How he wished he could live in the country with his mother and spend his life doing anything other than follow the plan his father had pounded into his head since birth.

"I'm off to scoop ice cream," Grant said, interrupting my thoughts.

His voice startled me and I was suddenly self-conscious about where my mind had wandered. It was almost as if my real Grant had caught me with my daydreaming Grant.

I brushed the dirt off my hands as I stood to give him a hug. "Have fun."

"Impossible. I hate this job so much. The kids are sticky and whiny," Grant complained.

"You sound a little whiny yourself," I teased. "It's a summer job. Not everything is fun. Besides, you said you wanted a future using your hands instead of sitting behind a desk," I said, referencing one of our hazy discussions while wrapped in each other's arms.

"Yes, but I want to use my hands for something more noble than scooping ice cream."

I reached out for him and trailed my fingers on the inside of his palm. "I wholeheartedly support a future using these hands to their maximum capacity. It would be a waste to trap them behind a desk."

"Any ideas?" he asked with a wide smile.

"I'm not the one that needs to come up with ideas. That's your job," I said, playfully jabbing his chest. "I'm pretty sure you've had enough people tell you what to do with your life."

His face dropped and the shine in his eyes faded. I realized that what I said was too serious. Or too true.

"I hate that he's here. Everything sucks with him around." Grant didn't need to tell me he was talking about his father. I knew.

"I've been given one path," Grant said. "Go to school, work in finance, ultimately take over my father's firm. But I feel like there are hundreds of possibilities for what I could become and I'll never get the chance to figure it out."

"Yes, you will. Start now," I said, holding his hand tenderly. "Go try everything. It's your life and you're about to go away to college. Your father can't control you forever."

"I wish that were true." Grant stared off into the distance.

I put my hand on the side of his face and turned his gaze back toward me. "You're making excuses."

Grant pulled my hand away from his face. "Tess, you have no idea how much power my father has. I don't have to live in the same city as him to be under his control. Look at my mother."

"What about your mother?"

"Does she look like someone who's living a life she wants, a life she chose?"

I thought about Kay. The woman I first met that day in Ms. Milton's sitting room was mesmerizing. Magnetic. But over the last week, that woman turned into a shell. It was as if all the light inside her had been snuffed out. I didn't know if Grant's father was to blame, but he certainly didn't help. She seemed more detached from the world than ever before. My voice was small as I said, "But you don't have to be like her."

There was a hitch to his voice as Grant said, "I don't know how to be any different."

"Pick something. Right now. If you could have any job, what would it be?"

Grant looked over at the rocking chairs on the back porch of his mother's house. "I'd like to make things like that. Chairs, tables. The idea of making furniture. I'd like that. I had this whittling kit when I was a kid. It was my grandfather's. One summer, I worked every day on this little wooden horse carving. I loved it. But I guess it's a big jump to go from a wooden horse to furniture."

"But it's not. You could do that, Grant. Or you could try, at least. This fall, when you're at Princeton, find some furniture maker or whittler or somebody and offer to sweep their floors in exchange for lessons."

"You make it sound so easy."

"It is easy. You are in control of your life, Grant."

He sighed. "I'm not, Tess. My father would say, *That's a hobby, son. And a stupid one at that. You can buy perfectly fine furniture.*"

"So don't tell him."

"He'd find out."

"How would he know?"

"He knows everything."

"I hope not everything." I leaned against his side. "Promise me you'll think about it? It's good for you to have some secrets from your father."

He grabbed my hand and kissed my palm. "All you do is make me think about things, Tess. I can't stop thinking because of you."

"Good. I'm glad I've been a good influence this summer."

"I hope it isn't just this summer." I couldn't tell if he was trying to have a serious conversation or not. We hadn't talked about what would happen when he left for college, even though I knew it filled both of our thoughts.

"I love you, Tess," Grant said, kissing my cheek. "I'll see you later." He walked away, not waiting for me to respond.

I still hadn't reciprocated those words, and yet Grant continued to deliver them freely. He told me he loved me every time he saw me. He said it tenderly and he said it casually. He'd cup my face and stare into my eyes and list all the ways he loved me. And when I stumbled on our walk through the fields, he'd even tell me that he loved my clumsy feet. I didn't feel like I deserved this kind of love, but I was grateful for it.

After Grant left, I finished my work in Kay's garden. While gathering my tools to return them to the shed at the side of the property, I heard a man's voice. I thought Grant forgot something, but I quickly realized that it wasn't his voice. This one was deeper and full of anger.

I quickly stepped inside the shed, but kept the door open enough that I was able to see two figures emerge onto the back patio.

Kay was wearing a black silk nightgown with lace on the straps and a coordinating robe that hung off her shoulders, dragging on the ground. It was after noon, but recently this had become Kay's standard wardrobe. I rarely saw her in anything other than the clothes she slept in the night before, and she barely left the property. There were no more afternoon teas with Ms. Milton or trips to the local nursery for gardening supplies.

Kay was wringing her hands. Her voice was shaky and tears stained her cheeks. Richard Alexander was standing behind her. He wasn't comforting her. He wasn't even standing close enough for them to touch. He was a few feet away, arms crossed, in a stiff suit without a bead of sweat on his face on this ninety-degree day.

"Shut up, Kay!" Richard screamed. I unconsciously stepped farther inside the shed and hid myself. I could still see them, standing on the patio, but I hoped they couldn't spot me. I made it a practice to avoid angry men, a lesson my mother had instilled in me all my life.

I studied Richard, wondering how he had so much control over his family. At first glance, he looked like any other businessman. He was always wearing a dark suit and his ties were either gold or red. His hair was cut short, but peeks of gray gathered around his temples. He was average sized, but his presence was huge. I saw the precision of his jaw as his face remained neutral, reactionless to the tears of his wife.

It was so stark, the difference between Richard and Grant. His son had easy smiles and hair that swooped over his eyes constantly. He laughed freely and approached even the most mundane activities with joy. I couldn't imagine Grant ever raising his voice. I couldn't imagine crying in front of Grant without his arms immediately sweeping around me. Maybe Kay and Richard's dynamic was a natural progression after decades of marriage, though my only role models were my grandparents, who certainly never acted this way. I suppose passion fades, but for my grandparents, passion wasn't replaced with anger. I saw my grandparents holding hands when they walked into the grocery store. My grandfather would kiss his wife's cheek when he left for work. They would bicker occasionally, mostly about stupid things like dirty dishes or what they wanted to watch on television. But I never heard my grandfather yell like that, with such repulsion, at my grandmother.

For the last two weeks, Richard had been around more, arriving late at night and leaving early in the morning. I usually saw him when I arrived for work. Sometimes he would acknowledge my presence with a head nod, but more often than not, he walked past me and the gardens to his car as if we were all invisible. Grant thought Richard was coming around to check up on his "summer punishment," but I wasn't so sure. Richard didn't seem very interested in his family.

I'd never seen a tender moment between Richard and Kay. And it seemed so strange, while Grant and I were stealing moments when we could touch each other, here were two people, married, with the freedom to connect in any way they wanted to, and they chose to stay apart.

Kay spoke, words punctuated with choked sobs. "How could you, Richard? I thought there were limits to your behavior."

"I won't be lectured by you, Kay. You don't know what you saw. Leave it alone."

"I know exactly what I saw," Kay said, pointing her finger at Richard's chest. "How long has it been going on?"

"I'm not going to answer that. You're hysterical."

"No. I'm your wife. Or have you completely forgotten that?" Her attempted sarcasm was undermined by the way her voice cracked.

"Do you really want to have a discussion about marital duties? I thought we'd abandoned those obligations long ago."

"Richard, this crossed the line. Even I have my limits."

"I don't care," Richard said casually, with a shrug. And that one statement destroyed Kay.

Kay screamed and fell to her knees, sobbing, "You've humiliated me."

Richard stalked toward her, standing over her quivering body with a look of disgust. Eventually, he bent down and grabbed her arms tightly, pulling Kay upright like a rag doll. I saw the white of Richard's knuckles as he gripped Kay's arms.

She winced in pain as he squeezed tighter. "Enough with the theatrics, Kay. I'm going back to D.C." Richard released her arms and turned to walk away.

There was surprising strength in Kay's voice as she said, "I'm done, Richard. I'm no longer participating in this charade of a marriage. You'll have to find someone else to parade around parties so that your clients can think your home life is just as controlled and successful as your financial portfolio."

Richard turned and lunged toward Kay. His hands circled her neck, and even from here I could see they gripped too tightly. My breath stopped, afraid for what was going to happen next. His hands squeezed once more around her throat before releasing, leaving Kay gasping for air. "Do not threaten me," he spat.

He pushed her forcefully away, her body bouncing on the edge of the teak lounge chair before rolling onto the patio. "If you leave, what do you think will happen, Kay? How will you pay for this house?"

"This is my house. My parents gave me this house." Her words were ragged, anger and fear altering her voice.

He scoffed. "Your parents had this house mortgaged upside down. They left this house to us, *the happy couple*. And that's exactly what you will continue pretending to be if you want to stay here. Because you couldn't even afford the taxes on this property without me, not to mention what it takes to maintain a home like this."

Richard left, the roar of his engine and the whirl of his tires over the gravel filling the country air. Kay was immobile, her body shaking as silent tears fell steadily down her face. Minutes passed and I stood there, silent inside the shed, not sure what to do. A part of me wanted to rush to her side, to make sure she was okay, but another part of me worried how Kay would respond knowing there was an audience to that very private moment.

Eventually, Kay took a deep breath, smoothed the hair around her face, and stood to walk inside. I waited a few more minutes before leaving the gardening shed. I debated heading straight home, but I felt an urge to check on Kay. Grant wouldn't be home for hours and I couldn't imagine her being alone.

I walked into the kitchen, stepping quietly and peering around the corner. She was sitting at the kitchen island, a mug of something in front of her. She took a sip and reached for her camera. It was one of those big, fancy cameras with lenses that could come off and on.

I cleared my throat and Kay looked up. Her eyes were puffy and red, streaks of navy-blue mascara trailing down her face. She swiped at her cheeks and then ran her hands through her short, blond hair. She was almost childlike in her fragility. I wanted to wrap my arms around her. I wanted to call the police and report Richard. I saw enough to know that this wasn't the first time Richard had laid his hands on Kay. I wondered how far he had gone in the past. Maybe the grabs and shoves I witnessed were the extent of the harm, but I suspected they were just the beginning.

She fiddled with the camera, removing one lens before attaching a new one. "I'm going to take pictures of the gardens. They've never looked better. Are you done for the day, Tess?"

I nodded. I looked at her upper arm and saw lines of blue bruises already surfacing. Her neck was streaked with red marks. She followed my eyes and quickly pulled up her robe, wrapping it tightly across her chest.

"Whatever you saw, Tess, forget it."

I walked closer and spoke, almost whispering, "He hurt you."

"I said forget it, Tess." Her voice was firm, but the shake in the background was unavoidable. She straightened her body, trying to act more in control of the situation than she was. "It is not your concern."

She was right, it wasn't my business. But I was worried. And not just for Kay. I wondered how much Grant knew. And then a sinking feeling settled in my stomach. I wondered if Grant more than knew. I wondered if Grant had experienced this version of his father.

"Do you want me to call the police?" I asked.

"Oh, Tess. Don't be an idiot."

I recoiled. I couldn't understand how Kay could stay married to a man like that. How she could leave her son in that situation. None of it made sense to me.

"Do you want to talk about it? Whatever upset you?" I asked, not knowing the right thing to say or do.

"No. I do not want to discuss my private business with an eavesdropping teenager."

Her words stung. I had overstepped some imaginary line of decorum. The woman I met at the beginning of the summer, who would spend hours chatting with me about nineteenth-century British gardens and laugh about Ms. Milton's extensive china collection, was gone. At that moment, I was her employee and I'd seen too much.

"I'll be going, then. I'll see you tomorrow, Mrs. Alexander."

She stopped me before I could leave the kitchen. "Oh, Tess," she said, as if using my name as a retaliatory dagger. "I saw you two. You and Grant. I know there is something going on."

I stammered awkwardly. I thought we were so careful. But

it was clear I had been stupid. And maybe Kay was trying to show me that she could reveal my secrets too.

"Am I supposed to apologize?" I asked defiantly.

"What do you think?"

"I don't know the rules. There are so many in this life that I haven't been told."

Kay waved her hand dismissively. "No one ever knows the rules. We all play along, hoping we have it right. To answer your question, no, you do not need to apologize."

I treaded carefully as I asked, "Are you going to tell Ms. Milton?"

Kay was quiet for too long. I thought she was contemplating her answer, unsure whether she wanted to punish me for witnessing the scene with Richard this morning. But she shook her head slowly and her body turned rigid as she said, "Madeline is very busy these days. She has more pressing issues on her mind." She spat each word in a way that made me nervous. Kay continued, "Besides, I suspect you'd like to keep this relationship a secret."

I nodded. "I don't want to cause any trouble for my mother. She can't know."

"Understood," Kay said. She took another sip from her mug, this one longer and slower. Her face grimaced slightly before she set the cup down, strong fumes wafting in my direction. It was evident she was not drinking tea. "Does Grant love you?" Kay asked.

I was too innocent to think of answering her with anything other than the truth. "Yes," I said proudly.

"And do you love him?"

I hesitated because it was something I had been thinking about for weeks. Trying to put my feelings for Grant into words seemed impossible, but if there was one word to describe how he made me feel, I suppose *love* was it.

"Yes," I whispered. "But I haven't told him yet."

"Smart."

I flinched, not knowing what she meant.

Kay continued, "It gives you the upper hand. You need to control the situation."

"No," I murmured. "That isn't it at all." The notion of trying to exert control over someone else—especially when feelings like love were involved—made my stomach turn. But for a brief moment I wondered, is that what I had been doing? All those times when Grant whispered those words into my ears, when his eyes pleaded for a response, and I gave him nothing in return? Had I been unconsciously trying to create some type of even ground in a situation where I felt completely unsettled?

"Well, if it isn't your intention, it should be. Don't be stupid in matters of love, Tess. Once you give your heart away, it's impossible to retrieve. And one day you'll discover that you're destroyed by the loss."

I wasn't sure if Kay was speaking about my relationship with Grant or her own relationship. But I tentatively said, "Grant would never destroy me."

"Yes, he will. You're naive and you two are being reckless. You need to be careful, Tess."

The idea of protecting my heart, when it was completely in Grant's hands, seemed impossible.

Kay looked intensely into my eyes, unsettling me. "Alexander men are not kind, they are not honest, and they do not know how to love."

"Grant is nothing like his father," I began to protest.

"Grant may be a boy, but he's turning into a man. As hard

as I try, as much as I love him, I can't stop him from turning into an Alexander man. My husband is much too powerful for me to stop that trajectory."

My heart ached for Grant, for the fact that neither of his parents saw the person I did. And for Kay and the fact that she had resigned herself to a life of such misery.

I took a deep breath, trying to stand taller when the entire conversation made me feel so small. "Life is full of surprises, right? Maybe Grant will surprise you, Kay."

She shook her head and stood to leave. "It is more likely he will surprise you, Tess. Protect your heart."

She slid a photograph across the kitchen counter. It was Grant, with his arm draped around my shoulders. I had no idea Kay had taken the photograph or how her fancy camera zoomed in without us detecting her presence, I just saw how happy Grant and I were together. I stared at the photo for a moment longer, before slipping it into my back pocket.

I looked at that picture every night, tucking it between the pages of the book I read. By the end of the summer, it was worn from my touch. Until the day Grant left and I tore it apart, knowing that Kay had been right. He did surprise me. He did break my heart.

But someone kept us whole. Someone kept that picture. No matter how many years passed or how hard I worked to rebuild my broken pieces, Grant Alexander's love was always going to ruin me.

PART II

Grant

Nine

JULY 2021

Tess's voice echoes in my head. "Someone knows about us," she says.

My hand fumbles the phone. I grip it tighter and rub the stubble along my jawline. She sounds exactly the same. Her voice quivers just like it did at seventeen.

Except we aren't kids anymore. My mind spirals as I try to figure out who could know and what that could mean.

"There's a photo of us, from that summer," Tess says. "Grant, we need to meet. Soon."

Just then my wife, Cecilia, walks into the kitchen.

I turn my back and stare out the window. My voice is low as I reply to Tess. "Now is not a good time. Can you text me the details? I agree we should discuss this in person."

Tess harshly whispers, "Fine," and I hang up.

I rest my hands on either side of the sink. This is fixable. At least that's my hope. Although I always seem to make a mess of things involving Tess Murphy.

"Who was that?" Cecilia asks, walking up behind me, eyes narrowed.

"A campaign donor." The lie slips easily out of my mouth.

"I feel like our lives revolve around donors these days," Cece says with a sigh. "There's so much to do before tonight, Grant. I need your focus for two minutes."

I don't respond quickly enough, and Cece says my name again. I close my eyes, trying to erase Tess's ghost so that I can concentrate on my wife. There is a donor dinner tonight, hosted in our home, and Cece is already irritated.

"I'm sorry," I say, a smile plastered across my face. "You have my undivided attention."

There are delivery trucks lining our driveway and strangers moving throughout the rooms, rearranging, preparing, and following the party planner's orders.

Cecilia is slamming kitchen cabinets louder than the builder's soft-close finish ever intended. This is her way of telling me she is upset about the bodies cluttering our home.

She turns toward me, lips pressed together tightly, and I can't help but laugh. She's trying to be supportive, but Cecilia craves privacy and these constant invasions of our home have been bothering her for months. Last week it was a photo shoot for some magazine, tonight the party, and I'm sure Stuart has planned a dozen or so additional events between now and November.

"Anything bothering you, Cece?" I ask, watching her move around the kitchen, adjusting a vase of flowers, wiping the marble counters.

"Why would anything bother me, Grant? It's a beautiful summer day. You are the Republican nominee for governor. Everything is perfect." The way her pitch escalates at the end of each sentence suggests she feels otherwise.

"Everything?" My head tilts sideways. "Because it seems like something is bothering you."

"I'm fine." She eyes me critically. "Is that what you're wearing today?"

I look down at my khaki pants and golf shirt. "I feel like my answer should be no, but I'm not sure why."

"You can change before the party tonight. I'll lay your clothes out on our bed. I want to make sure we coordinate this time. The picture from the event last week was a disaster."

"You are going to lay out my clothes for me? Am I your third child?"

Cecilia's eyebrows shoot up and I quickly say, "Never mind. Don't answer that. Besides, no picture of you has ever been a disaster."

I watch Cecilia's eyes wander as she nervously nibbles on the inside of her cheek. "Cece, what's going on?"

Cecilia sighs deeply and I see the concern streaking her eyes. "Nothing important. There are a million things to do before the party tonight and the boys leave next week for camp. It's hard to get anything done with these people around." She whispers "these people" with the judgment and disdain used by gossiping grandmothers.

"I'll talk to Stuart. No more of these big events at our home."

She nods, but none of her concern disappears.

"The boys are old enough," I say, attempting to decode what's worrying her. "Ten-year-olds should be spending the summer in the woods, not on a campaign trail."

We decided early in the race that if I won the nomination, the twins would spend the summer at sleepaway camp in Maine so we could focus on the campaign. Cecilia reluctantly agreed.

I reach for a cinnamon roll on the platter of pastries someone has brought in. "Declan and Hudson are going to have the time of their lives. And Stuart is going to keep you so busy you won't have time to miss the boys."

Cecilia gives me the look she usually reserves for the end of the day, after I've done something to piss her off. "Grant. Don't be ridiculous. They are our sons and six weeks is a long time to be apart. I am going to miss them so much."

I lean my head backward, pausing before I respond. "We are *both* going to miss them like crazy, but this is the best solution for everyone."

She looks at me like I'm some clueless dad from the fifties. Sometime in the last decade of parenting, I was relegated to the position of sidekick. Oftentimes, the incompetent assistant, rendering my parenting opinions irrelevant. It's a dynamic of my own creating, I realize. Long hours working when the boys were infants led to Cecilia doing it all, because I was too slow with the diaper changes or I didn't know that the boys liked baseball better than football that week.

I get it. But it feels like shit to be useless to your own family.

I take a giant bite of the cinnamon roll, Cecilia watching my movements, her nose scrunching upward.

"You shouldn't eat that," Cecilia says. She decided to give up gluten a year ago for who knows what health-related reasons, which basically means that I eat as many sandwiches as I can during the day and graciously accept whatever grain-free dinner she gives me at night.

"I know," I say, diving in for another bite. "That's why it tastes so good." The frosting sticks to my lips and I grab Cecilia's waist before she can run, pulling her in and briefly brushing my mouth against hers.

"You're purposefully glutening me, Grant." She squirms away and I try to ignore the fact that my wife flinches when we kiss.

I fake a smile and say, "Yep. Do you think you'll survive?"

"Barely," Cecilia whispers.

And then my wife, with her regimented exercise routine and daily diet and closet organized by color and season, surprises me. Cecilia leans forward and takes a bite of the cinnamon roll in my hand.

She closes her eyes as she says, "That's delicious."

All of a sudden, it feels like we're thirty again, before kids and campaigns and bread substitutes that taste like Styrofoam. Back when Cecilia would look at me across a room, raise her eyebrows, and I never knew what kind of trouble she had in mind, but I would always hope it was the naked kind.

I lean forward, whispering into her ear, "What if we did something else crazy? Let's sneak away, take a drive to the mountains, maybe grab a pizza on our way. The weather is too nice to be stuck inside." I'm tired of polling numbers and conversations with strangers. I want one small break for one morning before the whirlpool of our lives resumes.

Cecilia raises her eyebrows and my hope soars for a moment. "Except we have two children asleep upstairs and a house full of strangers," she says.

"I know. It's perfect. Built in babysitters. Come on, Cecilia. We need this." It's an understatement because the intensity of the campaign has only magnified the long-simmering issues in our marriage.

It looks like she's considering my suggestion, and I feel the tension in my body begin to disappear. Mentally, I'm already driving down Route 15, watching houses fade away from view as the Blue Ridge Mountains roll across the horizon. But then Cecilia's shoulders hunch, tenseness overtaking her, and I realize I'm wrong. She's not considering the suggestion; she's criticizing it.

"I'm not leaving our children with a bunch of campaign interns. The last thing I need is a day away from my children right before they leave for six weeks. Besides, you need to prepare for this fundraiser."

And just like that, the bristly version of Cecilia is back, listing all the practical reasons why we can't ignore our responsibilities. We used to steal moments away all the time. She'd meet me at the office with takeout and a bottle of wine. I'd sneak home in the middle of the day to hold the twins while she showered, and she looked at me like I was a living hero. We liked making each other's lives better and spending time together. Now a kiss on the cheek falls somewhere on the nightly checklist between teeth brushing and phone scrolling.

There is a litany of things we should discuss: how she really feels about the campaign, the tidal wave of change on the horizon if I win the election, why we seem to piss each other off more than make each other laugh. But we only make time to talk about logistics and the kids' schedules. Maybe it's better this way, because if we're too busy to talk, then I don't have to worry about the truth slipping out. And she won't have time to notice that my entire body seizes every time Tess's name is mentioned.

Cecilia returns to her standard morning routine, setting out bowls of oatmeal for Declan and Hudson that they will complain about but eat reluctantly, the momentary chink in her rigidity repaired.

"I'll see you this afternoon, Grant. Don't forget to change

your clothes." She starts to leave the room, but I reach for her arm, stopping her.

"Cece, I know this campaign is a huge sacrifice, especially for you and the boys. I promise I will spend my life making it up to you. We just have to get through the next few months and everything will be different."

She pauses, sweeping the wisp of blond hair that has escaped her ponytail behind her ear. "Oh, Grant. I love that you believe that." She walks away before I can respond.

I debate following Cecilia but know there's no point. I've been married long enough to understand there are fights best left ignored.

Dispirited, I walk toward my study, hoping to find my campaign manager, Stuart. We were going to work out of my house today to minimize distractions before the donor dinner tonight.

Stuart's known me for years. We met at St. Albans, as scrawny and insecure boys navigating boarding school, with parents rarely around, left alone too often. Stuart fell hard for D.C., a political junkie through and through. He lives and breathes campaigns, bouncing around from one to another. He's too experienced to be my campaign manager, but we both know this is just step one in his plan. I'd be lying if I didn't admit that his plans excite me.

When he first approached me four years ago about running, I said no. But Stuart was persistent. And a pain in the ass. He wore me down, and last year I announced a leave of absence from my hedge fund to start the campaign. Stuart has been by my side for most of my life, except for the one summer that changed everything.

I walk into my study, staring down at my phone, wondering

if I should call Tess back. Wondering if I should finally tell Stuart everything.

"Cecilia seems pissed," a deep voice rumbles from inside the room.

My fist clenches instinctively, surprise and then anger in my eyes. It isn't Stuart; it's my father.

"Why is your wife pissed?" Richard Alexander asks with amusement in his voice. "Did she find out about your old girlfriend?"

"What do you *want*, Richard?" I ask, my disdain cloaking pure hatred. He still has the ability to rile me up.

The last time I saw my father was the twins' ninth birthday party. Cece rented a laser tag company to set up a course in our backyard. I was watching the boys, in their mock spy gear, rolling around and laughing with their friends, when my father put a hand on my shoulder and said, "A bit juvenile, don't you think?"

I did not think so. I thought it was a fucking awesome party, one I would have loved as a nine-year-old. When I told him all of this, it devolved into a screaming match having very little to do with birthday parties and more about the pain and mistakes that fueled our hatred. Cece thought the presence of the boys' third-grade class and their families would cause us to act civilly, but it didn't.

I used to understand Cece's attempts to maintain a connection, but after a while, I resented her efforts. Because I never acted the way Cecilia wanted me to act, and she didn't seem interested in how I actually felt. Thankfully, Cece doesn't try to orchestrate family reunions anymore. Left alone, my father and I are content with zero contact. Which is why his appearance in my study is so jarring.

"Can't a father visit his son's home?" he asks. He is pretending that there is some semblance of normalcy to our relationship.

I stalk across the room and point to the door. "I don't have time for this. Leave."

His steel eyes meet mine. His voice is quiet but full of force. "Close the door, son. We have things to discuss."

I wonder when a day will come when I can tell my father no. I never could do it as a child, but I thought that would change as an adult. It hasn't. My house is full of eavesdropping strangers and there is a fragile campaign in the balance. I close the door, hoping that my life is moving closer to the day of standing up to this man instead of further away.

I sit behind my desk and lean forward. "What? Just say whatever you came to say and then leave."

My father takes his time, settling into the chair across from mine, leaning back with smug satisfaction and commanding more space than he actually occupies. He's always been such an imposing figure in my life. His dark hair is mostly gray and there are deep lines creased in his face, but it's his permanent expression that makes everyone around him sit taller, speak less. There's no joy in his face, only business. Everything is a job. To a boy, he was terrifying. To some grown men, I suppose there is something aspirational about my father's demeanor. But to me, a product of all that misery, it's just sad.

Richard shakes his head as he says, "Only you, Grant. Only you could bungle this kind of opportunity."

"Do you want to issue general criticisms or get into specifics? What opportunity have I handled so poorly?"

"You're going to lose to that country trash," he says, waving his hand dismissively into the air.

The Summer We Ran

Everything about him infuriates me. I stopped trying to make him proud long ago. But he can't even acknowledge the work I've put in to get to this place. Any success I've had in life, from school to career, could have been better. I should have graduated with highest honors instead of honors. Nothing was ever good enough. But it's not the assumption that I'm going to lose the race that makes me stand and scream at him.

"She's not trash," I say, and I'm immediately eighteen again, having the same fight that destroyed everything I loved.

He laughs. Because my attempt to defend Tess now is just as pointless as it was then. "You sound like your mother. I never understood what either of you saw in that girl."

"Don't bring up my mother," I snap, aware that no walls could ever contain our exchanges.

"Your mother was a drunk. Don't try to defend her, Grant."

My eyes widen and it takes all my restraint not to wrap my hands around his neck. "Don't ever talk about my mother!" I shout into his face.

He stands. "I wouldn't make an enemy out of me, Grant. I know secrets that could destroy your future."

"Secrets that would destroy *our* futures. That's the problem, right? Our names tie us together despite the fact that both of us wish otherwise."

"You're ungrateful. For all the opportunities I've created for you. None of this life would have been possible without me."

This isn't the first time I've heard him proclaim his greatness. I used to try to reason and defend myself. But now I know it's pointless. "You've never understood that I don't want it. I never wanted any of the so-called opportunities you created for me."

My father scoffs, a response he practices frequently in sterile boardrooms and oak-walled studies. "Grant, everything you have—the beautiful wife, the adoring children, the money, the political ambitions. That's all because of me. Because I provided and planned and created access for every single detail of your life. You've never appreciated my power to give. But you understand my power to take it all away. I could make just one phone call and destroy you."

"Do it," I say, holding my fist behind my back so that he can't see it shake. For a moment I wonder what would happen. Because he's right, about his control over my life and how quickly everything could disappear. My stomach churns.

He reaches for the door handle and smiles. "No. *My son, the governor* has a nice ring to it. I'll keep quiet for now."

"What does that mean? Did you say something?" I ask too quickly.

My father's eyes widen. He smirks as he says, "No. I didn't." He tilts his head sideways, examining my face as I try to hide my concern. But I could never hide anything from my father.

"You have a leak, don't you?" he asks. I look away, frustrated that he seems to always be right. "It's a good thing I have a plan, Grant."

"Whatever you planned, forget it," I say. "I can handle this."

He laughs, a short, loud bark that echoes throughout the room. "I've lost count of how many messes I've fixed. You could never handle anything involving that girl."

"Stay away from me," I say, voice rising. "I don't want your help."

"It's not your choice," Richard says.

He leaves and I wonder why he even came. After a year of not seeing each other, when I am focused on the biggest development in my professional life, why does he reemerge?

But then it's clear. My father has never been able to go long without asserting his control. I watched him do it to my mother for years, only I was a boy and didn't understand the nuances of their relationship. His tactics may be different, but he might as well have slapped me across the face. He's in charge and I should be afraid.

My face is cradled in my hands, my body leaning against the wall for stability, when Stuart walks into my office, quietly closing the door.

"Don't let him back in here. Ever again," I say.

"I'm sorry. I didn't see him until it was too late." Stuart's face is full of regret. He doesn't know everything, but he knows enough about the dynamic with my father to realize that this isn't a distraction I need right now.

I blow a slow stream of air out of my mouth, trying to exhale all of the feelings of anger and inadequacy that accompany every interaction with my father.

Stuart wants to go all the way to the White House. He's been saying it since his first campaign. He's gotten one candidate to the top of the ticket but suffered a painfully close loss. When he approached me, said I was the horse he was betting on, I felt a sense of pride. Stuart can get me onboard with even the most dreaded campaign tasks with one whisper of "you're my winner." That's how Stuart's dreams became my dreams. Because if I was the governor, or the president, it would finally erase my father's claims that I was a failure.

I don't want to let Stuart down, and yet, in every step of this campaign, it's a fear I confront.

"What was the fight about?" Stuart asks. His face is neutral and his question is genuine. If Stuart overheard our discussion, he wouldn't have been able to hide it from me.

"It's always the same," I say, trying to recover. "My father doesn't believe in me."

"Well, he's wrong," Stuart says. "I'm looking at the next governor of Virginia. You will beat Tess Murphy."

I force a small smile, hoping Stuart is right. I'd like to be more than a mistake my father fixes. But my father is rarely wrong. I can't admit that when I lost a fight with Tess more than two decades ago, it was the most painful loss of my life.

Ten

JULY 1996

"Lower your voice. Grant is upstairs," my father said.

"I'm done following your instructions, Richard." Her slurred speech echoed down the hallway.

I'd been sitting on the steps for fifteen minutes, waiting for my parents to leave. They always attended Madeline Milton's summer solstice party, but for some reason, my mother wanted to stay home.

"Pout if you want, but we have to attend Madeline's party. There is no way to explain your absence." The door slammed as my father left, his frustration reflected in the roar of his engine as he revved it once and then twice, waiting for my mother to join.

A long beat of silence was interrupted by the piercing sound of breaking glass, followed by a primal scream. I rushed into the kitchen. My mother's wineglass was in pieces, an empty bottle remained on the counter. Her eyes were glassy as she looked up. I scanned her body for physical injury, but there was none, only a wounded expression across her face.

"Mom?" I wanted to know if she was okay or if she needed me or if she'd finally had enough. But I never asked any of those questions out loud. Instead, I stared at my mother's quivering chin and watched as the tremors eased away, replaced by a plastered smile and a dismissive tone.

"Go back upstairs, Grant. Your father and I are heading out," she said with annoyed resignation.

I wanted to punch the wall. When would it stop? When would my mother finally stand up to the man who made her miserable?

"It doesn't sound like you want to go," I said.

"My wants became irrelevant years ago." My mother took a deep breath, smoothing her black evening gown. "I'll be fine," she lied.

She kissed my cheek and walked outside. I heard the slam of a car door and the scattering of gravel.

I'd been waiting all day for the moment when my parents finally left and Tess and I could meet up. I should have been excited, but instead I couldn't shake the feeling of unease. Something was wrong with my mother. She'd always been moody—periods of joy followed by days holed away. But lately, it seemed as if any trickle of happiness or confidence disappeared into never-ending fights with my father and glass after glass of wine.

My mother always described Madeline Milton's summer solstice party as the social event of the year. The fact that my father was forcing her out tonight made zero sense. Usually, she was pleading with him to attend and he was complaining about "unnecessary demands on his time," but tonight he seemed eager to leave. My parents cared more about social obligations than they did about each other, but maybe that was how all marriages ended up.

I took a moment to clean up the shards of glass before I headed out. No matter what was happening with my family, I wasn't going to let it ruin my night alone with Tess.

She insisted on keeping our relationship secret, especially from her mother, who would be working the party. When the barn manager got fired earlier in the summer, she said her mom grew even more anxious, constantly reminding Tess that any mistake, no matter how small, could ruin this job with Ms. Milton.

And I knew Tess took this threat seriously. She was afraid of how her mother would react to our relationship. Even though Tess resented her mom's intensity and desire to shape her into something she wasn't—a feeling I completely understood—she never wavered in supporting her mother's insistence that they protect this opportunity.

I once asked Tess why this particular job was so important. She immediately got quiet and pulled away, eventually saying, "I know you don't understand, and I don't think it's something I can explain to you." It was the one time I felt a crack in our connection, so I dropped it and never asked about it again. And reluctantly agreed to keep hiding in the shadows.

When I finally made it to Tess's cottage, I knocked softly. My knuckles barely finished brushing the edge of the wooden door when it was flung open, her bright face filling the room. It should have been impossible to hear my knock over the laughter and music streaming out of Madeline Milton's home, but Tess must have been waiting.

"Hi," she chirped, raising onto her tiptoes to kiss my lips

briefly before grabbing my arms and pulling me quickly inside. Tess's dark hair spilled down her back as she looked over her shoulder, her chestnut eyes sparkling. She smiled and I felt my pulse quicken.

I'd heard people describe a feeling of coming home, a comfort I'd never associated with any physical structure that my parents occupied. But I had that feeling when I was with Tess Murphy.

She was giddy as she showed me around the cottage, but it was only one open room, with a small loft, full of discarded furniture. Nothing matched. It was the house of the broken and forgotten. I couldn't imagine sharing a space this small with my mother. Space was a prerequisite for our family.

But it was evident Tess loved it. She made me take my shoes off before giving me "the tour," which took approximately forty-five seconds. My hands were on her waist as I trailed behind her, smelling the shampoo in her long hair, finding it difficult to concentrate on the amazement of a "real claw-foot tub" when her body was inches away from mine.

We ended up at the window, looking out at the lights glowing from the main house and the noises of partygoers piercing the night air.

"What is this party?" Tess asked. "My mother said they flew in lobsters from Maine and the basement was filled with crates of champagne. Have you ever gone?"

One of my eyebrows raised as I responded, "A party with a bunch of drunk old people? No thanks."

Tess sighed as she said, "I wonder what it tastes like."

"Champagne?"

"No. Lobster."

"You've never had lobster?"

Tess turned around, putting her hands on my chest. She craned her neck upward as she said, "No. Where would I ever eat lobster?"

I leaned down and kissed her lips. "You'd like it. Lobster's sweet. Surprisingly so. Like someone else I know."

Tess rolled her eyes. "No one would ever describe me as sweet. Rude, smart, outspoken, reckless. That's how I'm described."

"All of those are true," I replied, feeling Tess's fingers playfully tickle my ribcage before I continued, "but you're also sweet, Tess. Not many girls would spend an hour with somebody's mom discussing new hybrid rose varietals. You made her day. She seemed almost excited this afternoon, which is a rarity." I didn't mention that my mother's excitement vanished the moment my father pulled into the driveway.

Tess's face scrunched up as she considered her words. "She seems lonely. And sad? I don't think she likes her life, but she's afraid to leave."

"I know," I said, pausing, because talking about my mother seemed like a betrayal. Tess saw that my mother was unhappy, but there was so much more she didn't know. I was conditioned never to reveal the deeply hidden secrets of my parents' marriage. We did not discuss the screaming fights I overheard or the marks on my mother's arms. We smiled for photographs and made jokes at parties about family vacations that never happened. I was so used to pretending that the darkness didn't exist that it seemed impossible to talk about, even with Tess.

I looked out the window, my voice quiet as I continued, "She used to laugh all the time. Now I only see her smile in her garden. Or with you. You make her feel better, and sometimes I think I make her feel worse."

"I can't imagine you ever making someone feel worse," Tess said as she squeezed my hand.

I thought for a moment, about how Tess was always so excited to see me, her eyes sparkling, the electricity of her body vibrating before she melted into hugs that lasted longer and longer, glances across the room that conveyed entire paragraphs of meaning without any words uttered.

We'd spent every day of the last five weeks together. We'd talk about easy stuff like the fact that Scottie Pippen was the true MVP of the Bulls. But sometimes we'd slip into conversations about more serious stuff. Tess would ask me what I wanted to do in life. She didn't expect me to rattle off the elite schools I needed to attend to ensure a future of success like my father did. She didn't accept my vague reference to a career in finance, the same answer delivered by dozens of other kids at St. Albans. Instead, she pushed and prodded, asking what made me happy and whether I wanted to change the world or disappear into a completely different identity.

When I answered her honestly and said, "I have no fucking clue," she smiled and said "Totally." And then we would talk about the possibilities in front of us and the dozens of ways our lives could evolve. For once, I felt like the person listening to me cared about what I had to say.

Being with Tess made me realize that I didn't have that kind of relationship with anyone else in my life. Stuart was a good friend, but we never talked about anything other than lacrosse scores and the idiots on our team. Most kids had people in their lives, parents, who showed interest and wanted to connect with them. Not me. I got forced smiles when I walked into a room, exasperated sighs at every question I asked and every suggestion I proposed. My parents made me feel like a burden they shifted back and forth, oftentimes strategically depending on the dynamics in their battles. I didn't know how to fix them.

But Tess I cared about. When she said she'd never had lobster, that seemed like a problem I could fix.

"I have an idea," I said. "Come with me?"

Tess eyed me suspiciously but nodded. "Okay. But I hope this doesn't take too long. We have one night with our parents all out and I want to take full advantage of it."

I swallowed slowly, my mind swirling with the possibilities for how this evening could unfold. Ever since our picnic at the river, I'd been slow and careful with Tess. And every day she tested my restraint in ways akin to torture. The way she was looking at me right now made me realize that my restraint didn't stand a chance tonight.

On a lobster hunt, we walked around the back of the Milton house. The place was busy, people coming and going. They had a temporary kitchen set up in the barn and waitstaff were moving back and forth, bringing platters of food to the main house. I was wearing a white IZOD polo and khaki shorts, blending in with the waitstaff uniforms. Tess waited beside the barn as I grabbed a plate and filled it with lobsters. No one noticed, or everyone was too busy to care about two lobsters when there was an ocean of food to be served.

"Grant, what if someone sees us?" Tess asked as we walked back to her cottage.

"No one is paying attention to us. They are all too wrapped up in themselves." I scanned the party. Most of the guests were inside, the early-evening temperatures too hot to be enjoyable. But I looked up and found my father standing on the stone terrace. He was smoking a cigar, his standard smugness visible from across the property. I was too far away to be noticed, and besides, I looked like the staff. In my father's world, there was never a reason to acknowledge the people he found beneath him. I knew that most days, I was in that category.

At least he was giving my mother some space, I thought, relieved that she was nowhere in sight. Tess's eyes were glued on the entrance, taking in the guests' arrival. The driveway was full of cars, a team of valets moving vehicles into the south field. Most people really dressed up for this party, and as Tess's eyes got bigger, I realized that she'd probably never seen anything like this.

I elbowed her side. "You're staring."

"Look at those cars, Grant," she said, pointing at the line of Jaguars and Mercedes parked in the circle. "Can we watch for a minute?"

"Watch what?" I asked.

"The outfits. Look at that dress," Tess squealed, pointing to a bright pink gown that seemed to swallow its resident.

"Kind of ridiculous, huh?" I said, wondering how a dress like that made sense in the middle of a bunch of hayfields.

"Ridiculously amazing," Tess said and sighed.

I glanced back at the terrace and saw Madeline Milton walking toward my father. He smiled in her direction, and Richard Alexander rarely smiled. My father said something and Madeline's head rolled back as she laughed. How could my father charm everyone around him except for the people he was supposed to love?

"Come on. I've seen enough," I said.

I could tell by the dreamy look on her face that Tess disagreed. She wanted to stay and take it all in because she hadn't been around these people long enough to watch the luster fade and understand their vicious circle of masking flaws with finery.

Tess pulled her eyes away from the guests and looked into mine. "Are you going to show me how to eat those things?" she asked, pointing at the lobsters.

"Of course."

Back inside the cottage, we sat at the table and I cracked the shells, removing the lobster meat. She took a few bites and I asked, "What do you think?"

"It's chewy. Kind of like shrimp, but a little sweeter. You were right about that." Her mouth pulled to the side and she gulped forcefully, indicating how she really felt about the food.

"Not your favorite?"

"I guess I'm more of a fried-chicken girl." She picked up a lobster and looked at its face as she said, "You are not my thing."

I laughed. "What else is your thing, Tess?"

She thought for a moment before responding. "My mother's Brunswick stew is pretty good."

"What's in that?" I asked.

"A little bit of everything. Pork, chicken, lima beans, corn."

"That sounds awful," I said, cracking a claw. I watched as Tess's face fell. I tried to recover quickly. "I mean, not awful. Just not the same as lobster."

The conversation turned silent as we finished the rest of the lobsters. Once it was clear we were done, Tess picked up our plates and brought them over to the kitchen. She grabbed a garbage bag from under the sink and poured in the shells. She was removing the evidence of our dinner, and her elongated silence killed me.

"I'm sorry about what I said, Tess. I'm sure your mom's soup is great."

Tess sat on the couch and I walked over to join her. She looked at me and sighed. "I'm fried chicken and you're lobster. You get that, right, Grant?"

I nodded and shrugged. "Yeah. It's one of the things I like the most about you."

"Why?" Her arms were folded tightly across her chest and her eyes were focused. I didn't want to fumble an explanation this important.

"Everyone in D.C. is trying to be someone else. Everyone at those parties"—I gestured toward the Milton house—"is pretending that they are more important than they really are. That world is exhausting. You are not."

"You like me because I don't exhaust you?" Her eyebrow shot up and I knew I hadn't gotten this right.

I swallowed before I continued. "Yes, because being with you is the most natural, the most real, I have ever felt in my life. You don't put on an act, Tess. You're confident and fearless. I feel like the best version of myself when I'm with you. Like there is a world where I don't have to pretend to want the life my father demands. Where I can make choices and mistakes."

Tess's eyes danced as she asked, "You feel all of that because I like fried chicken more than lobster?"

"Probably half the people at that party like fried chicken more than lobster. I feel all of that because you aren't afraid to admit that you like fried chicken more than lobster. You aren't afraid of saying the unpopular thing."

"Some people, my mother in particular, would say that I talk too much. That maybe I should keep these opinions to myself."

I shook my head. "No. Please don't ever change who you are, Tess."

"We're really different people, Grant."

"Different is not bad, Tess. Besides, I need more fried chicken in my life."

"I don't try to be anything else because I don't know any better. This summer is a whole new world for me."

"Do you like it, Tess?"

She looked down at the floor. "Not the food. Or the rules. Or the fancy furniture. I've never been more uncomfortable. I'm always on edge that I'm going to mess this up for my mother. I know how important this job is to her. And I guess it's important to me too. I'm ready for her to have a regular job, not wondering if her hours are going to get cut, and whether we can afford stuff." Tess turned her head away as she said, "Stuff that you never have to think about. We have big differences, Grant."

She was right. She did things, like wrapping up half of her sandwich in a paper towel and putting it in her bag. Or smoothing out the tinfoil and folding it into a neat square. I'd notice her doing these things but never stopped to think about why. Especially when I would so easily have thrown a half-eaten sandwich into the trash.

Tess leaned her head on my shoulder as she said, "But the thing I like the most about this summer is you."

I laced my fingers with hers and lifted her chin as I said, "I love you, Tess. I love you exactly the way you are."

She swallowed, the weight of my words seeming to sink into her brain.

I had never said these words to anyone before Tess. It wasn't a phrase my parents used, not with me and not with each other. I'd certainly never told a girl that I loved her, and I didn't completely know what it meant to love another person, but I couldn't imagine feeling more for someone than I felt for her.

I held my breath waiting for her response. The same reaction I always had after I said those words to Tess. I wondered if she felt the same way. I wondered if I scared her with how I felt. I wondered if it was a mistake to say those words out loud.

She grabbed my hand and led me upstairs to the loft, where she slept. We climbed the ladder without speaking. At the top, I was surprised to see a space that was purely Tess. The walls were sloped with white-painted boards that she had covered in pictures ripped from magazines, held up with strips of masking tape. There were pictures of her favorite bands, Pearl Jam and Stone Temple Pilots and Alanis Morissette. There were pictures of New York and Paris and an article titled "Things to See and Do in Washington, D.C." She had a whole collage of gardens and flowers. There was a shelf overflowing with books and stacks of them beside her bed. I saw some novels she'd mentioned as her favorites and a few books I grudgingly suffered through in high school English class. There was also a whole stack of history books about U.S. presidents. Half of those books were ones my father had been nagging me to read for years. There was a pile of clothes in the corner and three empty Dr Pepper bottles on top of her dresser.

I realized I was staring at the room and Tess was staring at me. I turned toward Tess, my face full of joy at getting to see her space. She smiled, leaning in to my body, reaching her arms up so she could loop them around my neck.

I swallowed nervously. For once, she had her arms around my body and she was completely calm. I knew what that meant, because I told Tess she had to set the pace. There had been a few times when we'd gotten close, when I'd wondered whether this would be the day, but then I'd see Tess hesitate. And I would stop. Because the last thing I wanted in the world was for Tess to have any regrets when it came to me. I wanted her to trust me completely.

The Summer We Ran

That night could have been like those other times, except it wasn't.

Tess looked into my eyes and whispered into my ear, "I am 100 percent ready."

Eleven

AUGUST 2021

I order a beer, because when you're sitting at a rooftop bar in the summer, the Washington, D.C., humidity blanketing every porous surface, it's a requirement to order a beer. But as soon as the waiter brings over the frosty mug and I take a sip, I regret my decision.

This isn't a relaxing afternoon to unwind. I'm no tourist, gawking at the White House. I already feel anxious about the idea of this meeting and the conversation that's about to take place. The beer tastes bitter sliding down my throat, a sourness sitting in my stomach. I push the mug away and stare down at my phone, my knee bouncing up and down uncontrollably.

"Grant."

I look up and Tess is standing in front of me. Her hands rest on her narrow hips. Time isn't kind to some people, but Tess doesn't fall into that category. She looks exactly the same as she did twenty-five years ago, except she's traded cutoffs and

T-shirts for power suits in jewel tones. Her long black hair is twisted into a bun at the nape of her neck, but a few strands have managed to escape, sweeping across her cheek. Her lips are pulled tight and her face is flushed. I'm not sure if it is from the heat or the anger.

"Want to join me?" I ask, motioning to the empty seat across the table.

When she speaks, I'm surprised by the resentment in her voice. "No. I don't want to join you, Grant. I want nothing to do with you, but we're both in this mess, so we have to find a way out." Tess's eyes survey the nearly empty bar before she eases into a chair, her nervous energy impossible to ignore.

She tries to plan for the unpredictable. This meeting location, in a touristy section of town away from political insiders, is as careful a meeting spot as possible for two people who look like they're grabbing a quick drink before returning to work.

I close my eyes briefly. "Yes, Tess. You made that clear. Then and now. I'm well aware you want nothing to do with me."

She's sitting ramrod straight, legs crossed at the ankles. Grateful for the beer in front of me, I take a sip to break the tension. I sigh deeply. "We don't have much choice in dealing with each other now. Show me the picture."

Tess reaches into her purse and pulls out her phone. She slides it across the table. I'm confronted with an image I've never seen, yet it feels as familiar as morning coffee. My young arm is wrapped around Tess's tanned shoulders.

If I were more in control, I would have remained expressionless. But that was never the case with Tess.

I smile as I ask, "Do you remember that day? We were in my mom's backyard. I think we were about to sneak off to the river. Just like every afternoon that summer."

"Don't do this, Grant." Her eyes are pleading when she speaks.

"Do what?"

"Start dredging up these buried memories. It's not good for either of us."

She's right. I push the phone back across the table. "Where did this picture come from?"

"I have no idea," Tess says, sighing. "My campaign manager received an anonymous email. Someone knew about us and held on to this picture for twenty-five years. Who would do that?"

Ever since Tess called and told me a secret photograph existed, I have been trying to answer that question. Shaking my head, I say, "I don't even know who took this picture."

Tess shifts uncomfortably in her chair. She looks away as her fingers twist the hem of her skirt. Tess fidgets when she's nervous. I know this about her, but I don't know why she's nervous.

She finally looks me in the eye and whispers, "Your mother took the picture, Grant. She gave it to me that summer."

My eyes narrow. "What?" I knew Tess kept things from me, but I didn't know she had secrets with my mother.

Tess seems to sense my spiraling confusion. She speaks quickly as she explains. "Your mother took that picture and gave me a copy. But I didn't keep it. I threw it away when you left. I haven't seen that picture in twenty-five years, Grant."

I stare at her, pushing aside doubts about whether she is telling me the truth. Because even though decades have passed, Tess is still the easiest person to read. Her eyes are focused and her lips are still. If she were lying to me, I'd be able to see it on her face.

"What did she say?" I ask.

"Who?"

I look at the ground. "What did my mother say when she gave you that picture?" I'm not sure whether I want to hear Tess's answer, but when you lose someone you love, you cling to stories about them, especially those you've never heard.

"She told me to be careful," Tess says quietly. "She seemed to know you would break my heart." I watch as a glassy sheen appears in Tess's eyes before she blinks it away.

I swallow. It's been years since I've allowed myself to think about my mother and those final weeks of her life.

"I've always disappointed the people I love," I say, unable to meet Tess's eyes.

"Grant." Tess whispers my name. I look up and something seems to have softened in her. "Your mother would be proud of you."

"No, she wouldn't," I quickly reply. "You don't even know me, Tess. Stop the bullshit." My words come out harsher than I intend. But Tess knew my mother better than most, and *proud* wasn't a word my mother used in describing her son.

"You're right," Tess says, swallowing, an iciness returning. "I don't know you. And if Kay Alexander were here, she'd tell us to clean up this mess."

I nod. "She would." I lean forward, resting my forearms on the table. "Any ideas on how to fix this one?"

Tess winces. "I have an idea. But you aren't going to like it."

"We have to start somewhere."

Tess looks upward, running her fingers through her thick hair. She meets my gaze and hesitates before saying, "I think your father is involved. He could have found Kay's roll of film. Maybe he had a copy of the picture and kept it all these years."

I shake my head. "I didn't even know she took this picture. How would he know?"

"Grant, it was sent to my campaign. You know what your father is capable of. The games he plays with the people he loves."

"My father doesn't love," I say, trying not to think too hard about that reality.

"Ask him if he did it," Tess says.

"I already spoke to him. He hasn't done anything. The picture didn't come from him."

"He wants to destroy me," she says, a tremble in her voice.

It's a reasonable fear. I've seen my father destroy lives to get what he wants. I'm just not sure he thinks Tess Murphy is important enough to factor into his plans.

She continues. "You're protected, Grant. You always were." Her voice teeters between tough and frail. "That's the part of this that you never seemed to understand."

I look around the empty bar, momentarily concerned that someone may have overheard Tess, my eyes darting over to the bartender across the room, who is busy slicing limes, unconcerned with our conversation.

"If this leaks, I'm the one who will be judged," Tess continues. "I'm the one who will lose my career and family. And your life will remain the same." She may have lowered her voice to a whisper, but the intensity persists.

"I don't know why I'm surprised by any of this," she says. "I could never trust you."

"You want to talk about trust? After what you did?"

"What exactly did I do, Grant? Please tell me. Because the way I remember it, you were long gone. I'd love to hear your judgment of actions you weren't even present for."

We aren't fighting about the present anymore. She's ripped off the Band-Aid of a wound decades old and I've waited years to have this exact conversation with her. "You didn't give me a chance."

She quickly replies, "You didn't earn it."

She's right, but her words bite. We exchange a look, knowing we've both hurt each other too much for one lifetime. I can see her mind working. She's trying to put together pieces of a puzzle that neither of us can solve. I used to love watching her think, delighted by the complicated pathways of her world. But now, it's like watching the clock on a bomb wind down.

"Are you sure this wasn't your father?" Tess asks.

I nod. "I've had plenty of experience with my father's manipulation. Anonymous emails aren't his style. His blackmail is a little more straightforward. I don't know who sent that picture, but it wasn't my father."

She leans against the back of the chair, seeming to relax for the first time since she arrived.

"Relieved?" I ask.

"No. We still have no idea who is manipulating us. We're just as fucked as before."

A small smile creeps across my face. Because she's right. But even in the midst of this crisis, I can still appreciate the bluntness that is pure Tess. Once, I had a front-row seat to her magnificence. Now I'm just a distant spectator like the rest of the world.

Tess motions for the waiter and orders a glass of sauvignon blanc. We sit in silence until she gets her drink. After she's taken a few sips and I've downed about half of my beer, we both find ourselves willing to converse.

"Who do you think it is?" Tess asks.

"I've been racking my brain. I can't remember anyone else

that summer." I find myself clenching and unclenching my fist. "That was part of the problem, I suppose."

"How is your campaign reacting?" she asks. I raise my eyebrows in surprise. There is an unspoken rule that Tess has broken, asking about the details of our campaigns. But I suppose when we both showed up for this meeting, we knew the rules no longer applied.

I answer truthfully. "I haven't told them anything. How much does your staff know?" I'm hoping that Tess has guarded this secret just as closely as I have.

"I told my campaign manager, Mara, that I worked for your mother. That's it. She knows there's more to the story. She threatened to quit, but for now, I've convinced her to stay." Tess takes a small sip of her wine before continuing. "No one else knows anything about that summer."

"Not even your husband?"

"Don't mention my husband, Grant. And I won't bring up perfect Cecilia."

The last thing I want to discuss is "perfect Cecilia," as she is often referred to in the media. In fact, I'd be happy if "perfect Cecilia" disappeared forever. I much prefer the version of my wife that I first met—the one who danced on bar tops and took spontaneous road trips in search of the best nachos. Cecilia easily slips into the mold of the ideal candidate's wife—beautiful, polished, intelligent—but I miss her messier side. When she had tousled hair and wrinkled T-shirts because we stayed up too late playing poker with our friends, or trying to re-create a recipe from our favorite restaurant, or christening a new piece of furniture.

When we started a family, our priorities changed, and I'm so grateful that she's such a dedicated mother. I just wish responsibilities didn't erase fun. Because we used to have so much fun together, and now we review our calendars over oatmeal.

I look at Tess, and despite the fact that there is a twenty-five-year hole in our relationship, I know that she'd never morph into some sterilized version of herself. Even on the campaign trail, she's been relatable and candid. The media has been replaying a blooper of Tess eating a hotdog, mustard dropping onto her blouse, and the toddler sitting at her side handing over his bib. Tess's giggles with the child have gone viral. I've watched that clip too many times. But Tess isn't my wife. She's just someone I used to know who haunts my past. And threatens my future.

"You know my wife's name," I point out sheepishly.

A flash of embarrassment streaks her face, and then Tess's stoic exterior resumes. "Of course I know her name. It would be very hard to miss the Republican Party's Most Photogenic Couple."

"I'm sure we'll be replaced with another couple by the end of the summer."

"I'm not so sure about that. The public loves blondes. Golden couples." Tess self-consciously pushes away a wisp of her dark hair. "And those twin boys. You have children." There is a slight hitch to her voice, signaling that those words were difficult to escape from her mouth.

I nod slowly.

"It's hard to imagine you as a father," Tess says.

"Is it?"

"Yes."

"Because I'm not eighteen anymore?"

"Partly," Tess says softly. The expression on Tess's face is unfamiliar. It isn't one of the easy smiles I memorized the summer we were teenagers or one of the focused faces I see in her print ads. Her eyes drift past my shoulder, her face almost wistful. I can't let myself imagine what she is longing for.

I lean forward. "You and Mountain Man are pretty popular too." Tess's eyes narrow and I hold up my hands in surrender. "I didn't say his name."

"Let's not discuss our families."

"What should we discuss?" I ask.

"A plan. Until we know who has the photo, I think we should keep quiet. It's possible that nothing more comes of this, right?" I understand the desperation in Tess's voice, hoping for the unlikely.

"Maybe. But if there are more pictures, Tess, or this gets leaked to the press—"

She cuts me off. "I know. It could get worse."

We both stare off into the distance. I wonder if she is imagining the dominoes of disaster that I am. It was necessary to erase that summer from our history, because of what happened, and because we both had to find a way to move forward. If the truth begins to unravel, I'm not sure either of us will be able to recover from those revelations.

Tess absently twirls her wedding band. I thought I'd be the person to put one of those on her finger. And yet, here we are, sitting across from each other, strangers and enemies.

"I should go," Tess says.

I nod. She's right, we've been sitting together too long. But I want to keep talking. I want more time. That was always my problem with Tess. I never knew when to stop.

I stand as I say, "When I saw that photo, it made me feel like that boy again. Our lives were so different."

"Were they?" Tess asks rhetorically. "We're still the same people."

I think she's joking, but she's not. "No. We're not the same as those kids."

"I am," she says defiantly, as if she's convincing herself that there's truth in her statement. We are standing on opposite sides of the table, our faces inches apart.

"Your confidence is the same, that's for sure," I say.

She rolls her eyes like a teenager, and it's unsettling that one look can transport me back in time.

"You have the same . . ." There's a grin on Tess's face, but she hesitates.

I can't figure out what she is about to say. A slight nod signifies that she's stopped herself. This is a different Tess, because the girl I knew never thought before she spoke.

"You're right. You're a completely different person." Tess's face is serious. "And I wonder if I ever really knew you."

Her words slap me. Of all the lies she must have told herself throughout the years, this must be the biggest.

I stare intently. "You knew me. You knew me better than anyone."

Tess swallows. She must know I'm right.

"We made so many mistakes, Grant." Tess's voice hitches and I see the corners of her eyes fill. "I've been wondering if all of this isn't exactly what we deserve. Maybe this photo coming out is our punishment. Maybe we should have to finally explain our lives to the ones we love."

I understand what she means, because I've thought the same thing over the last few weeks. But hearing this, my stomach drops. Because there was a time when Tess was the one I loved and there was never a need for explanation.

I shake my head and gently say, "We were kids. We did what we thought was right." I reach out to grab Tess's hand, but she pulls it back quickly, wrapping it around her purse strap.

"Don't make this harder than it has to be," Tess says, wiping away her tears.

"I'm sorry." I look away. "I keep forgetting I hate you."

"I know." Tess nods, agreeing, and the sadness of this situation sweeps over me.

I want to reverse time and protect our teenage selves from the heartbreak we suffered, erase everything that happened. But at the same time, I know those months with Tess were the best of my entire life. I'll never feel that way about myself again. I can't help but wonder if she feels the same. Except I'll never know because Tess and I are experts at avoiding the difficult conversations we should be having.

Tess walks toward the exit but stops and turns back, asking, "Why did you run, Grant?"

I shrug. "I was asked."

"Your life was always that simple."

"I never understood why some people make things more complicated than they need to be," I say.

Tess's shoulders scrunch upward. It's the same motion she'd make that summer when we disagreed. We were teenagers discovering that the same world looked very different through two sets of eyes. It makes me answer honestly.

"I ran because I wanted to do something outside his control."

"Your father," she says softly.

I nod. When Stuart approached me about running, I was drunk on possibility. Someone outside my father's influence believed in me. Of course Richard came around acting as if governor was a piece in his master plan. There's no part of my life he won't try to manipulate, but not even my father is powerful enough to buy off every Virginia voter. I want the job and I want the feeling of worthiness that comes with each ballot cast in my favor.

"How'd you switch from woodworking to politics?" Tess asks.

I grin. Of course she remembers some stupid teenage idea I confessed at a time when Tess gave me hope that anything was possible.

"This seemed more realistic," I say, smiling. "Why did you run, Tess?"

"I've always wanted this. You know that."

"You wanted to conquer the world. I didn't know governor of Virginia was one of your stepping stones. When I saw your name on the short list of the potential Democratic candidates, I almost dropped out."

"Why didn't you?"

"Because I never imagined that this would happen," I say, gesturing at the space between us. "I never thought we'd be running against each other. Once that became more likely, I was in it too deep to leave."

A small smile creeps across Tess's face. "You didn't think I'd win the nomination? You underestimated me."

I can't help but smile. "I forgot how much you enjoy being underestimated."

Tess cocks her head to the side, looking out over 15th Street and across to the White House. "I didn't want to conquer the world. I wanted to change the world. I thought you knew that."

That summer, I saw Tess's heart search for ways to make the world kinder than the place she knew. Mostly by trying to fix my broken family. I thought she'd eventually realize it's impossible to force change upon others.

"If you get what you want, I lose," I say.

Tess's face crumples before I realize that I've said those words before. That was the last thing I told Tess when she left my room that day years ago. I see the devastation on her face and realize, Tess never learned. She's still making the same mistake, hoping for change that will never come. Tess does the same thing she did twenty-five years ago. She runs away.

Twelve

AUGUST 1996

"Are you going to miss her, Grant?" my mother asked.

I nodded, knowing she was talking about Tess. Even though Tess wanted to keep our relationship a secret, it was impossible to hide it from my mother.

"She's everything to me," I said. It should have been an embarrassing admission, but it was so true it was impossible to hide.

My mother smiled as she tried to smooth the comforter on my bed. My room was a mess, even more so than usual. There were piles of clothes in every corner, a locker room's worth of old sports equipment accumulating in the center, and a stack of school papers and yearbooks that seemed like things I should keep but would probably never look at again.

I had a duffel bag filled with the clothes I thought I'd need for college. My mother bought a bunch of sheets and towels that seemed too nice for the amount of time they would spend on the floor of my dorm room. After four years of boarding school, packing was routine. I didn't think too much about it. My mother should've had a similar reaction, but every time I mentioned leaving, she cried. She seemed to have red-rimmed eyes most of the time these days.

"Are you going to miss me?" my mother asked, a childlike quality to her voice.

"Yeah," I said automatically. "I've had some practice missing you, though."

The words came out before I realized their impact. Yet it was true, after boarding school, I was used to being away from my mother. We both knew that even when she was around, she wasn't completely there.

I tried to recover. "I've loved being here this summer, Mom. I want to spend more time here. With you."

"Yes. Maybe. We will have to see what your father says about that." She smiled politely, the kind of expression you use around strangers—not your son.

Long ago, I gave up on trying to understand my parents, but something was bothering my mother more than her usual moods. My father had been spending more time at the house. Even though he was technically here, I saw him less, if that was possible. His car was in the driveway. His briefcase was on the kitchen table; muffled voices escaped from his home office; occasionally, he left ties on the back of the couch. There were signs that he was around, but we never saw each other. Forget having any type of father-and-son chat before I left for Princeton, which was fine with me. I'd rather not feel like I'd failed college before I'd even started.

But mostly, I knew he was around because of the yelling. I never thought I'd long for the stretches of silence between my parents that used to be their primary mode of interaction. I'd developed a few coping mechanisms, mostly Dave Matthews played as loudly as my Walkman allowed. I heard them start to argue and turned on the music, muffling my father's shouts and my mother's tearful screams in return.

When I was younger and they would fight, I'd run into the room, begging them to stop. I'd stand in front of my mother, a ten-year-old protector. But after a while, I realized that she didn't want my help; instead, she'd hide from me for days afterward, my care regulated even more so to the nanny. I suppose I was the worst reminder. Eventually, I realized it was better if I stayed away from their fights and stopped trying to protect her.

In a school assembly one year, we had to watch this movie about an abusive boyfriend. It started with a push, and then escalated to a slap, and one day he strangled his girlfriend. The whole point of the movie was that something small can turn into something bigger and girls needed to look out for warning signs in relationships. At least that was what the guidance counselor said before she moved on to a discussion of the food pyramid.

My life was filled with warning signs, but my experience wasn't anything like that movie. My father was always a steady level of asshole. He grabbed, and pushed, and occasionally slapped, but he didn't care enough to escalate it further than that. It was almost as if we were beneath him. Or maybe he knew that his image depended on my mother staying and me being able to fake a smile when needed.

When they settled on separate homes and boarding school for me, it was a relief. If we were all apart, no one would get hurt.

"Will you be okay when I'm gone?" I asked.

"Of course," she replied, almost reactively. "It is not the child's job to worry about the parent."

This was always how these conversations ended, curt directives from my mother reminding me that this wasn't a topic we discussed.

"Go see your girl, Grant," my mother said. "I'm going to lie down for a bit."

I nodded, heading down the stairs and through the kitchen. I didn't want to waste a single moment with Tess. As I left out the back door, I noticed the pile of wine bottles, wincing at the thought that I took out the trash yesterday.

I started walking toward Tess's cottage, hoping I would find her alone. Her mother had been working late hours. Tess shrugged when I asked what her mother did all day. I knew feeding the staff that worked at the Milton property was a big job, but she'd been doing that since the beginning of summer. It was only recently that Tess's mother had been working late nights, researching recipes for elaborate meals with multiple courses. Tess thought her mother was trying to do everything she could to impress Ms. Milton before the end of the summer, since she still hadn't gotten an extended offer to work in the fall. When I asked Tess what would happen if her mother didn't get the job offer, she would shudder.

Tess didn't want to go back to living in her grandparents' old trailer and she didn't know if her mother could get her job back at the resort. This summer was a gamble for them, with stakes that were so foreign to me.

I was thankful that Tess's mother was busy, because it meant more time for us to be alone. We spent most nights in the field between the two properties. Lust taking priority, followed by hours of lying on our backs, staring at the stars, our conversations competing with the cicada songs.

This day, I jogged over to the Milton property, immediately regretting my choice. I should have driven, but Tess was so nervous about my car being seen. Instead of showing up like a normal human being, I appeared at her doorstep dripping in sweat.

I knocked, but there was no answer, so I walked around the back of the cottage. Tess was lying on a towel spread in the grass with headphones on. She had a stack of mixtapes, probably songs she recorded off the radio.

I walked up behind her, my figure casting a shadow over her body. She sat up and pulled off her headphones, a giant smile spreading over her face.

My eyebrows raised as I asked, "Aren't you hot?"

"Melting. Isn't the weather going to cool off soon?"

Tess was wearing a pale blue bikini. Her dark hair was piled on top of her head. There was a copy of *Seventeen* magazine in her hands, which she tossed to the side.

"What are you reading?"

"Embarrassing shit about silly girls."

I laughed. "Doesn't seem like your type of magazine."

Last week, Tess was reading *The Grapes of Wrath*. For fun. She had stacks of books that she tore through these past couple months. Since she wasn't sure where she was going to school because of the uncertainty with her mother's job, she was making sure she'd read every possible book that might be on a summer reading list. And she smiled when she said that.

Tess picked up the magazine, flipping through it casually. "It isn't my typical choice, but there was an article I wanted to read."

I grabbed the magazine and eyed the cover, asking, "The story about Claire Danes?"

"Nope, the headline below that. 'My Surprise Summer Romance.'"

"Pick up any good tips?"

"Lots." Tess flipped to the story. She read aloud, sarcasm dripping from each word. "'How to keep the spark alive when the weather chills,' 'Body warmth is more powerful than weather warmth.' It's an encyclopedia of information."

I laughed and grabbed the magazine from her hands, tossing it aside. "We don't need this." I leaned in for a kiss, but she pulled back. "Are you worried, Tess?"

She shook her head quickly and I pulled her onto my lap. She nooked her head under my chin and I wrapped my arms around her tightly.

"I know we have only a few days left before I leave for Princeton, but we're going to make this work."

Tess responded with a quick "yeah."

I wanted to say more, but I'd spent countless hours reassuring her. Nothing I said seemed to make a difference.

After a few moments of silence, Tess tentatively asked, "Are you excited?"

"Yes and no. I want to get away from them." I gestured over the hill toward my mother's house. "I want to be on my own, without my father snooping over my shoulder. I think life will be different at Princeton, but my father has this way of being everywhere, even when he's not physically in a room. I'm afraid it will be the same as it's always been."

"You can make it different, Grant. It might not be easy, but if you don't break away from your father now, you never will. Promise me you'll figure out what you really want. Don't let him be the voice in your head."

"I'll try," I said, because it was impossible to tell Tess no. There was nothing I wanted more than to break away from my father, but I didn't think she had any idea about the extent of his power. "What about you?" I asked, hoping to change the subject. "Excited for your senior year?"

"I'd just like to know where I'm going to school. My mother keeps insisting that missing the first week of classes isn't a big deal. She's sure that Ms. Milton is going to offer her a job any day and we can move here permanently. But it's driving me crazy. It's not the way I thought my senior year would start."

"Do you want to go back to your old school?" Even as I asked the question, I hoped her answer was no, because I didn't want to lose even a single day with Tess.

"Not really. My mom said I could go back to Hot Springs and stay with a friend of my grandmother's. But I said no."

I smirked when I said, "Because you don't want to leave me?"

She scowled, poking me in the rib. "Because it would be stupid to start one school and then transfer after two weeks. And I know I can catch up on a few weeks of missed classes. Plus my grandmother's friend is bossy and smells weird. And I don't want to leave you."

"That's a lot of reasons. I'm glad I fit in there somewhere."

Tess looked down, her chocolate eyes shaded by her long lashes. "You more than fit in, Grant. It's going to be so strange not talking to you every day."

"We can write, we can talk on the phone, and as soon as orientation is over, I'll take a bus to visit you."

"Grant, please don't make promises you aren't going to keep."

"I won't. Don't you want me to visit you, Tess?"

"Of course. But I also know you're going to be in a new, exciting place. Sitting on a bus for six hours to visit a high-schooler isn't going to be your priority."

"Tess, you are my priority. There is no party, no new place that is ever going to feel more exciting than you."

"Okay," she said quietly, almost in a whisper.

I swallowed and said the thing I'd been thinking for weeks but had been too scared to vocalize. "Sometimes I think I feel more for you than you feel for me."

"Because this body is irresistible," Tess said, skimming a hand down her legs before laughing loudly.

This was the way Tess masked her insecurities. She was unbelievably beautiful. And yet she seemed convinced that she wasn't enough for me. So she made jokes. Occasionally, she'd point to pictures of blond models on the covers of magazines, all boobs and legs, and say, "That will never be me. Are you sure you don't want that?" I'd stare at her dark eyes, her long hair, and her smooth skin and know the mystery of Tess would always amaze me.

I looked away. "Tess, I'm serious." I knew she was trying to make light of this conversation.

"I'm sorry. I won't joke." She took a deep breath and then looked into my eyes. I was silent, waiting for what she was going to say. "Grant, I love you, but—"

I reached for her and cut her off with a kiss. I didn't care what else she had to say. I'd waited weeks to hear those words out of her mouth. I tried to tell myself that it didn't matter if she said it back. But I felt a wave of relief that Tess Murphy, the most beautiful, frustrating, inspiring person I had ever met, loved me back.

Once we started kissing, it was the same as it always was with the two of us. Her body was a magnet and I couldn't pull myself off, even though it was the middle of the day and we were outside.

I rolled her over and propped myself up, elbows on either side of her body as I kissed her lips again and again.

She put her hands on either side of my face, staring into my eyes. "I love you, Grant Alexander. Exactly as you are. Even your off-key humming on our walks."

I bent down and crushed her mouth with mine, knowing that there was no one else that loved me without wanting something more, to change me, to use me. I knew without a doubt that being loved by Tess was the best gift I would ever get.

She nibbled on her lip and her eyebrow cocked upward as she pulled off her top and slid her bikini bottom down. I reached into my back pocket for a condom. We came together quickly and fiercely, our bodies having spent weeks practicing this reciprocation of movement. I watched Tess's face as a chorus of I-love-yous echoed between our mouths, stolen declarations between frantic kisses.

When she wrapped her legs around me tighter, the sun beating on my back, her hair tumbling in every direction, I lost myself, hearing Tess's breathing reach a fever pitch, her body tensing around mine.

We lay there, tangled in each other, the hot sun beaming on our exhausted bodies. Eventually, I reached for the towel and draped it over Tess before gathering my clothes.

As I got dressed, Tess looked up at me and said, "Promise me something, Grant."

"Anything."

"I'm not your obligation. I'm your want. You want to be with me and write me and call me. If that ever changes. If you meet someone else. If my life is too small for your new world, don't stay with me out of obligation."

"Tess, you are the most amazing person I've ever met. Being with you is a privilege."

She grabbed her bikini top and slipped it over her body. "For now," she said on an exhale.

"What does that mean?" I sat next to her as she finished getting dressed.

"It means we're in a bubble here," she said, gesturing around us. "I'm Tess and you're Grant and there's nothing else."

"I don't think that's because of our location. That's because of us."

"Grant, we work right now because the outside world doesn't matter. But in a few days, all of our differences are going to be magnified."

I shook my head. "None of those differences matter. For the first time in my life, my world makes sense. It makes sense with you. I'm not going to let anything mess that up."

As my arms wrapped around Tess, I thought I'd made a promise I could keep.

Thirteen

SEPTEMBER 2021

Two loud voices boom into the campaign headquarters followed by peals of laughter. Since the boys got back from camp and classes began, Cecilia has made it a habit to bring them for a visit after school. She says we have months to make up for. I'm grateful for the few minutes every afternoon we get to spend together, since most days I'm working long after they've gone to bed.

They grew inches while they were gone at camp, coming home with a trunk full of filthy clothes that no longer fit. I expected Cecilia to take the whole trunk and dump it in our trash can, but instead she sat on the floor of the laundry room, eyes glistening. When I asked her what was wrong, she said, "I'll never get those months back. They're gone. They're so different and I missed the change."

She's right. Almost two months without their parents and they did come back different kids. They eat dinner like animals, but otherwise, all the changes have been positive, at least what I see. They're confident and independent, and maybe that's part of Cecilia's sadness. The boys don't need her as much. I feel a pang of guilt. There's a finite number of summers with your children and we lost one because of this campaign.

Having them home has increased the hectic nature of our days—coordinating the schedules of two active boys, one active campaign, and a couple who largely communicates through assistants. I hoped Cecilia and I would grow close over the summer, working together on the campaign without children's demands constantly distracting us. Instead, it was the opposite. We grew further apart. In some ways, the boys returning made it easier. At least we have an excuse for barely seeing each other.

I could blame Stuart because he wanted to double our coverage by scheduling us at separate events. But when it was just Cece and me in the house at night, we didn't recap our days or laugh over the antics of my staff. We climbed into bed and rolled onto opposite sides, a sea of space between our bodies. Marriages have phases, and passion comes and goes, but Cecilia has long acted like sex with her husband is a task she needs to check off her list, somewhere between yoga class and planning dinner. I stopped trying after too many nights of feeling like her obligation rather than her desire.

Before I agreed to run, I asked Cece if she ever thought about divorce. It's a word I never wanted to utter, and the shock of it rolling off my tongue immediately made me feel queasy. Stuart kept harping that a strong candidate needed a solid marriage. I nodded along, in the reflexive sort of response that was expected. But the more questions Stuart asked about the state of our relationship, the more fear I felt about our future. We'd been distant for years, blaming it on my career and the demands of raising twins. Still, I surprised us both with the question because we were so good at pretending to be okay.

She shook her head and relief washed over me. While we weren't the perfect couple, I wanted the family I never had and to keep trying to be the husband she needed. *We can do this,* I thought, until I saw Cece's chin quiver as she said, "The boys are too young."

Most days I feel like an expired piece of meat hiding in the back corner of the fridge. She'll kick me out eventually. But I hold out hope that I can fix this. Maybe she'll change her mind and love me again, even the rotten parts.

Declan runs up to me and wraps his arms around my waist as his backpack falls to the floor. He speaks so quickly that it's hard to follow the play-by-play excitement of fifth-grade gym class and the joke his teacher told about fractions. On his last breath he exclaims, "Mom let us get ice cream after school. I got rainbow cotton candy. Two scoops. Hudson just got vanilla."

Hudson sits in my office chair and spins around as he says, "I like what I like."

Declan is by his side immediately, spinning him faster and faster.

I turn to Cecilia and whisper, "What are the odds one of them pukes?"

"High," Cecilia says on a sigh. "Boys, please stop spinning."

Cecilia has a quiet power about her, evident by the fact that the boys follow her instructions. If I had asked them, they would have laughed and spun faster, ignoring me until I walked away.

I want to be a better father. I want them to listen to me and care about me, and sometimes I think they do. My worst fear is that one day my boys will look at me with hatred instead of with admiration. I might spend too much time in the office, but I tell them I love them every night before bed. I try to make up for the fact that I never heard those words from my own father. It's not enough, but it's a way I can try to be better every day. And I remind myself that they're lucky to have Cecilia. It makes a huge difference to have that kind of love and stability in your life, especially when your father works too much.

"Do you think you'll be home for dinner tonight?" Cecilia asks.

Stuart wants to meet and I'm surprised he isn't already in my office. He wants to spend the evening discussing the strategy for the second debate.

I shake my head, seeing the flash of disappointment on Cecilia's face, but she quickly masks it and smiles at our sons. "Well, since it is just us, how about we pick up some burgers on our way home?"

Hudson says, "Cool."

Declan declares, "This is the most epic day ever. Ice cream, cheeseburgers, and unlimited Minecraft. I love my life."

Cecilia laughs as she says, "Ice cream, cheeseburger, and then homework and baths. Nice try, Declan."

"Worth a shot," Declan says as he high-fives Hudson.

They may be twins, but they are polar opposites. I often wonder how much genetics plays into who a child becomes. Are there parts of me that are unavoidable because of my parents? But if my twins teach me anything, identical genes seemed irrelevant to their strongly emerging personalities. Seeing their differences is a comfort.

Stuart walks into my office, a cell phone to his ear. "As deep as you can fucking go," Stuart says into the phone, before hanging up and noticing the audience in my office.

"Sorry," he mouths to Cecilia before walking toward Hudson and spinning him faster in my chair.

"Me next," Declan pleads.

My wife rolls her eyes. "Time to go, boys." Cecilia herds the boys toward the door, straightening the pens they knocked over and pushing my chair back in place.

A few seconds of hugs and bets about whether they can eat two whole cheeseburgers, or maybe even three, and my office is quiet again.

"What was that call about?" I ask Stuart.

"Nothing," he says.

I cross my arms, waiting for his answer.

"Fine," Stuart says. "That was a buddy at the RNC. He's doing me a favor."

"What kind of favor do we need from the National Committee?" I ask.

"The kind of favor I don't want to discuss with you," Stuart says.

"When has that answer ever worked, in the history of all political campaigns?"

"I've already dealt with enough bad news today," Stuart says. "You're not going to like my answer and I don't have enough patience to cater to your emotions right now. We need to get started on debate prep."

"What bad news?" I ask, frowning.

Stuart walks to the window and stares outside. "We are down six points. Tess Murphy is likable Teflon and I hate losing. We are adjusting our strategy."

I knew we had dropped in the polls, but I didn't realize the drop was that big. No wonder Stuart is on edge. "Am I included in this strategy discussion?" I ask.

"Yes. But the national party guys have more experience. We need their help."

"Is that what your call was about? This new strategy?"

Stuart nods.

"Talk, Stuart. I'm the candidate. I want to be in on it," I say, leaning back in my chair and crossing my arms.

"We need dirt." Stuart sits on the edge of my desk. "We need to make Tess Murphy unlikable."

I immediately start shaking my head. "No opposition research. That's not how I want to play this. We focus on our campaign, our platform."

"Okay," Stuart says in a sarcastic way that obviously means the opposite.

"Stewie, I'm serious. No dirt digging. No negative ads. I've been clear that's not the way I want to win."

"Either we do it and control the narrative or the national party does it on their own, without our input, and we have no control." Stuart starts pacing the room. "There is no such thing as a clean campaign anymore. Especially not against a candidate like Tess Murphy: married to her college sweetheart, career public servant, committed to the cause."

Stuart leans forward, his arms perched on either side of my desk. "You win as the family man. Voters have to like you more, and that's not easy because she's incredibly likable." He leans back and says, "And don't call me Stewie. I hate that."

I smirk briefly, but then the weight of Stuart's words settles. He's right. Everyone falls for Tess Murphy, even the people who should hate her. I know this firsthand. But I also know the danger of opposition research, and the secrets it may uncover.

"No," I say, forcefully. "I'm firm on this. No good comes from digging up dirt on Tess Murphy."

Stuart shrugs. "You had no problem with negative ads on the other Republicans."

I swallow. I need to tell him. I need to tell him everything so that he can manage this situation.

I shake my head as I confidently say, "We have to consider the gender dynamics. We attack her and it will look bad."

Stuart seems to think about this. "We'll make them reactive. When she attacks, we respond. But we have to be ready to respond. We need to start the opposition research."

"Table it for now. We can deal with that if and only if she attacks."

Stuart starts to lose his cool. "You have no idea how these things work. You're a newbie. I love that, but you have to trust the political experts."

"Stuart, I'm not willing to negotiate on this. No opposition research. It's not how I'm going to get elected."

Stuart's eyes narrow. "What do you think your father is going to think of this approach?"

My jaw immediately tightens at the mention of my father, my teeth grinding back and forth. "You don't work for my father. You work for me."

"He's incredibly well connected. You might need to get past your hatred so that we can use his influence."

"No," I say flatly. "Mention him again and I'll find a new campaign manager."

"Fine," he says with an eye roll.

Stuart doesn't push because he knows it's pointless. I've never been good at letting people in, and Stuart gave up trying years ago. We've known each other since we were boys, he attended my wedding, sent cigars when the twins were born, and yet I've shut down every attempt at emotional conversations with one-word answers and shoulder shrugs, especially when it comes to questions about my father. I've kept our friendship superficial because that's the only way I knew to hide my family's dark secrets. And now, I try to keep our relationship professional, because we both want to win, and explaining why I hate my father isn't going to help that goal.

Stuart continues, "The opposition research is happening. They've started digging into Tess. I should have the report by the end of the week."

"Well, tell them to stop," I say, stumbling over the words.

"I can't." Stuart speaks slowly, his eyes narrowing into slits. "Winning this election matters to more people than just you. Get. On. Board."

I pace the room, my thoughts spiraling as I feel Stuart's focused eyes examining my every move.

"Spill it," Stuart says. "Why do you care about the Tess Murphy opposition research?" he asks quietly.

"Because I knew her," I blurt.

"What?" His response is almost a laugh until he sees the panic on my face.

"I knew Tess," I say, as I swallow slowly.

"You cheated on Cece?" I watch as anger sweeps across Stuart's face, his mind jumping twelve steps ahead.

"No. I've never cheated on Cece. You know I wouldn't do that."

There are lines I'd never cross after witnessing the destruction between my parents. "This was before I met Cece. Tess and I were kids. It was the summer before Princeton."

"Start talking," Stuart says. His face is pale. I watch as shock turns into something else. He's hurt. This secret must feel like a betrayal of our friendship, but it seems too late to fix that mistake.

I use the same story Tess repeated to her campaign. I tell Stuart that I met Tess when I was eighteen; she worked for my mother one summer; I haven't seen her since.

Stuart listens, except he's known me most of my life. He knows that my story could never be this simple. He's uncharacteristically silent as he waits for me to finish.

"That's it. That's why I don't want opposition research."

Stuart shakes his head slowly. "In all the campaigns I've worked on, something has always come out. A secret. Some housekeeper paid under the table, a teenage arrest, drug use. Everybody has something to hide. But I naively thought that running my friend's campaign would be different."

"You never asked if I knew her."

"I didn't know that was a question I needed to ask. Don't worry, I'll update my candidate background questionnaire. Going forward, I will ask if any of my candidates screwed the opposition."

"You're crossing a line, Stuart."

"Really? You don't think it would have been a good idea to tell your campaign manager, your friend, that you know the opposing candidate? That you had sex with the opposing candidate? Jesus, Grant. This is some grade-A idiot shit, even coming from you."

"She worked for my mother for a few weeks. It was one summer. You're jumping to conclusions."

"I need to know the whole story. Now," Stuart commands.

"That's it. You have the whole story, Stuart."

He shakes his head, unconvinced. "Who else knows?" Stuart asks, his chin jutting forward.

"Tess and her campaign manager." I hesitate before continuing. "And my father."

"Tess's campaign knows? Fuck." He draws out every syllable of his favorite word.

I quickly cut off Stuart's spiraling. "Tess's campaign manager was sent a picture of us, from an anonymous account. Tess admitted she worked for my mother. That's it."

"At least you two agree on your lies." Stuart's voice deepens as he continues. "This is going to be everywhere. It will destroy your campaign. There is no such thing as one isolated photograph from an anonymous account. You are staring down the tunnel of a blackmail campaign."

"I don't think so," I say, my voice sputtering. "Tess and I have been in touch. Her campaign hasn't received any other pictures."

"Oh, you've been in touch with Tess. That's nice." Stuart folds his hands, his body and words making a mockery of my statement while his eyes narrow. He looks like he wants to murder me.

"I met with her once. I thought it was necessary."

"Listen," Stuart growls. "It was necessary to tell your campaign manager the truth. Meeting with the opposing candidate is never necessary." He pauses, annoyed that he has to take a break to breathe. "You lied. You need to start talking. If I'm going to manage this, I need to know everything."

My forehead immediately starts to dampen. A part of me wants to explain. Because maybe then I could begin to alleviate the gnawing guilt of that summer. But I know I can't. All of the worst moments of my life are tied up with Tess. If I admit one part of our relationship, everything unravels. It's not just about the campaign anymore. It will destroy my future and the dreams Stuart shares.

"Do you think I'm an idiot?" Stuart says. "If she worked for your mother, you would have told me. If you had something to hide, you would freak out about opposition research. You hid this for a reason and I'm trying to figure out just how epically it's going to blow up in our faces."

I hang my head, knowing Stuart is right.

It's then that I notice Stuart and I are not alone. He was too angry and I was too defensive to notice that Cecilia slipped into the room and is standing behind my heavy office door.

I don't know how long she's been there, but she's heard enough to create a tightness across her face, her slender hands clenching into fists. She looks as if she's deciding whether to slap me or run.

Cecilia stutters, "Declan left his backpack." She bends over to pick it up.

I lean in to Cecilia's ear and whisper, "There's nothing to tell. It was one summer. It meant nothing."

She takes a step back, her eyes slowly moving from my feet up to my face. "You sound like your father," she says, knowing the devastation of those words.

"I can explain," I stutter.

She closes her eyes. When they open, I see a streak of pain quickly disappear as she surveys the room. "Yes. We will speak later," she says.

She walks away. There is an audience of campaign staffers outside my now open office door. I reach for her arm. She hesitates but then kisses me on the cheek because of the room of people pretending to work while they gawk at this scene. Her voice is clear and her eyes are narrow as she says, "I'm taking our children home. You should change your plans and join us for dinner. And you will tell me everything."

I nod.

Cecilia tosses Declan's backpack over her shoulder as she says, "You can pick up the burgers, Grant." She leaves, exchanging pleasantries with the staff on her way out, and never once looks back at me.

There's a brief look of guilt on Stuart's face. He knows this isn't good for my marriage, but his remorse quickly evaporates.

"Sit down," Stuart says, slamming my office door. "We need to come up with a plan."

I shake my head. "I need some space, Stuart."

He laughs too loudly. "No. You need to tell me the entire story of your relationship with Tess Murphy and then we need to prepare for the second debate."

"I can't," I say, my voice as unstable as my body feels.

"Yes. You. Can." Stuart speaks to me like I'm a child he needs to teach a lesson.

I stand, but Stuart corners me at the door, blocking the exit.

"Leave me alone, Stuart. I'm serious. I'm done." Each word is louder than the last. As if my voice is yet another thing I'm unable to control in this rapidly deteriorating situation.

Stuart holds up his hands. "Sorry I'm blindly trying to win a campaign for a candidate who doesn't seem to care."

"Then quit!" I scream.

"No," Stuart says. "Dropping out would be a career-ender for me. You can't imagine the scrutiny I'm under since the last election. If I botch this, I'll be lucky to get a state rep campaign."

"You made it seem like you were doing me a favor."

"I am, Grant. I'm the best. But I lost the last election and I'm trying to prove to the entire Republican Party that I can be the kingmaker they need. Besides, I've won with bigger shit shows than this. Leave. We'll talk tomorrow."

I know everyone is staring as I walk toward the front door. They expect an explanation, some reason why their boss who barely raises his voice to get everyone's attention at team meetings just screamed at his campaign manager. But I'm all out of words.

Except Cece needs an explanation tonight. Maybe it's time I told her what happened that summer. Because it feels impossible to hide the truth any longer, and then she'll finally know that all this time, I've just been pretending to be a good man.

Fourteen

SEPTEMBER 1996

My bags were by the front door, ready for the drive to Princeton. I wasn't sure whether my sense of dread was over leaving Tess or spending six hours in a car with two people who hated each other. The night before, I heard my parents arguing, insisting that they could each take me alone, fighting about who was the better parent. I fell asleep to my Walkman at full volume, drowning out their voices.

I woke up as the sun was rising and looked out back, sure I was going to see my mother in her garden, pruning flowers before the trip away. But the garden was empty.

I shuffled down the hallway, past my father's shut door. He must have been asleep, which wasn't like him. He was usually up all hours of the day.

My mother's room was on the opposite end of the house. My parents had slept alone in separate wings of the house for the last few years, their physical distance mimicking the emotional wall building between them. Her door was cracked open, so I stepped inside, finding an empty bed.

I glanced at my watch. It was a few hours before we were supposed to get on the road. I wanted to see Tess. To hold her and tell her for the thousandth time that I would see her soon. That I would talk to her that night. That even though everything was changing, nothing was going to change about how much I loved her.

Before I left my mother's room, I noticed her bathroom light was on. I called out softly, "Mom, you up?"

No response.

I knocked on the slightly ajar bathroom door. "Mom?"

When I stuck my head inside, I saw her, lying in the bathtub, naked. Embarrassed, I whipped around and stood immobile in her bedroom.

"Sorry, Mom," I stuttered. "See you downstairs?"

But she didn't answer. There wasn't a sound coming out of the bathroom.

There should have been a warning sign that my life was about to shatter. Instead, there was a deafening silence.

I turned around and pushed the door fully open, stepping onto the cool, marble floor of the bathroom, expecting to wake my mother out of a stupor. To move through the motions like any other morning, my mother hungover, our mutual awkwardness resulting in stifled conversations ignoring any acknowledgment of reality. I reached for one of her obscenely expensive ivory towels, my fingers sinking into the lush fibers. I couldn't believe this was how I was going to spend my last morning at home. Pretending I didn't see my mother drunk in the bathtub, shielding her nakedness so that my teenage-boy eyes didn't wither into my skull, hoping that things would get better once my father and I weren't such a daily bother.

I held up the towel, squeezing my eyes shut. "Here you go." I waited for her reply, but it never came.

"Mom, you need to get dressed. We'll be leaving soon," I said, hiding behind the towel and hoping that this momentary embarrassment would be a memory easy to erase.

I waited too long, too many moments of silence with no response before I slowly lowered the towel and looked into the tub.

Her face was unnaturally pale. I said her name again and she didn't move, not even when my voice turned to shouts, panic rising into my throat. I lunged forward, my arms diving into the water as the tepid temperature sent alarm bells ringing. She didn't just get in the bath. She'd been there for hours.

I held on to hope, a chance she'd be okay as I heaved her out of the bathtub, streams of water soaking my clothes. Her limp body slid out of my arms and onto the bathmat. It was the open eyes that would haunt me the most. I was used to vacant stares from my mother, but this was different. Bold, black pupils overtaking any trace of her blue irises, her lips slightly parted but no breath escaping.

I jumped back, drops of water spilling off my shirt. My heart raced from the terror and tragedy in front of me.

I ran down the hallway, bursting open the door to my father's room, because I needed help and had no idea what to do.

"Dad," I stammered. My voice sounded unfamiliar, like a child creeping into his parents' bed after a nightmare.

My father rolled over and groaned. "Grant, get out of here. I need to get some sleep."

My whole body was shaking, my voice cracking as I said,

"Dad. It's Mom. Come. Now." Each word was an instruction, a plea.

I ran back down the hall, gasping for breath as I heard his footsteps behind mine.

I stood outside the bathroom door, my face soaked with tears I had no control over.

My father walked into the bathroom and I watched his body still, his eyes close briefly, and then open as he stared at the ceiling. "Shit," he whispered.

He bent down, checking for a pulse, and then straightened. He walked out of the bathroom without even a gesture toward me and headed down the hall to the phone. I heard him pick it up calmly, methodically, taking a deep breath before dialing.

"I need a favor," he said.

I had no idea why he wasn't calling for an ambulance or who was on the other end of that phone call. The calmness of his voice unsettled me almost more than my mother's body had.

I stumbled into her bathroom, not knowing where else to go or what do to. Her skin was white, blue undertones seeping through. Her open eyes almost seemed like she was pleading for help. And if I could, I would have done anything to help my mother. But I couldn't.

I stared at my mother and knew she was dead.

Suffocating my fear, I gently brushed my hands against her eyelids to close them and give her some deserved peace.

My father walked back into the bathroom and put one hand on my shoulder. "You shouldn't see this. Let's wait outside." He said it like we were waiting for a movie to start.

I lunged at him, fists swinging wildly. "Did you do this?" I screamed. "Did you kill my mother?"

He pulled me tight, holding my arms against my sides as he

rocked my body back and forth. He shushed me like I was a baby, which was probably the last time he'd held me that close.

"Your mother was sick, Grant. I'm so sorry. I'm going to take care of this. I'm going to take care of you."

"You have never taken care of me!" I shouted.

"You have no idea how much I have done for you. Let me deal with this situation and then we'll have a talk." He sighed, like he was exasperated by my display of emotion.

"*This situation?*" I screamed. "She's dead. Your wife is dead. And you're treating it like some corporate takeover. You're disgusting."

"No, I'm doing what must be done. I take care of the problems and messes that others leave behind." He gestured around the room, finally pointing at my mother.

"If she was a mess, it was because of you," I accused.

For the first time that morning, I saw emotion streak across my father's face. He was wearing a matching set of plaid pajamas and looked vulnerable in a way I thought impossible. I rarely saw my father out of his suit.

His voice was low as he said, "We loved each other once, you know. Then we didn't. We came to an arrangement that worked for us both. But your mother was unhappy. I never thought it would go this far."

It was the only time he ever acknowledged responsibility for my mother's pain.

Tears flooded my eyes and I shoved him away, racing downstairs and out the front door. I kept running. I ran away from him and the icy coldness that surrounded his lack of emotion. My lungs burned as I thought about my mother and how long she must have been lying in that frigid tub. Was she waiting for him? Did she slip and hurt herself? Did she drink too much and find her body easing under the water? Or was it possible that he did something to her? He was the coldest, most calculating person I'd ever known, but would he hurt his wife while his son slept down the hall?

I kept running, thoughts spiraling through my head, unsure whether I would ever know the truth. Whoever my father called on the phone would help him put a tidy bow on the unfortunate situation of his wife's death.

My mother may not have been perfect, but she was the only love I had known. As a boy, when my father's sharp words sliced me to the core, she swooped in with tight hugs and assurances. As I got older and more hardened to his demeanor, she still tried to smooth the rough edges of our life, justifying my father's outbursts by explaining that his work was stressful. Every bruise on her face, her arms, came with a story about an accident or delicate skin. I saw past these excuses, knowing my father's true nature, finding her complicity unsettling. Now I wondered if it led to her death.

My mother was the only love I knew, before Tess. Maybe that's why I found myself dripping in sweat, panting at her front door. When it opened, Tess's mother was standing there. She opened her mouth to speak, but something about my face must have stopped whatever she meant to say.

"Tess," she called quietly.

A sleepy Tess walked toward me. Her eyes were red-rimmed and puffy. Did she know?

"Grant, I can't say goodbye again. It's too hard," Tess said.

I shook my head and choked out the words. "She's gone. My mother is gone. She's . . . dead."

Her arms wrapped around my body as I slowly slid to the hard floor. I heard unfamiliar screams, and it wasn't until Tess's voice intertwined with those sounds, repeating, "I'm here, I'm here," that I realized the sounds were coming from me.

"Don't leave me," I whispered.

"I'm not going anywhere," she said, and I believed her.

We sat like that, clutching each other, for much of the morning. At some point, her mother left for work. But Tess stayed. Her small, warm frame clung to my side as my body shook. I barely spoke. Maybe I thought if I acted like time was frozen, I could undo this morning. But that wasn't possible.

Eventually, Tess's mother came back to the cottage. She said Ms. Milton got a call from my father. I'd been gone long enough that even Richard Alexander felt the need to express some concern.

Tess hadn't asked a single question, seemingly knowing that there was nothing about this morning I was able to explain. She sat beside me, providing the support I needed without even asking.

But Tess's mother was different. Her voice was gentle, but her eyes were full of concern as she said, "Ms. Milton said your mother fell, Grant."

"She's lying. My father is a liar," I said, nostrils flaring. "Don't believe anything he says."

Tess's mother reached for my hand. "They're worried about you. Your father is going to send out a search party if you don't go back soon."

I stood and nodded. "I'll get out of your way. I don't want to cause you any problems."

"Mom, what's wrong with you?" Tess asked. "Grant, stay. You don't have to go back there."

"Yes, he does. He needs to be with his family. And I don't need to explain to Ms. Milton why he is here," Tess's mother said.

"His mother died," Tess whispered harshly. "There are more important things than your stupid job."

I watched the unspoken conversation unfold between Tess and her mother as their eyes narrowed and the room filled with tension. Last week, Tess's mother had been offered full-time employment at the Milton estate. Tess had enrolled in the local high school. It was everything they had worked for all summer. It was too much for them to lose.

I placed a hand on Tess's shoulder as I said, "It's okay. She's right. I have to go home." My voice cracked and Tess wove her fingers into mine.

"I'll go with you." Tess squeezed my hand tighter.

"No, Tess. You stay here," her mother said. "You are not family."

"Yes, she is." I stared at Tess, our eyes locked. "Tess is my family." At that moment, I never doubted the truth of that statement.

She wrapped her arms around my waist, melting into my body. We were a unified force, oblivious to everything around us, including our mounting differences.

"I'm not leaving him," Tess said. "He needs me."

Tess's mother looked away, her eyebrows drawn together as she said, "I have to get back to work." She walked toward the door and said, "I'm sorry for your loss, Grant." As she left, she mouthed, "Be careful." I assumed it was directed at Tess, but it felt like a warning we all needed.

Tess and I walked slowly back to my mother's house. The sun was shining brightly, like peak summer, but the air was crisper, hinting at the fall to come. Everything was green and lush, rolling fields melting into the hills. It was a beautiful day, the landscape coming to life, and I was dead inside.

Tess was gentle, asking me simple questions. But I couldn't respond. I didn't know how my mother died. Even when she died. As we walked up to the house, I knew I needed answers. The shock of that morning hadn't worn off, but I felt more prepared to confront my father with Tess at my side.

I expected to see a swarm of emergency vehicles, but instead, there was a single sheriff's cruiser parked in the driveway next to my father's green Jaguar. We found the sheriff and my father sitting at the kitchen table, chatting casually.

"Where is she? Where is my mother?" I demanded.

Richard looked up and sighed as he said, "Your mother's body is at the morgue." His eyes narrowed in on Tess. "Where have you been? With the gardener? Please send her home."

I felt Tess's body stiffen next to mine, Richard's cold voice creating even more tension in this tight corner of the room.

"She stays." I stared at my father, a silent standoff that he eventually ended by looking away.

"Why aren't there more police officers here?" I insisted. I forced my voice to be as steady as my father's, even though my insides were churning. "There should be an investigation. You need to figure out how my mother died," I said to the sheriff.

"There will be no investigation." Richard's tone was as dismissive as it was confident.

"Why not?" I screamed. "What did you do to her? She was fine last night. And now this morning she's dead in her bathtub. What happened?" I pleaded.

"Your mother hasn't been fine for a long time, son." It should have been a term of endearment, but the way my father said "son" seemed more like a warning. "Your mother's death was a long time coming."

I lunged for my father, shocked by his callousness. Even by

Richard's low standards, his lack of emotion over my mother's death compounded my pain.

The sheriff quickly set down his coffee cup and jumped up, inserting himself between me and my father. "Are you arresting him?" I asked, jabbing my finger toward my father's chest.

"Of course not, Grant." Richard turned away as he said, "It was an accident. Your mother fell and hit her head on the bathtub. It's a tragedy. That's what we will say."

Tess shifted from side to side. I could only imagine how uncomfortable she felt, being in this room, hearing these bizarre reactions.

The sheriff placed a reassuring hand on my shoulder. "I'm sorry for your loss."

Those were the same words Tess's mother had said. It was the phrase any decent human being would say, but it only highlighted the lack of emotion Richard displayed.

I stared him down. "I don't believe you."

Richard slammed a pill bottle on the counter. "This was empty. She took sleeping pills and then chased them down with a bottle of wine. She was reckless and now she's gone."

I couldn't speak, but my head shook back and forth. My father was an asshole, but was he right? I tried to remember my mother's actions leading up to that night. She was sad and drinking more and my mind spun with all the times I should have tried harder to slow her spiral.

"Neither of us deserve the disgrace of your mother's addiction," Richard said. "The sheriff has kindly agreed to keep the circumstances of her death confidential. As will everyone else in this room." I watched as my father glared at Tess. He raised his eyebrows as he said, "Understood?" He said it like a command.

"She didn't always drink this much," I said, my voice small. "What happened this summer?"

The muscles in Richard's jaw tightened. He hesitated, shifting from one foot to another. His eyes darted over to the sheriff, who took a step closer, clearly interested in his answer. "It's obvious, Grant." Richard sighed before continuing, "You're the reason."

I shook my head back and forth, feeling Tess's hand grip mine tighter.

Richard continued. "Your mother got to spend the summer with you, her only child, right before you left for college. It should have been the happiest time of her life. But the longer you were here, the more depressed she got. She saw your laziness—sleeping most of the day and, apparently, sneaking off with this common girl. Your admission to Princeton was almost rescinded because of that stupid prank. I told her that you were a spoiled child who wouldn't amount to much. She started the summer hopeful that you would show some worth, but we all know how she felt by the end of the summer."

I knew about his cruel tactics. I knew how he manipulated me. But the devastation of his words choked the air out of my throat. "That's not true."

He leaned forward, harsh whispers coming out through gritted teeth. "Covering up your mother's addiction is more for you than me. What kind of mother drinks and drugs herself into oblivion while spending the summer with her only child? What does that say about the mother? Or worse, the child?"

Once my father had finished, he gestured toward the door. "I'll walk you out, Sheriff." The conversation was over, and knowing my father, so were any future discussions of my mother's death.

I turned toward Tess, tears streaking down her face. A part

of me was embarrassed that Tess saw this side of my life. Another part knew I wouldn't be able to stand if she weren't at my side.

My mother's behavior *had* become more erratic, and I knew she was drinking more. Something happened that summer that seemed to send her over whatever edge she'd teetered on before. Maybe it was my fault. I watched her decline but was too consumed with Tess to ask what was bothering her. I was too focused on myself and let my mother die. Or worse, my father was right.

"I need to lie down," I murmured.

"Nothing he said is true," Tess stated. "She loved you." Tess cupped her hands around my face as she continued, "Grant, you did not cause your mother's death. You know that, right? This was an accident."

Tess kept repeating, "It was an accident, Grant. Tell me you understand that." But it sounded so distant.

I nodded, but clearly it wasn't convincing, because Tess vehemently continued. "Her bag was packed for Princeton. She was so excited to take you up to college. She told me she had a stack of gifts in her closet for the care packages she planned on mailing you this fall."

I didn't want to be the disappointment my father described. I wanted to believe Tess. But unfortunately, Richard Alexander was right about almost everything.

Tess followed me upstairs, where I collapsed onto my bed. I tried not to think about the empty room on the other side of the house or my father's words or the loneliness seeping into my bones. Instead, I focused on Tess's warm body wrapped around mine, the rhythm of our breathing falling into sync as the sky turned dark.

In the days following my mother's death, time moved forward, yet I remained immobile. I spent too much time lying between the rows of rosebushes, avoiding my father and staring at the sky. Tess had started school, but as soon as classes ended, she dropped her backpack and came running across the fields to meet me in my mother's gardens.

Princeton told me to take as long as I needed. A part of me didn't want to leave my mother's house, but I knew that staying here, surrounded by her memories, was making every day more difficult.

Tess was the only break from the darkness. I should have been excited about the extra time we had together, but I couldn't let myself enjoy it. The pain of my mother's death was still too raw, my guilt too powerful.

I needed to get away from this place; I just wish it didn't also mean getting away from Tess.

I bent over my mother's prize rosebushes, trying to take care of them when Tess was at school, but I had no idea what I was doing.

Tess suddenly appeared in the bright sun. "Am I doing it wrong?" I asked, staring at the rosebush.

"Ummm . . ."

"She would have told me. She would have said, 'Drop those clippers, Grant Alexander. That's flower butchery.'"

"You're right. That's exactly what she would have said. Let me help." Tess reached for the clippers, letting our hands linger, before she showed me how to prune back the dead growth.

"What size ice cream today?" Tess asked.

"Single scoop," I said, and turned back to the roses.

The day of my mother's funeral, I told Tess that I was tired of everyone asking how I was doing. No one wanted to hear the honest answer—that my mother dying was a pain that could never be healed and every tiny step felt like climbing a mountain.

Tess and I decided to create our own code. When I worked in the ice-cream shop, I could tell what kind of day a person was having based on their ice-cream order. A single-scoop day was pretty good: It meant that my mother was still gone, but I was able to get dressed. There weren't going to be any banana splits. Nothing about life felt celebratory.

"How about you?" I asked.

"Not bad. The teachers are acceptable and the other kids in my class mostly leave me alone. It seems like a lot of work to make new friends." Tess stared off across the field.

I elbowed her side. "Make friends. You are very likable. Trust me. I know."

"I'm new. And I say the wrong thing. You are an outlier in the 'Tess is likable' club."

"I am the president of that club," I said.

Tess flashed me a quick smile but then returned to pruning the flowers. She was quiet, and Tess was never quiet after school. When she fumbled the clippers and they fell to the ground, I knew something was wrong.

"What's bothering you, Tess?"

Tess winced. "It doesn't matter. We can talk later."

I pulled Tess down onto the grass next to me. "You're worried about something. Talk to me."

Tess shook her head. "I refuse to pile on to the Grant sadness sundae." Tess fidgeted with the garden shears, her eyes refusing to meet mine. I saw a nervous shake to her hand.

"Spill it," I ordered.

Tess sighed. On her exhale, she blurted, "I don't want to push, but I need to know what you're planning. I need to know how long you're going to be here and when you're going to leave me and how I'm going to do this alone."

I swallowed, clueless about how to respond. Because I didn't have those answers. And I'd never heard Tess so worked up. My voice was timid as I asked, "You feel all of this because you have to make new friends at school?"

"No," Tess quickly said, and then seemed to correct herself. "Kind of." Tess's face was pale when she turned toward me. "I need to talk to you. It's not a good time, I know that. I'm just not sure how much longer I can wait."

"Tess, whatever you have to say, I'm listening. You're scaring me."

"I think you should be scared. I'm terrified."

"Tell me." I tried to slow my racing heart.

Tess took a deep breath. Yet somehow, I knew whatever she was about to say was going to break up this bubble we'd been living in.

"I'm pregnant."

I should have tried harder, but I couldn't hide the shock on my face.

She started rambling about how she took a drugstore test in the high school bathroom stall. About how her periods had always been erratic. Tess kept apologizing and then she begged me to say something, anything.

"But we use condoms," I stuttered.

"Not the first time," Tess said softly.

"But that was your very first time."

Tess swallowed. "The irony is not lost on me."

"You're really pregnant?"

"Yes." Tess's voice hitched as she gasped for air before crumbling into tears.

I wrapped my arms around her and repeated, "It'll be okay."

"I'm sorry, Grant."

"Don't apologize. We did this together."

Tess's voice sounded jagged and erratic. "I know you miss your mom and this is the last thing you need right now."

"I miss her. Life feels like a tornado without her."

"I'm making it worse." Tess's sobs intensified.

"You're not making it worse. You're the only normal thing in my life right now."

"This is so messed up," Tess said, wiping her nose with the back of her hand. "I'm pretty sure a pregnant teenage girlfriend should never feel normal."

"It's okay. We will be okay." I couldn't tell if I was reassuring Tess or myself.

"I'm shocked and scared and so mad at myself for being so stupid. I got an A in biology. I know how this works."

"Tess, you've gotten an A in every class you've taken."

"So why did I make such a stupid mistake?"

"We were stupid, Tess. Together." I took a deep breath, an eerie calm coming over me. "Maybe this was meant to be."

"What do you mean?" she asked.

"We've known each other only a few months, but you feel more like family than I've ever known." Images of Tess filled my head. Every moment with her was better than the last. "It will be hard, but we can do this." I felt a glimmer of hope that had been missing for weeks. I spoke faster and faster, fitting in pieces of an imaginary puzzle. "I'll transfer to UVA. We'll get married, we'll have this baby."

"We can't afford a baby," Tess said, her voice measured and clear.

I nodded slowly. "My father will probably cut me off. But that's for the best. I don't want to have anything to do with him anyway. I'll get a job. I'll find a way to support us."

"No offense, Grant. But it takes a lot of scoops of ice cream to pay for diapers."

I flexed my arm and said, "I'm a very talented scooper."

Tess smiled out of obligation, because her face quickly fell as she said, "We can't do this."

I reached for Tess's hand. "It'll be hard, but we have each other."

"Grant, you're saying all the things that you're supposed to say. But you can stop pretending. There is no way we can have this baby. This isn't a hard situation, it's an impossible one."

"We don't have a choice, Tess. I didn't plan on starting a family now, but the best things in my life have been surprises." I kissed Tess on the cheek, indicating that she was one of the best things. I thought I'd always feel that way.

"We have a choice. I have a choice." Tess's words came out clearly and with conviction.

I immediately understood what she meant, and pain washed over me. My jaw clenched as I searched her face, trying to find the person I knew.

Tess scrambled to explain. "Grant, I'm a high school senior. If I have a baby, that's all I'll have in life. I can forget my plans to travel and see the world, to get an education and a job. I will have a child and I will struggle the rest of my life just like I've watched my mother struggle."

"You have a mother who loves you. Seems like a pretty lucky life to me." My voice teetered between bitter and broken, unsure which way to fall.

"Says the guy who has never struggled for a second of his life," Tess said, widening our divide.

"Struggle isn't only financial, Tess." My head fell into my hands. Everyone was slipping away. My mother. My Tess.

"I'm sorry," Tess said, inching closer to my side. "I don't want to fight with you."

"I know. We'll figure it out," I said with a stoic expression. We sat in uncomfortable silence.

"I don't want to have the baby," Tess whispered.

"What are you saying, Tess?"

"I think I should have an abortion."

My eyes narrowed. "But it's our child."

"We can't take care of a child."

"You won't even consider keeping the baby?"

"I don't know," Tess said. "I'm seventeen. It would change everything."

"Not all change is bad."

"Grant, my life is just starting. I don't want to give up everything."

"Please, Tess. I'm begging you. Don't make any decisions right now. I love you." I placed my hand gently on Tess's stomach. "We can be a family."

Tears flooded Tess's eyes. Her shoulders shook as choked cries escaped her lips. My eyes scanned back and forth, searching for something, anything, to comfort her.

It was then that I noticed we weren't alone.

My father stood at the edge of the garden. His eyes narrowed in on Tess and my hand on her abdomen, shaking his head in disgust. Tess buried her sobs in my chest as I instinctively clung to her tighter. At that moment, I foolishly thought holding the person I loved could keep us together. I should have known my father would find a way to break us apart.

Fifteen

SEPTEMBER 2021

I knock and hear a groan on the other side of the hotel door. Tess turns the lock and flings it open with an exasperated "Mara, I don't want to talk about it."

Except it's not Mara at her door. It's me.

"Grant, what are you doing here?" Tess pulls her robe tighter as I take a step into her hotel room.

"We need to talk," I say.

"You can't come in here." Tess blocks the doorway, pushing me backward.

"Do you want to have this conversation in the hall?" I ask.

Tess bites her lip, seemingly unsure what to do. The last thing either of us needs is some hotel guest walking by, seeing two political candidates standing together in the Ritz-Carlton hallway.

Hours earlier, the second debate was held in the grand ballroom ten floors below. I should be back in my home, a few miles down the road, but instead I'm standing in front of Tess, my eyes begging her to let me in.

"Fine," she says, gesturing me into the room before I glance over my shoulder, relieved there is no one else around. "How did you find my room?"

"I bribed the guy at the front desk."

"That was stupid. He'll sell that story," Tess quickly criticizes, before noticing the glint in my eye. A slow smile creeps across my face because I can't help teasing her. It's easy to slip back into our old dynamics.

She folds her arms across her chest. "What did you really do?"

"I overheard your campaign manager tell one of the staffers backstage. Something about making sure there were enough potato chips in your minibar." My eyebrows raise. I kind of love that Tess's junk food addiction stuck around. So much else disappeared.

"I'm glad my campaign security is so solid," she mumbles.

I walk over to the minibar and grab a beer before sitting on the sofa in her hotel suite.

"Exactly how long are you planning on staying?" Tess asks.

I cross my leg and rest my ankle on the opposite knee. "Can you ever relax?"

"Not around you."

I take a long sip of beer and lean forward. "Have you heard anything more?" I ask.

Tess shakes her head.

We haven't spoken—outside of our debate—since we met for drinks in Washington, D.C. If Tess's campaign received any other emails from the anonymous source, I hoped she would call. I'm relieved that's true.

"My campaign knows," I admit. "My wife too."

Tess leans forward. "Knows what, exactly?"

"That we met before," I say, taking another long sip of my beer. "That we knew each other as teenagers."

"And they believed that was it?"

"No. But I didn't tell them more," I say.

The night Cece found out, I made it home for dinner. We sat together as a family, listening to the boys debate battle strategies for their latest video game obsession. Cece nodded and smiled at all the right times and I wondered how she did it. How did she pretend to care about a ten-year-old's imaginary world when our reality was crumbling? I had answers for the various questions I assumed she would ask, practicing in my car mirror on the drive home. But after the boys went upstairs and Cece was done pushing around her sad fast-food salad, we sat there silently. Eventually she asked about Tess, except I could tell she didn't want to hear my story. "Tess worked for your mother? One brief summer? That was all, right?" Cece didn't look into my eyes, her rapid-fire words less questions and more pleas for confirmation. It was so easy to go along with it. And when Cece eventually looked in my direction, she seemed relieved that we were able to continue this lie. She left to check on the boys' bedtime routine and I felt more regret than relief. Cece was the perfect wife. She trusted me. She believed me. I was finally ready to open up and it was clear she didn't want to hear it. Perfection is difficult to abandon.

Sitting in front of Tess makes me wonder about that more. "Dean wasn't here tonight," I comment.

Tess stiffens. "His classes started."

My eyes narrow. "Does he know?"

"No." Tess shifts uncomfortably in the upholstered chair next to the sofa that I was occupying. "But he's upset. Campaigns aren't easy on marriages."

I look down at the ground, twisting my wedding band. It's impossible to know the inner sanctum of a marriage. The last thing I want to do is speculate about Tess's. I'm still harboring so much anger toward her, but that doesn't negate the amount of guilt I feel toward the innocent players in each of our lives. None of them deserve any of the pain that may be coming.

"We're being so stupid, Grant," Tess says, her eyes welling. "This is going to come out and it's going to destroy us both."

"It may not come out." I try to keep my voice steady.

"Who would keep your mother's photo? Who would care about our past?"

"I don't know." I place my beer on the coffee table and lean back. "Whoever it is, they probably want the same thing everyone always wants. Money."

Tess flinches. "That's not what matters to everyone."

"Really?" It's a challenge and Tess knows it. She doesn't take the bait, refusing to answer any of the questions she left me to wrestle with decades ago.

"We've already had one debate tonight," Tess says softly. "I don't want to start another one."

I reluctantly nod in agreement. Fighting with Tess brings back the worst memories of my life. The fact that it is my job now seems like cruel punishment.

Tess shifts uncomfortably as she asks, "Do you believe what you said tonight?"

Immediately, I know what she's talking about. I lean forward. "Yes. Every word."

Stuart and I don't agree about much these days. He still pushes for the full story on Tess and I still deflect. But we both agree that abortion is the most critical issue to my campaign. And we knew that it would be the central issue of tonight's debate. When the moderator asked Tess about her position, she said all of the expected things about a woman's right to choose.

When it was my turn, I was ready with my carefully rehearsed statement. "I guess I never understood how my opponent could say abortion is a woman's choice. My wife chooses our dinners, our vacation plans, and most of my outfits." It was a folksy comment, but the audience laughed. I continued, "Abortion shouldn't be a choice like dinner, and certainly not something as simple as saying it is a woman's choice. Being a father is the greatest privilege of my life. I can only imagine what it would be like if my partner made a choice that took that gift away." I tried to hide the cracks in my voice. Because it was supposed to be a debate about an issue, not a fight about a long-ago mistake.

Tess was quick with her rebuttal, pointing out the burdens unique to women—financial, medical, interpersonal—that childbirth brings. She spoke too quickly and I could tell that her response sounded like a recitation, whereas I hoped I connected with voters on a more personal level. At least, that was the feedback I got from my campaign. But I'm sure she has an army of people selling her false promises of victory at the same time.

I don't agree with Tess. But the last thing she said at the debate keeps echoing in my head. "We have to trust women," Tess had said.

Except I did. I had trusted Tess, which made her betrayal unbearable.

"We are very different people," Tess says. She seems disappointed, and I understand. Because maybe if we agreed, we could have saved ourselves from the pain that drove us apart.

"Yes." I nod. We are no longer on the debate stage. We are

sitting across from each other in her hotel room. "Different people who both decided to run for governor. What a frustrating coincidence."

"You really think it's a coincidence that we're running against each other?" she asks.

"Of course. Don't you?"

She looks out the window, the dark night lit up with the lights of the surrounding buildings. "Maybe," she says. "Or maybe it was fate forcing our paths to cross."

"We have a lot of unfinished business, Tess."

"No. We have history. That's it." Tess looks away and I wonder if she is trying to convince herself that there's nothing more between us.

"You haven't ever wondered about me? All of these years later, you haven't ever tried to look me up? To have one last conversation?"

She swallows, her eyes finally meeting mine. "Of course I have. But then I think about the last time I saw you. It was one of the worst days of my life. I know I never want to feel that way again. I push those feelings and that speculation away. Instead, I look around at the life I have fought so hard to create and focus on that."

"It was the worst day of my life too, Tess."

I extend my hand across the center of the sofa. Our fingers are inches away from each other's. Tess's gravitational pull has always been too hard for me to avoid. My fingers float toward hers and for one brief moment, our hands connect. She recoils quickly and stands, smoothing her hair, pulling her robe tighter, polishing away our brief moment of weakness.

"If there are other emails or more photos? If anyone finds out what really happened between us, will you tell me, Grant?"

"Yes," I answer, without hesitation. "I don't want this out. I don't want to win at your expense."

"Thank you," she whispers.

"I can't stop caring about you, Tess." I take a step forward, but she holds up her hands. I quickly nod, sensing that whatever transpired between us is gone. It has to be gone.

She walks me to the door. My hand rests on the doorknob as I ask, "Are you going to tell Dean?"

"Yes, I have to. Eventually. But it will destroy us. It doesn't ever seem like a good time to lose the love of your life."

I feel a sharp pain that I didn't know is possible after so much time has passed. "You're right," I say. "There's never a good time for that."

I walk down the hotel hallway, thankful for its emptiness. When I'm inside the elevator, I slump against the door, drained from the emotions that Tess stirs. I don't know what to do next, and every step of my life has been preplanned since birth. I glance at my watch. It's almost midnight. Cece will be waiting, wondering why my post-debate debriefing with Stuart took so long.

When the elevator doors open into the parking garage, I'm confronted with a familiar face.

"How long?" Cece harshly whispers. "How long have you been sleeping with Tess Murphy?"

"Cece, what are you doing here?"

"What are *you* doing here, Grant?"

"Did you follow me?" I ask regretfully, knowing I have no place to question her actions.

"I knew something was going on. Of course, I followed you."

I look out across the garage, wondering if there are cameras, wondering if it is as deserted as it looks, or if we have an audience.

"Get in the car, we can talk there," I instruct, walking toward Cece's Range Rover.

She cocks her head. "What are you concerned about, Grant? Getting caught fighting with your wife? Or getting caught leaving Tess Murphy's hotel room? I'm just wondering where I rank in your concerns these days."

I've never seen this kind of calculated anger from Cece. Not when I came home from my bachelor party so drunk I could barely stand. Not when she was delivering the twins and the doctor told her she needed to work harder.

I stare at the ceiling and close my eyes briefly. When I open them, I'm met with her icy stare. "Cecilia, I can explain."

"I'm not an idiot. It's pretty clear what's going on."

"It isn't what you think. The last thing I want is to hurt you."

"Really? You thought I'd be totally fine with a little extramarital affair? Is that what you thought, Grant?"

"No," I reflexively reply. But then I stare at the concrete pillar in front of me and figure maybe it's time to be truthful with my wife. "Honestly, I'm surprised you care."

Her fists pound into my chest and she screams, "You are such an asshole. Of course I care. You are my husband. MY! HUSBAND!" The last words are shouted across the rows of cars, Cece's voice cracking into a million pieces.

"I'll tell you everything," I say, opening her car door.

"Start talking." She slides inside and slams the door, the sound echoing in the empty garage.

I open the passenger door. "Let's go home. We can talk there."

Cece whips toward me. "There is no way you are coming back to my house."

"Our house."

"You are unprepared for the fight ahead if you think you can sleep with another woman and then call the home where I raise my children 'ours.'"

"I didn't sleep with another woman. I'd never cheat on you. You know that. And they're my kids too, Cece."

"What were you doing in another woman's hotel room?" Her eyes turn into slits.

I try to explain. "Talking. We were just talking."

"You never had sex with Tess Murphy?"

I wince. "Not tonight."

"Is that supposed to make me feel better? When? How many times have you slept with Tess?"

"I don't know, Cece. But the last time was twenty-five years ago."

"Grant." She says my name like a curse. "Nothing you're saying makes any sense."

I look out the car window. "Sometimes it feels like you've never understood me."

"Because you don't talk to me!" she shouts. "Do you talk to her? Is that it? We've built an entire life together and you seem so willing to just throw it all away. What do you have with Tess Murphy?"

How can I explain Tess to my wife? How do I say that there's another woman who knows me better? Even after everything that happened, sitting next to Tess in the hotel room tonight made me realize I'll never love another person with the same intensity. "We have a connection," I confess. "Even after all these years. It's hard to explain."

"Please try, Grant. I've been married to you for twelve years. I'm the mother of your two sons. Please tell me about your connection to the girl you dated when you were a teenager."

Cece seems to sing the last sentence, making a mockery of my feelings.

"I don't want to hurt you, Cece," I deflect. I also don't want to hurt myself by admitting the truths only Tess knows.

"Too late," she replies.

"I've known Tess since I was eighteen."

"I know. She worked for your mother. You told me that." Cecilia doesn't try to hide her annoyance. "But what I'm trying to understand is if you've also had some kind of relationship with her all this time."

"No. We haven't seen each other since that summer. I didn't contact Tess until the first debate."

"Grant, this is ridiculous. I don't know what happened that summer with Tess and I don't care. Guess what, I had a boyfriend when I was eighteen too. And I thought I loved him too. But then I grew up and I got married and I entered into a committed partnership like an adult."

"What Tess and I had wasn't a summer fling. It was real. My feelings for Tess are complicated."

"What are you saying?"

"I hate Tess. But I also need her in my life."

"You *need* your high school girlfriend? You *need* to grow up." Cece stares at me with a mix of confusion and disgust. I don't blame her.

"She was never just some girlfriend." I try to explain. "There are things about my life that only Tess understands."

Cece recoils. "How can I understand you when you don't tell me anything?" She swallows, her jaw moving back and forth before finding her words. "Where exactly does this leave us?"

"I don't know, Cece. I haven't known where we stand for a

long time now. This campaign only seemed to make things worse."

"Say it."

"Say what?"

"You need to tell me it's over."

I close my eyes. "Sometimes it feels like we haven't had a relationship worth fighting for in a long time."

She flinches and I immediately regret the harshness of my words. "And whose fault is that, Grant?"

"Mine. Ours." Cece glares and I hold up my hands. "Mostly mine. I know I haven't been an easy man."

It's hard to admit that we drifted apart. We were too busy or negligent or exhausted to put in the effort required to maintain a marriage. Because if you avoid the daily tending, one day you wake up surrounded by overgrowth and can't find the person you fell in love with. It's almost sadder than a scandal, because we had thousands of daily opportunities to make things better and now it's too far gone.

There's a softening in Cece for a minute as she says, "Remember when you took me to Gold Cup and we wore those ridiculous hats and passed around that thermos of mint juleps while the horses raced?"

I can't for the life of me figure out why she's reminiscing about this date, but I nod because of course I remember that day.

"It was our third date," Cece says, staring into my eyes. "It started pouring down rain and you grabbed my hand and we ran barefoot through the fields back to your car. We were drenched and our legs were streaked in mud and you told me you loved me. I thought, this guy doesn't know what love means. He's had too many cocktails and he wants to see me naked. But then I thought about earlier that day when I overheard you talking to Stuart. He was being an asshole, telling a story about some idiot at work, and you defended this stranger. You told Stuart that he never sees the good in others."

I don't remember anything about the conversation Cece overheard, but it sounds right. Stuart is one of the most judgmental people I've ever met. *Ruthless but right,* he would say. In my experience, people's actions reflect their past. I saw how my mother's pain and sadness took root, growing all kinds of behavior that was easy to criticize. I try to ease my regrets by being easier on others than I was on my mother.

Cece smiles. "That's what I loved about you, Grant. You looked for the good despite being surrounded by a lot of shit in your life. I thought to myself, this guy may not know what love means, but he's worth showing."

I don't deserve any of the kind things she is saying right now. I reach for her hand, but she pulls it back quickly.

"I spent so many years trying to show you love, Grant. After a while, I realized it was pointless. You may hate your father. But tell me how you are different from him?"

I shake my head. "I am nothing like him, Cecilia."

"Really? You don't work long hours, avoiding your family? You don't close yourself off from the people who are trying to love you? I know there is more to the complicated relationship you have with Richard. I don't know why you despise a man who you have so easily become."

"My father is a monster. You cannot compare me to him." My voice quivers slightly.

"Why not? You say he's a monster, tell me why. Open up to me. I'm your wife." She spits the word like a knife slicing through the air.

"I can't talk about my parents."

"You shut down every conversation about your father. And you won't even mention your mother or let yourself remember good memories. And when I've begged you to let the boys visit the country, to see where you grew up, you've said that stepping foot in that house is like walking through fire. But I have no idea why."

"I'm sorry, Cece. I've never been able to share that part of my life with anyone."

"She knows, doesn't she? Why can you open up to Tess Murphy but not to me?"

"I don't have to open up to Tess. She knows because she was there."

"There for what?" Cece asks.

"There when my mother overdosed." I don't mean to shout, but I do.

Cece looks up, her round eyes meeting mine. "Your mother fell. She hit her head. You always said it was an accident."

"She drank and took too many pills and then she fell." I find my voice shaking as I continue. "The morning I found my mother's body floating in her bathtub, Tess was there for me."

Cece swallows. "You never told me you found your mother's body."

I take a deep breath as I continue, admitting my deepest scar. "It was my fault. I caused her death."

"You can't know that," Cece says reflexively.

"I do," I say, refusing to elaborate, relieved when Cece doesn't ask for more. She's used to my two-word answers.

"Why didn't you ever tell me?"

"There's so much about that time in my life I never told you, Cece. Too much. It's my fault we're in this place."

"If you had let me in, I could have been there for you too," she says, and I wonder whether she's right.

I close my eyes. "You don't deserve this. You deserve better than me."

"You're right," she says, my worst fears culminating. Cece knows who I am, and it isn't the person she wants.

She inserts the key into the ignition and gestures to the door. "Please get out of my car, Grant."

"Where are you going?" I ask.

"Home to the boys. There's a babysitter waiting."

I step out of the car. Before closing the door, I lean in. "Cece, I know I've asked too much of you. But I have to ask one thing more. This can't get out. It would destroy my campaign to answer questions about Tess."

"It destroyed your family, Grant." Her chin quivers as she continues, "You're right, you left our marriage a long time ago. And you kept the most important parts of yourself out of reach. I can't love someone I don't know." She finally meets my eyes, a look of fierce determination across her face. "But I will always protect our boys. That's why I won't make it public. They will never hear about your messes."

"Thank you," I say, and carefully close the door.

The truth of Cece's words linger in my shadow. She's right that I never knew how to love, how to be a good husband. Ever since Tess, I've never known how to trust another person.

But more so, Cece is right about my father because somehow, I've begged my wife to stay silent and I realize I've never been more despicable. I've never been more like my father. And just like him, I'm all alone.

Sixteen

SEPTEMBER 1996

I rubbed the sleep out of my eyes as I sat up in bed, clearing my throat. It was eight in the morning, entirely too early to be awake, but someone was pacing the hallway, the old floorboards creaking louder than any alarm clock. I assumed my father was preparing for another lecture.

"What do you want?" I called out, hoping he went away.

The door creaked open. It was Tess. As she timidly stepped inside, I felt a thrill of excitement until a pit in my stomach grew and I quickly looked around for a T-shirt to throw on. "I needed to see you," she said.

I needed to see her too, but after our last conversation, I had no idea where we stood. All summer, it felt like I'd finally found my match, but the way Tess told me about her pregnancy made me question if she felt the same way. I debated asking her to leave, but when I looked into her eyes, I knew that was impossible. The draw of Tess Murphy was too strong.

I swung my legs out of bed and moved toward her. I wrapped my arms around her waist and gently lifted her up, kissing her lips before a wave of panic settled in.

"I'm sorry. Did I squeeze too tight?"

She shook her head. "No, Grant. I'm fine."

"What are you doing here?"

"Your dad let me up."

"He did?"

She nodded. "He's downstairs." She looked up at me, her round eyes wide. "He says you're leaving this afternoon."

I reached for a pair of shorts and slipped them on over my boxers. "That's what he says, but I'm not going anywhere with him. I can't go to Princeton."

Tess walked over to the bed and gestured for me to sit beside her. I followed, and she reached for my hands. Her voice was gentle. "You have to go, Grant."

I shook my head defiantly. "Tess, I can't leave you. I've told him that a dozen times. I'm not going to Princeton."

"Princeton is an opportunity you don't throw away."

"I got into UVA. It's closer, it's a good school. I can start next semester after we've gotten settled in Charlottesville."

"Grant, it's not going to work."

"What's not going to work?"

I watched as tears started falling down her cheeks. She looked into my eyes and my breath caught, afraid of what she was going to say next.

"I can't raise a baby," Tess said through choked sobs. "I don't want to raise a baby."

"What does that mean?"

She sat quietly, waiting for her body to calm and her voice to return. She took a deep breath before she announced, "I'm having an abortion. I thought a lot about what you said, but I haven't changed my mind." She handed me the slip of paper with an appointment time at some place called the Whole Woman Clinic.

Somehow our hands fell apart. I didn't know whether my grip loosened or she pulled away.

"Don't I get a say in this?" It sounded too much like an accusation.

Tess stayed calm as she answered, "No. You don't."

I turned away, immediately pacing the room. I wanted a conversation, a decision made together. But instead, it felt like Tess was giving instructions that I was meant to blindly follow.

My hands ran through my hair, pulling it in opposite directions. When I turned to face her, my fists were balled, my jaw moving back and forth as I tried to find the words to respond.

Tess walked toward me, her calmness quickly evaporating. She pointed her finger at my chest and said, "You don't get to be angry with me either. It's my choice, Grant. You have to respect that."

"But I don't. I don't respect your choice."

"I can see that."

I reached for her, pulling her body against mine. "Tess, I'm begging you to change your mind."

Her hands pushed against my chest, creating space between us. "No, you're not thinking this through clearly."

"You're scared. You're letting fear make decisions. You can't live life like that." I cupped my hands around her face, staring into her eyes with desperation.

Tess reached up, placing her hands around my own and removing them from her face. "I'm not scared. I'm realistic. I know what this life will be like and I love us too much. I love myself too much."

Her words felt like a slap. "What about our baby? What about me?"

She turned away, walking toward the door. "I want you to try to see this from my perspective. I want you to trust me."

"If you decide to kill our baby, how can I ever trust you, Tess?" We were in separate corners of the room. I'd never felt farther apart from Tess.

"I'm not killing our baby, Grant. This is me. This is my body. This is my future."

"There's nothing I can say to change your mind?"

"No."

"I don't know if I can get past this, Tess."

"I don't know if I can either."

"What does that mean?"

"You should get going. Your father was eager to leave."

"What about us?"

"Is there an 'us,' Grant?"

"I thought so. But you seem like a stranger today."

"Why? Because I'm not doing what you want?"

My whole body deflated. "But there is a part of me in there too."

"I love you, Grant, but I need you to respect my decision. I'll be waiting for you if you can."

"If you get what you want, I lose." I pleaded, "Tess, I can't lose any more. Please don't do this to us."

Tess's chin quivered before she turned and ran out of my room, her footsteps moving too quickly down the stairs. As the front door slammed, I picked up the closest object I could find, a lacrosse cleat, and hurled it against the wall.

It punctured the plaster, leaving a hole and a trail of dust. I felt my legs shake and I slumped onto my bed.

The realization that I'd lost Tess settled in. She'd been in my life only a few months, but I couldn't imagine her being gone. Especially now, when each day felt lonelier than the last, the pain and confusion over my mother's death deepening.

I thought about what Tess said and whether I could move past this moment. Could I imagine a life with Tess, knowing that she chose to end her pregnancy when I so desperately wanted her to have this baby?

I reached for my pillow and smothered it over my face, muffling my screams of frustration.

It was then that my father barged in, throwing the door open and kicking aside piles of clothes, his eyes focused on the hole in the wall.

"Clean up this mess and get in the shower," he ordered. "We're leaving in an hour."

"I'm not going anywhere with you."

He sighed, seemingly annoyed that he needed to parent for a moment. "You are better off without her."

"No, I'm not. I'm nothing without her. She's the only person I've ever loved."

He rolled his eyes. "That's not love."

"You have no idea what it means to love another person," I screamed.

"And you're the expert? At eighteen?"

"I have to fix this. Maybe Tess is right."

"About the pregnancy?" Richard asked, vocalizing the topic both of us avoided.

I nodded. "I don't want to lose the baby, but I don't want to lose Tess more."

The Summer We Ran

"You can't take care of a baby, Grant." His tone made me want to prove him wrong, but doubt crept in. Maybe we were too young. I had no idea what a child needed and no real example to follow.

My stomach dropped, realizing that without Tess, I was all alone. My mother was gone and I could barely stand to share the same space with my father. Whatever it took, I needed Tess in my life. Even if it meant going along with her plans.

I walked toward the door as I said, "I have to go get her."

"Sit down, son."

"No. I need to find Tess. I love her."

"If it's love, it's the cheapest love you are likely to encounter." My father walked to the window, his arms crossed. This was the position he assumed when he was about to impart some pearl of wisdom about the way the world worked. I'd never wanted to hear a lecture less.

"I paid her to have the abortion." My father's words echoed in my ears as my vision started to swirl. I shook my head, but he continued. "If this had been a girl at Princeton, it probably would have cost double. Be smarter, Grant." He threw a box of condoms at me.

I stared at the box, my mind reeling with what my father had said. "What are you talking about?"

"That girl. The one you've been running off with all summer. The one you were so careless with? I took care of that problem for you."

"You paid Tess?"

"Yes. You can thank me later."

None of what he was saying made sense. There had to be an explanation. "Tess took your money?"

"Of course she did. Girls like that always take the money," he said with disgust.

"Not Tess."

"Yes, Tess. The money matters more than you. Remember that. Next time you think about putting your future in jeopardy because you think it's love, remember that it's not you they love. It's the money."

I charged at him, unable to believe he'd go to these lengths, to make up a story like this. "Tess wouldn't do that. You're lying."

"Do you want to see the bank records? I paid her, but honestly, Grant, paying for your mistakes is getting tiresome. I won't be here to clean up the messes forever."

"I never asked you to pay Tess. I never asked for anything," I spat, scrambling to wrap my head around all of this.

"And yet, I did it anyway. Maybe that's love."

"I want no part of that love." But I was beginning to deflate, the fight within me dissipating as the truth settled in.

"Get ready and get in the car. We're going to be late. It's a long drive to New Jersey."

I was frozen. The devastation of my father's revelation sent me into a dark spiral. My mind started replaying every moment of the summer as I questioned how I was so wrong about someone I thought I loved so much. My voice sounded flat, but my insides were rolling as I asked, "How much?"

"How much what?"

"How much money did you pay Tess?"

"Fifty thousand dollars." My father waved his hand dismissively, as if he were discussing the cost of a nice dinner.

Waves of nausea churned in my stomach. "That's how much our baby was worth."

"No, Grant. That's how much your future was worth."

I was struck by the irony that Tess and my father agreed about something. Maybe they were more similar than I ever knew. The two people who should have been the closest in my life, my girlfriend and my father, both disgusted me. I thought I felt alone the day my mother died. But this day was worse. Sitting on my bed, I realized that I'd never had someone I could fully trust. And I wondered what made me so fucking unlovable.

PART III

Tess

Seventeen

OCTOBER 2021

I've been holding it together, but I'm about to break. It's not just the schedule, which is relentless. Or the scrutiny of my every movement, which is constant. It's the worry that fills my mind, building each day as we get closer and closer to the election. Have I done enough to win? Who am I disappointing today? Am I the right person for this job?

This is what I think about when I'm brushing my teeth and when I should be sleeping, my mind churning with a million what-ifs. It's exhausting, physically and mentally. And I did it to myself.

But at this moment, it's my feet that are truly at their breaking point. I cannot walk another step in these heels. In my office across the campaign headquarters there's a pair of flats hiding under the desk. Twenty more feet, and then I'm in the promised land.

"Turn around," Mara instructs, blocking my path. "I need you to head out for another stop."

"No," I say, my eyes fluttering as I exhale. I take off the four-inch heels that allow me to make eye contact with most of the population and walk barefoot into my office. "I am done for the day."

Mara follows, doling out instructions to the campaign staff as she stares into her phone. "You are *almost* done for the day. I need one more thing from you and then I'll leave you alone for the night. Or part of the night. We need to be on the road tomorrow at four in the morning."

"Mara," I moan. "I have nothing more to give."

She shrugs, her lack of sympathy unsurprising. I signed up for this and Mara knows it. We got a slight bump in the polls after the second debate. Then, when Grant and Cecilia announced their separation, it became a bigger bump. Although Mara has been quick to point out that the dissolution of Grant's marriage hasn't impacted his campaign enough. "It's because he's a man," Mara has said too many times.

Maybe voters care more about Grant's qualifications than his personal life and that's why his divorce isn't destroying his campaign the way Mara feels it should. But more likely, Mara is right. Men can escape consequences women will always bear.

It's probably a good thing Mara has kept me so busy, because otherwise my mind wanders too often to Grant. I know he's always feared spending life alone.

I overhear a staffer ask if Dean is going to be attending our event tomorrow morning.

"No, he can't," I quickly reply.

Her face tenses. Dean's presence is important, she harps, especially now that Cecilia is off the campaign trail. I agree. I need Dean. Except it feels like he resents this election. We speak every day. I tell him good morning and ask if he had butter or cream cheese on his bagel. When I'm home, he hands me my reading glasses and tells me good night when he turns off his lamp. There's an undeniable chill in the air or simmering grievances, it's hard to say. We discuss mundane logistics, but we don't talk about anything of substance. He says he needs to focus on curriculum changes instead of campaign activities. I tell him I understand completely even though I miss my husband. Maybe I wouldn't feel so broken if he were by my side.

I've been attending all of my public appearances alone. The official statement is that Dean's classes resumed and he can't attend campaign events. He's a dedicated high school teacher. It's an excuse that seems to be generally accepted.

I finally make it into my office and toss my heels in the corner. Mara trails behind, walking comfortably in a pair of brown loafers that I've never envied until this moment.

"The article on the first spouses is set to run at the end of the week," Mara says. "Since Cecilia is out, it's a huge opportunity for us. Dean comes off great, personable, funny, humble."

"That's good news," I say, as I crawl under my desk in search of my flats.

"Yes, but he never gave the magazine your mother's recipe. I need you to send it in."

"Why? Can't they run the article without the recipe?" I pick up my heels and throw them into the trash can. I'm never wearing them again.

Mara walks over and retrieves the heels as I slip into comfortable running shoes. "No. It's the whole point of the article. We need the recipe and you need these shoes for tomorrow."

"I'm not wearing those shoes tomorrow. I'll be lucky if I can walk tomorrow. And if Dean didn't send the recipe, there's a reason. He probably couldn't find my mother's cookbook."

"Ask him. Or make up a recipe. I don't care. Just give me something to send to this reporter."

"Does this really matter?" I sigh, shoving the heels into my bag and grabbing my coat to leave.

"Yes. Voters need to like you. People with family recipes are likable."

"Fine. But after I sort out this recipe thing, I'm taking the rest of the night off."

Mara nods. "I'll pick you up at four in the morning. We have to be in Virginia Beach for breakfast."

"Do not come to my house a minute earlier than four, Mara," I shout, as I walk toward the door.

"Wear the heels," Mara yells in response.

By the time I am home, my exhaustion has reached a peak. I walk through the front door and glance in the mirror hanging in the hallway. I'm a mess. The hair that earlier today had been pulled into a neat, tight bun is now hanging wildly, strings having slipped free. The basic makeup I applied this morning is gone, washed away by the day's effort.

I want to collapse in my bed, but I know Mara will show up on my doorstep if I don't send her this silly recipe. I walk into our garage and it's a mess, even more so than usual. Boxes are open, their contents spread across the concrete floor. I can't remember the last time I was in here.

I start digging through the piles, hoping to find the faded blue cover of the cookbook that sat on my mother's kitchen counter her entire life. It should have been in the box that I packed for the hospital. When her breast cancer advanced and we were told she had days left, my mother asked me to bring her favorite things. We both knew she wasn't going to be cooking from a hospital bed, but the cookbook was a familiar comfort. In those final days, when she was so weak, she'd still have energy to flip through recipes and reminisce about her favorite meals. After she died, I packed up the cookbook and put it away. I never tried to cook any of those meals she loved, because my memory of her efforts was too perfect.

"Looking for something?" Dean's voice interrupts my nostalgia. I look across the chilly garage and smile at my husband. But he doesn't smile back.

"I didn't hear you come in," I say, pulling myself away from boxes and stepping toward Dean.

"I was working with the debate team tonight," Dean says. "I didn't think you'd be home."

Dean's eyes barely look up from the floor. I nervously fidget with the items in the open box. Why aren't we running into each other's arms? Why don't we know each other's schedules? Why aren't we together each night instead of two trains running in different directions? I want to scream these questions, but I swallow them down. Instead, I explain, "Mara needs my mother's recipe for that article. Did you find it?"

Dean shoves his hands into his pockets. "Yeah, I found it," he says.

"Did you forget to send it to the reporter?"

"I sent what I found to Mara." He walks over to a box in the corner and lifts the cardboard flap. I immediately recognize the cookbook with its fraying edges and dog-eared pages. Dean hands it to me and says, "I hope you find what you're looking for." Then he walks away.

I stare at the cookbook, unsure why Dean is acting so strange. He always keeps his promises, but Mara said she never got the recipe.

I slowly open the front page and see my mother's familiar

handwriting. It's been decades since I've looked at these pages. My mother wrote down a few of her favorite recipes for Dean, and that's what he always used when he would cook one of her meals. Her cookbook was more of an artifact, something I put away in a box, its mere existence providing more comfort than the recipes inside did.

As I start turning the pages, I realize that this isn't just my mother's cookbook. It's her treasure box. Tucked within the pages are notes from my grandmother, a card I made as a child, a rose petal pressed between wax paper.

My fingers flip through the pages as my heart aches with longing. I miss my mother and her calm practicality. I wonder what she'd think of me now. I wonder what advice she'd give. I wonder if she'd be proud.

Then I see it. My heart stops as I see the photograph tucked tightly in the pages, my young face smiling back at me. The photograph of Grant with his arm around my shoulders, a rip down the middle taped back together. For some reason, my mother smoothed out the crumpled, discarded picture that I clung to throughout that summer and thought was long gone. My mother kept it hidden in her most sacred place. And Dean must have found it. My stomach drops.

Dean did send Mara what he found. Except it wasn't a recipe.

I walk inside my house, the sky already dark on this late fall evening, to find him sitting at the kitchen table. He's cracking his knuckles and his leg is bouncing up and down. When he looks up, I see the red rims to his eyes and the stubble on his face. He immediately looks away.

I sit at the table and place the photograph between us. "Did you send Mara the picture?"

He nods.

"Why?" I ask softly.

"Why didn't you tell me about him, Tess?" Dean answers defensively.

Dean pounds the table, an uncharacteristic but justified reaction. I'm in no position to ask any questions. I should be pouring out explanations. I've opened my mouth a dozen times, ready to tell Dean the whole story, but every time I begin to explain my relationship with Grant, the words lodge in my throat, unable to escape.

It's the one thing we've never shared. Dean tells me when I have spinach in my teeth and he tells me when I look beautiful. He tells me when I'm being unfairly judgmental of his students' wardrobe choices and when I'm being fairly judgmental of his uncle's sexist comments. We usually fall asleep relaying all the minute details of our days. He's always thought that we told each other everything, but I left out a critical piece: the conversation I've been avoiding for most of my adult life.

"I was afraid," I answer.

"Of what?"

"What you would think of me."

"Why would I care about your teenage boyfriend?" he asks, incredulous.

"You wouldn't. But you'd care about the rest."

Dean swallows. "What else have you been lying about? I didn't think we hid things from each other."

I exhale and admit, "We don't. I should have told you about Grant."

"Start now," Dean instructs.

I pace the kitchen as I reveal these long-buried cracks of my past. "I met Grant the summer before my senior year of high school," I begin. "I worked for his mother. Manual labor in her gardens."

I try to say it casually, as if this were a banal moment of life, unworthy of mention until now. But Dean is not dumb. I spin my wedding band as I wonder if his trust in me will allow him to accept a simple story full of omissions.

Dean points to the picture of Grant and me, seemingly calculating his every move. "Why didn't you say something?"

"I should have. I was embarrassed. How does it look for me to have been an employee of the opposing candidate?"

Dean leans forward. "Maybe you don't announce it publicly. But why not tell me?"

"I should have," I whisper.

Dean stares through me. He isn't pushing, and that is almost more unsettling. My husband walks over to the window and I see his back muscles tense through his thin cotton shirt. I want to jump inside his head so that I can rehearse answers to his questions. But I can't.

"Why did you send the photo to Mara?" I ask.

"I waited," Dean says. "I found the picture, and I asked you questions about Grant. Every day, I asked you how you felt about the person you were running against. I gave you dozens of chances to talk. But you never did."

Our entire relationship, Dean's waited for me to do the right thing. Sometimes looking into Dean's face would be all the encouragement I'd need. My first year on the town council, I knew a staffer was falsifying expenses. But I also knew it was minor stuff. I liked this person. I told her I knew and I told her to stop. I thought that was enough. But Dean's perspective was more black-and-white than that. "You have to report what you know," he kept saying. I finally went to Accounting. It turned out those fake expenses were only a fraction of her theft. It was a huge scandal for the town and it would have continued undetected for years if I hadn't made that report. I beat myself up about it, knowing that I shouldn't have waited to inform Accounting. Dean could have rubbed it in my face that he was right. But he didn't. I'll never forget what he said to me. "You did the right thing in the end. I trust that you'll always get there, Tess. I know what kind of person you are."

I'm pretty sure Dean's been waiting for me to do the right thing. But maybe our problem is that our versions of right diverged. Because even though it may be misguided, I still feel like my relationship with Grant is my own secret. Even now, I'm fighting to keep it private, from the person I promised to share my life with.

Dean walks into the living room and sits on the couch. His face is neutral. He is leaning forward, elbows balanced on his thighs, gesturing for me to sit next to him. I accept the invitation.

"I'm going to give you one chance, Tess. I need you to tell me everything about your relationship with Grant. Otherwise, I don't know where we stand."

I stare at the ceiling as I pick at my nails, a nervous habit I've never been able to shake. Dean reaches for my hand to steady the anxious movements.

"Start with the photo, Tess. Explain the picture."

My voice is quiet and it's hard to look Dean in the eyes, but in this moment, I'm determined to tell him everything. I start at the beginning. "I dated Grant that summer."

"I figured as much. But why the secrecy, Tess? I don't understand why you didn't tell me this."

I take a deep breath as I try to explain to Dean, and maybe

to myself too, the deep wounds that summer inflicted. "Our relationship ended badly. After Grant, it was hard for me to trust anyone, especially someone in a relationship. In order to move on from everything that happened, I had to put it away. I don't let myself open the box of how I felt losing . . ."

I trail off, realizing what I almost said. But Dean finishes my sentence for me. "How you felt losing him."

I nod. "I was disposable. That's what I learned in my relationship with Grant. It wasn't until I met you that I felt deserving of love. You never asked me to do anything I didn't want to do. You respected me and my mind. Being with you was like trying on a new coat and I didn't want to take it off."

Dean's face is tense as he asks, "But were you pretending with me? It feels hard to know what's hidden, Tess. Do I know you?"

"Yes. What we have is real love." I try to convince him. I try to convince myself.

"Not much about us feels honest right now, Tess." When he finally speaks, Dean asks, "Did you love him?"

"As much as a seventeen-year-old girl can love someone." I don't know why I qualify my answer, because it isn't true. I exhale and correct myself, because Dean deserves complete honesty. "That's not right. I loved him. He was my first love."

This is when Dean stands up and walks away. I know his reactions are only going to get worse and I hate hurting him in the process.

I follow after Dean, my words pleading for him to turn around. "I should have mentioned our relationship earlier. This thing has spiraled out of control." I swallow away my tears and look up, surprised by the intensity of Dean's stare.

"Do you still love him?"

It's a hard question to answer. But I promised him the truth. "Yes. But I love you more." My cheeks are wet as my eyes search for Dean's. I need him to look at me.

But instead, he's staring off into the distance as he says, "I don't know if that matters anymore, Tess."

"Dean, of course it matters. It is the only thing that matters. I'm sorry I didn't tell you about Grant, but you are the most important thing in my life."

Dean finally looks in my direction. His face shows no emotion as he asks, "Why did things end badly between you and Grant? What happened?"

I swallow, because this is the question I was hoping to avoid. "It doesn't matter, Dean. We were kids and it's long over."

"If Grant didn't still matter, you wouldn't have hidden your past," Dean says.

"I love you. I love us," I plead.

"It's not enough!" Dean shouts.

My heart scrambles. It has to be enough. I have to find a way to show Dean that it's enough. "Tell me what you need," I beg.

"Tess, all I've ever wanted is for you to be the best version of yourself. I can't tell you what to do. I can't demand something out of you. But I think we both know we haven't seen that person in a long time."

"I should have told you about Grant. I never made good decisions when it came to him. I'm sorry Dean."

"I wish I could believe you," he says.

"You can. You know me, Dean. Please let me earn back your trust." I reach out for his hand, but he pulls it away.

Dean's arms are crossed, his jaw tight as he says, "You're still lying, Tess. Apparently, you've lied to me all along. About the most important part of our marriage."

Dean slumps onto our couch. "I don't care about some relationship you had decades ago. I could even get past the fact that you hid it." He takes a breath and continues. "What I can't get over is that even now, you're not telling me the truth."

Dean pulls a piece of paper out of his back pocket. He places it on our coffee table as he says, "This was in your mother's things too."

I walk slowly, my breath hitching as my eyes focus on the blurry picture on the table, a black-and-white image that forever changed my heart. I pick up the ultrasound photo and feel a wave of sorrow as I study the faint outline of a tiny nose and two clenched fists.

"In all the years we've been together, how many times have we talked about starting a family?" Dean asks. "How many times have I asked you to consider a child? Even when I begged, you wouldn't give an explanation beyond *I'm not cut out to be a mother*."

It's how I've always felt, but Dean wanted more information. He asked questions that were too painful for me to answer. I shut down every discussion with curt answers and frustration that I was even being asked for explanations.

"I kept pushing because it never made sense," Dean continues. "Your entire face lights up around kids. Children follow you at parties. You'd be the best mom, and yet you wouldn't even consider having a child with me."

Sometimes I feel like motherhood is an assumption women have to rebut. Just because I like kids doesn't mean I want kids of my own. I resent needing to provide an explanation. But this isn't a stranger asking these questions. This is my husband. I committed to sharing a life with Dean and I never shared my real reasons.

"You were pregnant once," Dean says, pointing to the ultrasound. "And you never told me."

I stare at the grainy photo printed on slick paper from the doctor's office. Dean's angry words echo, rightfully so, because everything he's saying is true, but I can't tear my eyes away from the image in my hands.

"Did you have a child with Grant Alexander?" Dean asks, his voice rising to match his frustration.

"I can't talk about that time."

"Why?" His shout makes me flinch.

"Because other than my mother, no one else knows what happened," I whisper. "I've kept this part of me hidden for so long."

Dean's lip curls. "You kept this from Grant too? Does he even know he has a child?"

I swallow slowly. "That's a conversation I need to have with Grant."

Dean stands. "He has some power over you that I don't understand. I've begged for answers for years. And even now, you don't care enough about us to be honest."

I open my mouth to explain, but no words materialize. I can't imagine telling Dean what happened before telling Grant. Dean is right. The power or love or guilt that Grant holds over me seems stronger than my now crumbling marriage. I had dozens of chances over the years to tell Dean everything. But I never prioritized the truth for my husband over the pain of revisiting my past with Grant.

Dean walks toward the front door. "I've given you so many chances, but I'm done giving you any more. I'm done with the secrets and the lies, Tess. That's not love." The door slams as he leaves. I fear he won't ever be back.

The empty room echoes. I could chase after Dean, beg, plead for him to come home, to come back to me. But I knew then and I know now that there are consequences for every choice. I'm all alone and it's exactly what I deserve.

Eighteen

SEPTEMBER 1996

My mother was pacing the small kitchen, her face red and cheeks wet.

"We need to pack, Tess," she yelled up to me.

I quickly hid the positive pregnancy test in my underwear drawer and climbed down the ladder from my bedroom loft.

"What's going on?" I asked, trying to focus on my mother when my mind was on Grant and our conversation in his garden. Grant now knew I was pregnant and, once he got over the initial shock, he said he wanted to keep the baby. He even wanted to move to Charlottesville so we could be together. I was a mess of emotions: surprised, confused, excited, terrified. Especially terrified of my mother's reaction; she was going to kill me. Grant was supposed to leave for Princeton any day now, which gave us no time to figure it out together.

"I was just fired," my mother said, and suddenly I stopped thinking about Grant and my pregnancy and tried to focus on her words.

"But Ms. Milton agreed to hire you permanently. I started classes here. What happened?"

My mother was pulling out a suitcase, throwing clothes inside. "I have no idea. One minute I'm peeling carrots for the dinner tonight, and the next I'm being told to pack up and leave. By tomorrow. No explanation."

I wasn't sure what would happen when I told Grant about the pregnancy, but now my mother was telling me we were leaving. And I didn't know how I was going to do any of this alone. Even though it had been only a few months, I couldn't imagine life without Grant Alexander. I didn't say any of this out loud. Instead, I listened to my mother grow more aggravated as she told me about her afternoon.

"Madeline Milton summoned me into her office and told me I was fired."

"What are we going to do?" I stuttered.

My mother stopped packing and stared at me. "I have no idea, Tess. The Homestead isn't hiring anymore. They're done for the season. I've got a little bit saved, but probably not enough to last us until spring." My mother shook her head as she quietly said, "Things are going to be very tight."

My chin quivered. Because if money was tight with my mother and I, it would be impossible with a baby in the mix. Despite what Grant said, there was no way we were capable of taking care of another person.

"Can't you apologize?" I asked. "I like it here, Mom. I don't want to leave."

"Tess, if I had any idea what I did, I'd be dishing out apologies." She leaned against the wall. "I've worked myself to the bone this summer, all for nothing."

She was right. My mother has woken early, stayed late, tested new recipes, managed the other household staff, and fulfilled even the tiniest request from Ms. Milton. We'd both been holding our breath all summer, hoping this opportunity worked out. And when Ms. Milton finally offered my mother permanent employment, it felt like all the sacrifices were worth it. My mother kept saying, "This is our fresh start." For the first time since my grandmother died, I saw hope on my mother's face. I let myself believe that maybe we could be like all these people around us. No longer scraping for every bit of security, but instead feeling as if we could merely exist in comfort. But I was wrong. And for the rest of my life, I knew that there was no easy path for girls like me. I would have to fight and scrape for every opportunity. It wasn't a life I wanted for anyone else.

I slumped onto the floor and started crying.

"Tess, I will figure this out. I know we both got our hopes up, but we're tough. We'll get back on our feet. This is just one setback."

Except it wasn't. My mother lost her job, we had no income, no place to live because my mother rented out my grandmother's trailer. And I was pregnant. I didn't know how we were going to solve any of these problems, but I kept those worries spinning in my head and instead whispered the name of the person I thought could fix everything for me. "Grant."

My mother sighed. "Tess, there will be other boyfriends."

"No. I have to see Grant," I hiccupped.

My mother shook her head. "I can't have you running over there right now. We have to pack."

I wiped away the tears from my cheeks. "You don't understand, Mom. I have to go talk to him."

"No," she said sternly. "There are more important things for us to deal with right now. Go upstairs and start packing."

I walked toward the loft, scheming how I could slip out later that night. I knew Grant loved me. Somehow, we would figure out what to do. I stopped when I heard a loud pounding on the door.

My mother mouthed, "Who is that?" and I shrugged because Grant was the only person who ever came over.

When she opened the door, it wasn't Grant. It was his father. Richard Alexander was standing outside and a sinking feeling came over me. What could he possibly want?

I swallowed nervously, waiting for him to speak, but he pushed my mother aside and stalked in my direction.

"Mr. Alexander, can I help you?" she politely asked, shifting from side to side. I didn't know how my mother knew Richard Alexander, but she seemed familiar enough to know that she should be nervous around him.

He spun around, his eyes shifting from me to my mother. "I heard you are without employment," he said.

My mother's voice shook as she responded. "Yes, sir."

"Do you know why you were fired?" he asked.

She shook her head. Richard looked at me. "Ask your daughter."

Her eyes widened as she turned toward me. "What did you do, Tess?"

"I didn't do anything. I promise, Mom," I stammered.

Richard laughed. He walked farther into our cottage and sat in a chair, making himself comfortable in a place that should have been unfamiliar. He had an ability to command a room, even when he wasn't invited into a space. It was a skill I would never master.

"Do you know about the relationship between our children?" he asked my mother.

"Yes," she quietly replied.

"And yet you did not stop it," he snapped. "You displayed very poor judgment."

My mother twisted her hands. "Mr. Alexander, I don't see what this has to do with my employment."

"After her employees were arrested at the bonfire, Madeline knew that she had to be extremely careful with her hiring choices. She cannot have people working in her home who would act so unprofessionally."

"I've been nothing but professional. All summer." My mother stared at Richard, her eyes conveying some unspoken message that seemed to infuriate him.

"Your daughter's behavior is a direct reflection on you, and I don't find *her* actions very professional. She's the reason why you won't be working here anymore."

My back was pressed against the wall. I wished I could disappear or reverse time, because my mother didn't do anything wrong. This was all my fault. I ruined this opportunity that we would never have again.

But my mother surprised me, and instead of backing down, she stood taller. "Tess has done nothing wrong. There's no reason Ms. Milton should question my professionalism. I'm sure I can speak with her and explain. I've worked very hard to earn her trust this summer."

For a brief moment, I had hope. Maybe my mistakes could be fixed. I should have known better, especially when Richard Alexander was involved.

"Madeline doesn't need your explanation. She trusts my judgment. I told her that you were not a suitable employee and she agreed. You and your daughter need to leave."

"You certainly are a powerful person," my mother said

quietly. She stared directly at Richard as she added, "And yet you're threatened by a teenage girl?"

"Your daughter trapped my son," he spat.

My mother immediately spoke. "Your son is a very willing participant in their relationship, Mr. Alexander."

I knew I didn't deserve her defense.

"She hasn't told you, has she?" Richard was asking my mother, but his eyes bore into me, never leaving my face. In that moment, I realized that he knew.

"What's he talking about, Tess?" She turned toward me with a puzzled expression.

"I was going to tell you," I muttered. I stared at the floor, fidgeting, not sure where to put my hands. Almost instinctively, they rested on my stomach. I looked up, my eyes meeting hers and watching her slow reaction. She focused on the hand across my abdomen as a shock of realization took over her face.

My mother shook her head slowly as she said, "Tess, please tell me you've been careful. Please tell me you didn't make my mistakes."

"I'm so sorry," I whispered, trying to blink away the tears in my eyes.

Richard stood, pointing his finger in my direction as he shouted, "Your careless daughter got pregnant."

I shook my head as I immediately protested, "I never meant for this to happen."

Richard scoffed. "I've known women like you. Women who see an opportunity like my son and manipulate their way into a future."

"Mr. Alexander, I believe a pregnancy takes two willing participants. I won't have you accusing my daughter."

I swallowed nervously, grateful for my mother's support but

suspecting that it would be short-lived. Her disappointment would soon take over. All my life, she'd harped on me not to repeat her history; she expected more for me. I never knew my father, and my mother's only explanation was that she was young and reckless. As a child, I wondered about him, but my mother and grandparents worked hard to make up for his absence, and I stopped asking questions about a person she didn't want to discuss.

"Your daughter *purposefully* got pregnant," he said.

Despite her small frame, my mother displayed surprising strength in front of Richard Alexander. She took a step forward as she spoke. "I'm not happy with the choices our children made. But firing me doesn't achieve anything. This pregnancy means that my daughter is in your son's life permanently, regardless of how either of us feel about that fact."

"No. This is all temporary and easily fixable." He walked toward me and handed me a card.

I looked down at the paper in my hand. It was an appointment, for a women's clinic, scheduled for the next week.

"What's that, Tess?" my mother asked.

"Her solution," Richard answered.

This was what I wanted, what I told Grant I wanted. I didn't want to have a baby at seventeen like my mother had. I dreamed of a giant, full life, and that seemed impossible with the responsibility of a small child. Even so, having an appointment scheduled made it all feel too real.

I looked out the window, my hand shaking. "I didn't trap him. Mom, I promise."

"I know that, Tess. Only foolish men believe that a person can be trapped," she said. I glanced at Richard and saw his face tighten.

I walked toward my mother and handed her the card. "I didn't mean for this to happen."

"I know you didn't." She studied the paper, her head whipping upward once she understood what Richard was trying to do. She grabbed my shoulders. "No, Tess. You are not going to let this man make a decision for you."

"I don't want a baby right now. An abortion is the only thing that makes sense, Mom."

This wasn't something my mother or I had ever discussed. Grocery bills and grades, yes. Maybe if we had more conversations about the gap between the life we had and the life I wanted, she wouldn't have been so surprised by my decision.

My mother's head shook back and forth. "I'm not happy about any of this. But you are not going to be forced into any decisions."

"She can't take care of a baby," Richard interrupted, reminding us of his presence. "And it's no wonder. Her own mother can't even take care of her."

"I think it's time you left," my mother said.

Richard turned toward me, dismissing my mother's instructions. "You and I both know that a baby would ruin your life. Grant's too. Take care of this problem and I'll return the favor."

"What does that mean?" I asked.

"You have an appointment." Richard pointed to the card. "Ten thousand now," he said, placing a check on the table. "Once you've taken care of your situation, I'll pay you the rest."

"Get out!" my mother shouted. "You cannot buy my daughter."

"Yes, I can," he said with little emotion. "You have no job, no income, no stability. I'm giving you both the chance at a future. The only reason I'm being so generous is because Grant is grieving. Your daughter will manipulate him into ruining his life and I won't have that." Richard glared at me as he said, "There is no future for you and Grant. But you get to decide if you want to fight for your own future."

"How much more?" I asked.

I hated the crack of a smile creeping across Richard's face. "Another ten thousand," he said.

I remembered Kay's advice, about negotiating better. I shook my head. "Fifty thousand," I said.

Richard rolled his eyes, dismissing my demand, but I remained firm. We stared at each other and maybe he realized that I had some power in this situation.

"Fine. Fifty thousand total," he said. "Ten now, the rest after the appointment. Tell Grant goodbye and then no more contact. Or no money."

Richard left, making the whole conversation seem casual when instead it was the lowest moment of my life.

Neither of us spoke, my mother and I staring at each other. I remained quiet until I couldn't stand to see the sadness on her face any longer. I ran upstairs and fell onto my bed, overwhelmed by the decisions, the threats, and most of all the thought of losing Grant.

I heard my mother's steps as she walked into the loft. The bed dipped when she sat on the side.

"Tess Murphy, you've made a very stupid mistake—"

I cut her off, moaning, "I know, Mom."

"Let me finish," she said in a sigh. "I've also made stupid mistakes. It's what you do afterward that defines your character. Do you take responsibility and change your behavior? I'm not going to tell you I'm disappointed, because you're hard enough on yourself."

I cried into my pillow. My mother smoothed the hair away from my face as she said, "I never should have brought you here."

"This is all my fault, Mom. We had a chance for a new life and I ruined it."

She wrapped her arms around me as she spoke. "We don't need chances from these types of people, Tess. We will start over. We will start over a thousand times if that's what it takes." She squeezed my hand as she said, "The three of us."

I shook my head. "You're right. It is up to me to fix my mistake. I'm not having the baby. I can't do it. And that amount of money..."

"Absolutely not," my mother protested. "We are not taking a cent from that man. It is your decision, but the money is not a factor, do you understand me?"

I sat up, wiping away tears and trying to smooth my tangled hair. "I need to see Grant."

"I understand," my mother said. "You two have a lot to discuss."

"No. I have to tell Grant goodbye."

"Tess, you need to slow down. There are too many big decisions that need to be made. Don't let his father control your life too."

"Grant wants to keep the baby. I don't." I swallowed as I continued, "Not just because of the money, which does matter, by the way. It's the best decision for my future. Maybe Grant will understand, but if he doesn't, then I know it's the end for us."

"Are you going to tell him about this afternoon? About the money?"

I gnawed on the inside of my cheek, thinking about how

much pain Richard had caused Grant. And the betrayal I knew Grant would feel. But mostly, selfishly, I thought about the divide between my life and Grant's and how it continued to grow. "I've watched them all summer, Mom. The money doesn't matter to them. I'd like to think Grant is different, but he knows his father buys his way out of trouble. He accepts what his world is like."

"And you don't want to be a part of that world anymore?" my mother asked, her eyebrows raised.

"A few times this summer, I let myself believe that maybe I could belong. Someday. Now I know it's a place I never want to return."

"Even if it means losing Grant?"

I nod. And yet I still hope that maybe someday Grant will realize he needs to leave that world too.

Nineteen

OCTOBER 26, 2021

The sun is barely rising as I walk down the street to my campaign headquarters. I've debated setting up some type of cot in the office since it would save time to sleep there, but it would raise too many questions. My house is a ten-minute walk away. The house where my husband lives. The reality is I'd feel more comfortable sleeping on a temporary cot in a rented office than under the same roof as my husband. And that's all my fault.

The first time he asked, I told Dean a lie, that I didn't want children. But that wasn't the complete truth. Every day since then, I've watched my lie snowball into something bigger, so that now it's impossible for me to unwind who I am and who I've pretended to be. I understand why Dean feels like our trust is broken.

I sleep in our guest bedroom; my only interactions with Dean are the dishes we shuffle between the sink and the dishwasher. He must have eaten chicken pot pie for dinner last night. I rinsed his plate after I finished a bowl of popcorn. I wonder if he has seen my mug of chamomile tea this morning. That way he'll know I came home at some point. He says he's getting an apartment, but he'll wait until the election is over to officially move out. It's a kindness I don't deserve. When Dean looks at me, I search for the love and pride that used to fill his eyes, but it's gone, replaced with resentment and disgust.

The streets of downtown Charlottesville are quiet in these early morning hours. It's a few minutes out of my way, but I make a detour through the pedestrian mall, peering into the dark shop windows decorated with brown craft paper and gourds and dried pampas grass. I think for a minute about the hydrangeas in my laundry room, hanging upside down to preserve the green and rust shades for winter. I'll use them for our Thanksgiving table, maybe adding in some orange winterberries.

I stop walking and close my eyes, trying to calm my breathing from the streak of panic that overtakes my body. I'm going to be alone at Thanksgiving. Dean will be gone. Maybe I'll be getting ready to take office or maybe I'll be trying to wipe away the taint from a giant political scandal. Either way, I'll be sitting by myself because I was too much of a coward to stand in front of my husband and tell him the truth. That I am my worst choices.

I try to steady my breath as I finish walking to the campaign headquarters. The lights are off and the building is dark. This is usually my favorite time of day. It is the peaceful hour before the chaos of when my staff appears. For whatever reason, I can't make myself go inside. I linger outside, debating turning around, but the idea of going home feels even worse. I take a step backward and collide with a familiar body.

"Grant? What are you doing here?" I try to create distance between us even though the feel of his firm chest lingers on my palms.

Grant isn't dressed in his usual navy suit, or even his "casual" look of khakis and a button-down, fleece vest optional. This morning, he has on a pair of worn jeans, the denim a light blue from years of washing. His faded black Princeton sweatshirt is frayed at the sleeves. His hair is mussed and his eyes are darting around anxiously.

"Can you come with me?" Grant asks. "My car is parked down the street."

"Are you crazy? I'm not going anywhere with you. We shouldn't even be seen together."

"I know. Tess, I've asked nothing of you in the last twenty-five years. I need you now. Please come with me."

I shake my head and turn to leave. As I glance back over my shoulder, I see Grant standing still. Maybe it's the clothes he's wearing, but all of a sudden I realize that the man I'm running against is gone. Standing in front of me is the boy I knew. I'm still so angry at him for leaving me alone at seventeen. He never showed me the trust or support I needed. But after decades of reflection, I know that the person I'm the angriest with is myself. Because when I see a glimpse of the boy I knew, I'm filled with guilt for my role in the pain I know he still feels.

It's the guilt that makes me turn around toward him.

We are silent on the short walk to his car. It's not until I've slipped into the front seat, feeling the buttery tan leather with my hands, that I ask, "Where are we going?"

He doesn't answer. Instead, he looks into my eyes for too long and starts driving. Wherever we are going, Grant doesn't need directions. He cruises through the streets of Charlottesville with ease, getting on the highway heading north. Minutes of silence pass, my patience waning and my anxiety rising.

The mountain range appears in the distance, amber and rust trees filling the skyline. "Where are we going, Grant?" I ask again.

"You know where we're going," he answers somberly.

"Stop the car. I'm not going back to your mother's house with you."

"We have to go. I need answers."

"Answers to what?" I question.

"I've been thinking about what you said. About the photograph my mother took. I need to know more."

I swallow nervously. I should have called Grant and confessed that it was Dean who found the picture in my mother's cookbook, but I didn't want to discuss everything that followed that revelation. I'm such a coward, hiding the truth from everyone I've ever loved. I take a deep breath, trying to find the courage to start being honest with Grant.

"I know who sent my campaign manager the picture," I admit.

Grant's eyes dart from the road to my face. "Who?" he asks.

"Dean. He found it in my mother's things. I threw the picture away, but my mother must have decided it needed to be kept."

Grant is quiet, and I wonder what he is thinking. I look out the window, remembering so many of the hills we are driving past. Finally, he says, "I guess the upside is that our secret is safe. There isn't some stranger that knows about our past."

"I guess," I mumble.

"Can I ask about you and Dean?" Grant says gently.

"Dean left me," I blurt out. I know this isn't information I should admit to my opponent, but in this moment, the person sitting next to me is just Grant and he understands the consequences of our mistakes. "I hid too much. Some people need the truth, no matter the pain it causes."

"I'm sorry, Tess."

"I keep making the wrong choices," I blurt. "I lose the people I love because I'm afraid," I say too quickly.

Grant swallows, and the reality of my statement takes over. "We both hurt people we loved," he says. He continues driving and we sit in silence as rolling hills fill the landscape.

"I'm sorry about Dean and the photo, but I still have more questions," Grant finally says. "I want to know why my mother took the picture. I want to know how she really felt about me that summer."

"Grant, your father said unforgivable things the morning your mother died. You cannot believe him. I know your mother loved you."

Grant's voice cracks as he says, "Except I've lived my whole life wondering why they didn't love me. Wondering if I somehow caused my mother's death. I haven't been back to that house more than a few times since she died. I need to go back now."

Even after all these years, I feel so much guilt knowing Grant dealt with this pain alone. "Then we'll go," I say, because he needs someone now. He needs me now. "We'll see what we find."

Grant nods. He is quiet as he moves his jaw back and forth. I don't know him anymore—he's practically a stranger, but I know every thought bouncing in his brain at this moment. Grant never understood his mother's death. He's likely spent his life wondering what happened in her final days, in her final hours, and this bit of information feels like one missing piece of the puzzle. There's more I need to tell Grant, but not when he's searching for answers about his mother.

I send Mara a text, letting her know that I need the morning off for a doctor's appointment.

Mara quickly replies: **It's not on your schedule.**

I roll my eyes because even before the sun has risen, Mara has memorized the schedule for the day. I reply:

I didn't know mammograms needed to be on the campaign schedule.

They should be. We can get a photographer over there and plug this into our women's health initiative.

Absolutely not. Let me have my boobs squeezed in peace. I will be in the office this afternoon.

You have other events this morning. Tess, we need to communicate better.

Agreed. We'll talk this afternoon.

I turn off my phone before Mara can send another message. There are a few people ahead of her in line to criticize my communication abilities.

Grant and I are silent for the rest of the drive. I find myself staring at the mountains, my mind replaying a movie of the last two decades and wondering if there could have been a different ending. When I hear the wheels roll over the pea gravel in his mother's driveway, the mild anxiety racing through my veins escalates. All I can think is that this is the place where I first met Grant. This is the place I promised myself I would never return. And here I am.

I look around at the meticulously maintained rows of boxwood hedges, the light blue door offset by the creamy brick-and-stone exterior. Grant parks the car and steps outside, stretching his back and arms as he moves. A part of me wants to stay inside the car. Being back in this place is harder than I'd imagined, but I walk to Grant's side anyway.

"Why did you keep it?" I ask as we both stare at the front door.

"My father wanted to sell, but it was my mother's family house. I made him hold on to it until I could buy it from him. It meant too much to her."

"I bet your sons love it," I say without thinking.

Grant surveys the house and property before he closes his eyes briefly. "They probably would, but I've never brought them here. There are too many painful memories." He stares at me in a way that suggests maybe he means me too.

We both hesitate before walking inside, knowing that there is an invisible line into the past we will cross once we open the door. "What do you need from me, Grant? Being here feels like a mistake."

Grant kicks at the gravel driveway as he speaks. "No one in my life knows about that morning. I want to hate you, but I can't, because you're the only person who understands. Having you here makes me feel less alone."

His words sting. There is so much anger between us, but I know our circumstances muddle those feelings.

Grant walks to the front door, but I stop him. I timidly ask, "Can we go around to the back?"

Grant nods.

I expect to see an overgrown tangle of bushes and vines, or

perhaps a sea of grass that could be easily maintained. Instead, I find the gardens just as I remembered them. It's fall, so many of the roses have already had their last bloom of the season, but the weather has been mild, so there are still plenty of flowers. The salvia provides streaks of purple against the green of the hydrangeas. The maples flanking each side of the garden have doubled in size, creating sweeping branches of bright red.

I have no idea how much money it must take to maintain a garden like this without anyone around to enjoy it. But clearly Grant thought the investment was worth it.

After staring for too long, we finally make our way inside the house, using the back door that was my usual entrance to the grand home. There are covers over much of the furniture, but not a trace of dust on any surface. No one has stayed here in years, but Grant has paid to make sure it's ready in case someone changes their mind.

"What are you looking for?" I ask.

Grant doesn't answer. He's walking through the rooms, likely taking in the life history that childhood homes preserve. He stares at framed photos, traces his hand over the polished wooden banister.

Finally, he says, "She used to keep her camera bag in her closet. The picture kicked this off. That's where I want to start."

He walks upstairs and I follow.

I wonder what he's thinking as we walk into Kay's room, a place that must be difficult for him to see. Her closet seems untouched, a time capsule of the mid-nineties. Stepping inside the space transports me back to when I was a teenager who longed for a magnetic woman's life.

Grant walks to the corner shelves and easily locates the camera bag. He looks inside and pulls out the camera. I don't see anything other than extra lenses. He opens the back of the camera, but it's empty. I suppose he was hoping for an undeveloped roll of film, a hidden clue that would answer his questions.

"She took so many pictures that summer," Grant says.

"I know. She said it was the best year for her garden. Even after all these years, I've never seen a garden as beautiful as your mother's."

He smiles. "She was happy outside, with you. Sometimes, when I try to remember those final weeks of her life, I see her with you. That summer, I'd look out my bedroom window and find the two of you talking, working side by side, and she was always smiling. I've got a lot of bad memories, so it's nice to have that good one."

I swallow as I step closer to Grant, unsettled by the way his body tenses when he talks about the past. "Some mornings she'd meet me on my walk over to your house. It seemed like we were the only two people awake. She told me that she liked to photograph the gardens at sunrise because that's when they were the most beautiful. I remember thinking the same thing about her. She was the most beautiful woman I'd ever seen. I wanted to be just like her."

I find myself walking over to Kay's vanity, sitting on the silky stool where she applied her makeup.

"She was going to give me lessons," I say. "I never did figure out how to apply any of this stuff." I pull open the top drawer and lightly touch the tubes and powders inside. "I hate wearing it for the campaign."

"You never needed makeup, Tess. Your face has always been perfect." Grant says it like he's reciting directions, but the compliment makes me feel like a teenager again.

"I've never felt perfect," I say, although that summer, Grant and Kay made me feel like it was a possibility. Ever since then,

I've chased the sense of belonging that slipped away.

I begin rummaging through the open drawer, thankful for something to occupy my hands.

I look up and Grant is staring at me. I realize that I shouldn't be touching his mother's things. Maybe he's upset. I try to remember where everything was located before my nervous hands made a mess. As I replace a tube of lipstick, the wooden divider in the drawer loosens. I try to push it back into place but knock it looser in the process.

"I'm sorry. I made a mess of this," I say, fumbling with the drawer's contents.

"Tess, I don't care about the drawer. Look at me."

Except I can't. I can't look at Grant. Because I see something hidden in Kay's drawer. Tucked underneath the felt protector holding her eyeshadows, there is a corner of a picture.

"Grant, there's something in here. Your mother hid something. Look." I stand up and point to the corner of the drawer.

He finally moves toward the vanity and sits awkwardly on the tiny stool. He lifts out the felt organizer and we both gasp.

Hidden in Kay's desk are pictures of Richard. Dozens of shots of Richard Alexander, with his arms around Madeline Milton, kissing.

"Madeline and my father?" Grant murmurs. "They were having an affair?" Grant's face seems divided between realization and shock. "Madeline Milton," he murmurs. "She was my mother's best friend. She stood beside me at the funeral, sent cards every Christmas and sterling-silver rattles when the twins were born. My mother grew up with Madeline. They always said they were more like sisters than friends."

I reach out and grab Grant's hand. All these years he's lived with the guilt that he caused his mother's death. A twisted manipulation by a father more focused on self-preservation than love. And Kay. I can only imagine how betrayed she felt by the two people who were supposed to love her the most.

Grant lifts up the photograph and I watch his face as pieces fall into place. Richard blamed Kay's death on Grant, when all along, Richard knew that his affair was likely what pushed her over the edge.

Then I remember, the fight I witnessed between Richard and Kay. Kay's drinking that seemed to escalate with each passing day. The perfect storm that resulted in a fragile woman's end.

"It was your father, Grant. The abuse, the affair. That's why she was drinking so much. He caused her pain."

Grant quickly turns toward me. "You knew about the abuse?"

I nod. "I saw him. I saw him grab your mother." I try to mask the regret in my voice, but it's impossible because I've often wondered why I never told Grant. I've wondered if it would have made a difference.

"Why didn't you say anything?" His voice cracks at every word.

"I was going to, but then—"

"Then everything changed," Grant finishes.

"Yes," I say, unable to trust what I might confess next.

He runs his hand through his hair. It's a movement I saw him do dozens of times that summer. His hair stands up in the same disarray. But there are subtle differences between the boy he once was and the man standing in front of me—flecks of gray in hair that is now closely cropped, lines of worry around once-carefree eyes, darker stubble dotting his jawline. I realize I'm staring too closely and look downward at the floor.

"My father and I were never on good terms." Grant seems to recognize the absurdity of his understatement, because his voice teeters on frantic. "But that summer he broke me."

Grant stands up and walks over to the window. "I never wanted to see him again. I cut him out of my life. We didn't speak until he showed up at my college graduation. For four years, our only communications were through bank transfers." It's clear his anger is still very raw, and I fear not all of it is directed at his father.

Decades ago, I would have tried to comfort Grant. But I know that there's no comfort I can provide for this pain.

He continues, "Eventually, it was too exhausting to stay that mad. We've had periods of civility, periods of complete silence, but we never talk about that summer. We never talk about my mother. I've always wondered what happened that night," he says. "Now I know."

Grant shakes his head. "I expect nothing of him, but I thought more of Madeline. She'd known my mother their entire lives."

I speak softly. "My mother always said Madeline Milton had two priorities: be the best and make sure everyone knows she's the best. It was never enough that my mom's food was delicious if it also wasn't the most talked-about food. She wasn't an easy person to work for. I know that. But how she went from a difficult, vain person to someone who betrayed her best friend, I have no idea."

"I wish I had known about the affair. Maybe I could have stopped him? Or confronted him? Maybe if I had finally stood up to him my mother wouldn't have felt so alone." Grant's eyes are pleading, and I realize this is the conversation that he can't have with anyone else.

"You were a kid, Grant. That wasn't your responsibility." I can't stop myself from walking toward him, reaching for his hand in comfort.

"I didn't make things easy for her that summer."

"She was sad that summer, but that wasn't your fault. The more your father was around, the more she fell apart."

His hand slips out of mine. I hear his fears surface as he says, "Or the more time she spent with me, the sadder she got. I may not have been the reason she drank so much, but she did it knowing I was in the house. Knowing I would find her."

I shake my head. "This is what I remember about your mother. I remember early dinners on the back porch. You made her laugh so loudly that I was worried they'd hear us over at the Milton property. I remember catching her staring at you with so much pride and joy in her eyes. I remember her teasing you about your messy room and your inability to pull a weed. Most of all, I remember the big smile on her face whenever she was with you."

I wish there was more I could say to reassure Grant without having to admit what I remembered most from that summer was how much I loved him.

He stares at me, short inhales making his breath jagged.

I continue, "We can't know what went on between your mother and father, but I know for sure that you weren't the person who made her sad. That was him."

He nods, but I can tell doubts are still swirling in his mind. My voice is firm and clear as I say, "You have zero responsibility for her death. You can't live another second of your life thinking that, Grant."

"All I do is think about that summer. Maybe if I'd done things differently, I could have changed her mind."

"You can't change someone's mind, Grant."

"I know. You taught me that lesson, Tess."

Twenty

SEPTEMBER 1996

I was lucky Richard Alexander made the appointment for a Saturday. I didn't have to miss school and my mother could drive me to the clinic.

She'd been surprisingly understanding. There had been moments of yelling and tears, but my mother said it was my decision.

I saw the way her lips opened and closed on the drive. There was something she wanted to say, but she didn't seem to know when or how to start. So it was a silent ride, both of our minds churning with unspoken emotion. When we pulled into the parking lot, she put the car in park but didn't turn off the engine.

The air had turned cool the week before and the warmth of the car felt cozy, a false comfort on a scary morning.

"We don't need his money. Cash is temporary. This decision is permanent," my mother said, staring forward.

We'd talked about Richard's offer for days. This wasn't the first time she'd made this argument.

My mother knew I disagreed. I never wavered in all of our discussions. That check would change our lives. I was firm as I said, "I'd be stupid not to take the money. I'm done being stupid about men."

My mother made it clear how she felt too. "This is your body, Tess. No amount of money can ever buy your body. Do you understand?"

I nodded and unbuckled my seat belt, exhausted by the repetitive conversation. My mother put her hand on my thigh, stopping me from leaving.

"I met your father at the Homestead." She inhaled, preparing herself for this memory. "His name was Jack. At least, that's what he told me. Sometimes I wonder if his full name was John or Jackson or maybe even Jefferson. Who knows? You don't think about asking for someone's full legal name when you have a one-night stand. Although that wasn't my intention at the beginning of the night." She mumbled the last part.

This was already more information than I'd ever gotten from my mother. I didn't speak, afraid to interrupt a story I didn't think I'd ever hear.

"I'd just turned eighteen, so I was living in the staff housing that summer. I thought I was so lucky to finally be out of my parents' place. But after a few weeks, I missed your grandmother's cooking, and sharing a bathroom with two dozen girls lost its appeal. It's funny how easily dreams can turn into disappointments."

My chin quivered. I wanted to hear this story, but I was afraid of what I would learn. Our relationship felt fragile, and

I didn't think I could handle finding out that I was my mother's regret.

My mother reached for my chin and turned my face toward hers. "You have never been and will never be my disappointment. You are my pride, Tess."

She shook her head. "I shouldn't tell you this story."

"Please," I said, my voice part whisper, part plea.

She took a deep breath and continued. "I was working in the kitchen, delivering room service that day. This room ordered pancakes and eggs and French toast. My tray was loaded. When I brought up the order, there was a line of beer bottles in the hallway from the night before. There were three of them, not quite men, but not boys either, staying for the weekend, a college graduation gift from their parents. They were dressed for a round of golf, but they all looked too hungover to enjoy anything."

My mother stared forward as I hung on her every word.

"I dropped off their breakfast order and cleaned up the bottles in the hallway. They weren't rude, but Jack was the only one who was nice. He helped me with the trash even though I insisted he shouldn't."

I saw my mother's lip twitch, as if a memory was triggered. "He had a great smile. Straight, white teeth that shone against his tan face. He flirted like it was a competitive sport, complimenting my hair, asking me questions about the area, telling me stories about their road trip to the resort."

I wanted to ask a million questions. I wanted her to paint his picture so that I could see that smile. I wanted to know if she saw bits of him in me, and which parts, and why she hadn't said any of this before. But I didn't interrupt. I let her keep telling the story she'd hidden for so long.

"He asked if I wanted to go see a band in town that night and I almost screamed 'yes.'" She sighed. "Sometimes guests treated me like I was invisible. I can't tell you how good it felt to be seen. I floated through work that day."

My mother seemed too practical to ever float, but I suppose she was a whole different person before me. A child changed everything.

"He bought me fancy cocktails and we danced and he held my hand the whole night. He talked about taking me on a hike the next day. And said his parents would love the restaurant at the hotel and he'd bring them back later in the summer. I assumed too much. I read into those tiny comments and thought that meant he planned on seeing me for more than one night."

My mother's eyes fluttered open, as if she was forcing away memories she wanted to forget.

"And then the next day, they ordered more room service. Except this time, he didn't help me gather the beer bottles. He looked away when his friends laughed about how good I was at my job. He left the resort and pretended like I never existed. Like he hadn't held me the night before and made me think my life could be something more."

I swallowed, knowing exactly how she felt.

"I've asked about him before," I said softly. "Why are you telling me now?"

"I was embarrassed. I should have been smarter. I want more for you." She rattled off these reasons like a grocery list. Then she took a deep breath and said, "Because, up until this moment, I didn't know if you could understand that mistakes can lead to the best moments in your life."

I shook my head. "You have to say that because you're my mom. I was a giant mistake and who knows what your life could have been like if you didn't get pregnant at eighteen."

My mother held my hand. "Having you was the best moment of my life. I can't imagine how empty I'd feel without you in my world."

The car felt too small for such a big conversation. I stared at the floorboard as I said, "You've struggled to make enough money and worked for assholes and now your daughter is pregnant. Mistakes don't lead to good stuff. They lead to more mistakes." I wiped away a tear from my cheek and saw my mother's glassy eyes mirrored my own.

"Try to see it a different way, Tess. I had parents who supported me and welcomed me back into their home. I've struggled, but I've never starved. I have a brilliant, kind daughter who is going to do remarkable things in her life. There are people who never experience a fraction of the love I've known."

She reached her arms around me and pulled me into a tight hug. "No matter what you do, today or any day, I will always love you."

I held her tighter. She showed me love that, up until that moment, I'd been too selfish to understand.

"Thank you for telling me about him." I kissed my mother's cheek. "Thank you for taking care of me."

I reached for the door handle.

"Do you want me to come in with you?"

I shook my head. "I need to walk in by myself."

She seemed to understand that I couldn't be ushered through this decision. I needed to make it fully on my own.

She squeezed my hand. "I'll be in the lobby when you're done."

My hand was shaking as I walked toward the building. There was a man standing at the entrance. At first I thought it was a protestor, but instead of shouting threats in my face, he handed me an envelope.

The Summer We Ran

It was a check from Richard Alexander for the remaining money I was owed. I wasn't important enough to justify his presence, so he sent a messenger. I shoved the check into my pocket and walked inside.

Twenty-One

OCTOBER 26, 2021

Grant stares at me from across his childhood bedroom. I brace myself for what comes next, because he's no longer talking about the pain of his mother's death. He's focused on our past and the decision that tore us apart.

"Can you honestly tell me you've never wondered?" Grant asks. "What if you'd kept the baby? We could still be together."

I'm an adult. Grant is the opposing candidate. And yet all of a sudden, I'm transported back in time. He forces me to juggle the sympathy I feel for a broken boy and my frustration at his lack of understanding.

"Because if I did what you wanted, we'd be together? Is that how you think love works? One person controlling the other?"

"I wasn't trying to control you, Tess."

"You were so idealistic. You thought our lives could go on with a baby. But it would have changed everything for me. You went on to Princeton and Wharton and got your fancy job and your fancy wife and your fancy house and nothing changed for you. But it changed everything for me. Everything."

"I know. That much money would change anyone's life," he bites back.

I recoil at his words, both in their bluntness and because they force me to face one of my biggest regrets. "You have no idea what you're talking about." I want to sound confident, but instead, my statement is a meek whisper.

"I know exactly what I'm talking about," Grant says. "My father paid you fifty thousand dollars to have an abortion and stay away from me. And you jumped at the money."

Grant is right. But I don't say that. Instead, I begin to defend myself. "Your father is an asshole."

"At least he's honest about who he is."

I've tried to be a good person. Maybe that's why I've devoted my life to making the world a little better. That check from Richard Alexander changed our lives, just like I knew it would, but I could never let go of the dread that I accepted it. Every grocery trip where my mother bought what she wanted instead of what was on sale, I had to ask myself if it was worth it. When I stepped on the UVA campus, I had to ask myself if it was worth it. When I married a man with a strong moral compass, I had to ask myself if it was worth it. I'm still searching for that answer.

I didn't want to be the person who took the money. But even more, I didn't want to be the person without it.

I continue my defense. "He got my mother fired. Did he tell you that? I was seventeen, pregnant, with no home, no money, and your father handed me a check."

"That's what he does, Tess. He finds someone's weakness and

jumps on it. You took that check and threw away our whole lives together."

"No, Grant. You did that. I hate myself for taking his money, but I didn't feel like I had a choice. I didn't want my mother's life."

"You didn't want a life with me either."

I stalk toward Grant, decades-long anger surfacing at his judgment of my decisions. "You knew me. But at the first sign of conflict, you ran. You didn't trust me."

"Why would I trust you? You took a bribe and killed my baby."

His words slap my heart. "I'm sorry you feel that way" is the only response I can manage.

Grant seethes. "You're sorry? Sorry for what? Sorry for taking the money? For having an abortion? For being the second love in my life stolen from me in a month? What are you sorry for, Tess?"

I try to explain, fearing that it's pointless. "I was young and stupid. I don't know what I thought would happen. We needed that money and it did create a whole new life for us. One I know we wouldn't have had otherwise. But I'm sorry you were hurt in the process."

"My whole life is made up of people who think my pain is irrelevant."

I'm frustrated that Grant thinks he is the victim. Because there were two lost kids that summer. "That's bullshit. I loved you and I thought our love was stronger than some asshole with a bribe. You knew who your father was. I took the money and I stood there that day you left and lied to you. I told you I couldn't be with you anymore because your father was willing to pay me more money than I ever could have imagined."

There are streaks of tears falling down my cheeks as I say the words that have been bottled inside for decades. "I will never stop feeling guilty for what that must have done to you. For how you must have felt. I know you felt alone, and I know my words made it worse. I'm sorry. I loved you so much and there has never been a harder moment in my entire life than the day I pretended I'd be okay without you."

"You didn't have to take the money. We could have made it on our own, Tess. I know we could," he pleads.

"You've never known what it's like to struggle. That's all I knew, and for the first time in my life, I was given an opportunity to escape."

"You talk about choice and control over a woman's body. But you were so quick to see that control sold off. I don't think I'll ever understand what you did, Tess."

"You don't have to." I want to repeat those words again and again in the hope that someday Grant will understand. "It was my life. I made decisions, and I am the one who has to live with the consequences of those decisions."

"That's not true. I still think about that baby. I wonder what kind of life she'd have. She would have graduated college by now. You took all of that away from me and you knew it wasn't what I wanted. She could have had a beautiful life."

"He," I say, letting the simple word slip from my mouth.

"What?" Grant stutters, looking as if he's been struck.

I walk toward the window of his room, unable to look into his eyes when I say, "He could've had a beautiful life."

"How did you know the baby was a boy?"

"The ultrasound," I whisper. I turn toward Grant and watch as his mind spins, trying to put together the pieces that have been missing for so long.

Grant shakes his head. "You couldn't have known that early. With the twins, we didn't find out until the middle of the pregnancy."

"I knew."

"Tess, what are you saying?"

I breathe in, knowing that the air can't be held any longer than the truth. "I didn't get an abortion."

"What?" Grant's entire body seems to shake in confusion.

"I took the money, but I didn't have an abortion."

"But you said it was your choice."

"It was my choice. But you weren't there. You never came." I can't stop my voice from turning into the pleas that a teenage girl was so desperate to vocalize. "I kept thinking you would reach out and I'd tell you and everything would be okay. I waited for you, and you never came."

"You never had an abortion." Grant's voice cracks.

"You left me all alone. I was seventeen and so scared, Grant."

"Tess, please, I'm begging you, tell me what happened. Do we have a child?" Grant is frantic.

"Grant, I'm not ready for this conversation."

"When, Tess?" he shouts. "You've lied to me for twenty-five years." His tone is even, but I see fury in his eyes. "I've waited long enough."

"I didn't lie to you. You believed what you wanted to believe, what you have the privilege of believing. I was the one who was pregnant and you left. You said you loved me, but that love was so quickly rescinded."

"I told you I wanted to keep the baby. You told me you made the decision for both of us. How do you think that made me feel?" Grant asks accusingly.

"You made me promises," I say, unable to stop myself from

jabbing his chest. "You said you'd be by my side. But when I didn't do exactly what you wanted, you cut me off. You never contacted me again. Didn't you wonder about me?"

"Every day," Grant says softly, closing the space between us. Tears drop onto my dress, leaving marks of darkened blue on the simple sheath. I think back to that summer. I look into Grant's eyes and his hand reaches out for mine. I then tell him everything that happened, a time I never want to relive. But I do it because Grant deserves the truth.

Twenty-Two

NOVEMBER 1996

Our apartment was nice. It was in a safe Charlottesville neighborhood with a good high school. My mom got a job at a bakery down the street and they were even letting her add a few of her own recipes to the menu. The hours were long, but we were both used to that. This job had fewer complications. No unpredictable schedule or ultimatums from scary men. She seemed happy, testing out recipes and settling into our new home, as if this new life was something she'd dreamed of.

And yet I was terrified all the time. I looked down at my stomach, still oddly flat, and wondered when I would start to show. I wondered if I would be able to finish my senior-year classes. I wondered what Grant was doing at that exact moment and if he thought about me as much as I thought about him.

I wondered if I made the right choice that day at the clinic.

I was led back to a small room for the procedure. I remember slipping on the paper gown, lying on the table, and staring up.

Someone had tucked pictures of flowers into the ceiling tile squares. I suppose they thought women lying on their backs would enjoy the distraction of pictures rather than counting the water stains. But I stared at those photographs of flowers, especially the roses that Kay loved so much, and I started to question my decision.

Then they turned on the ultrasound that was required before each abortion and I heard the whirling sound of the ocean followed by the repetitive pulse of a heart. I looked at the screen and saw the flickering beat inside me, prompting me to sit upright. "I'm sorry," I stammered. "I can't."

I came out of the clinic, expecting to see that same man waiting, seeking proof that I'd completed my end of the bargain. But instead, the only person waiting for me was my mother. I told her that I didn't have the abortion. She pulled me into a tight hug. "This may not have been your plan, baby girl, but we will figure this out. Murphy women are resilient."

My plan had been to become something more than my mother. All of the judgment that consumed my youth erased by the humbling realization that I'd be lucky to one day be as strong as her.

For a while, I expected Richard to call and demand his money back. But he never did. Maybe the fact that I went to the clinic was enough. Maybe the clinic kept the confidentiality obligations they promised. Although I knew Grant's father could find a way around those rules if he really cared. My best guess was that I didn't matter enough for Richard to follow up. I was out of his son's life and that was his ultimate goal.

But the money mattered to me. Because when I got an early acceptance letter to University of Virginia along with a tuition scholarship, I knew that money would cover the rest. I kept it in a bank account, ready to return it if Richard demanded, but hoping he stayed away because that meant I could go to college.

We hadn't done much decorating in the apartment, but the first thing I did was hang the ultrasound picture on the fridge. I touched it each morning as I took my vitamins and drank a glass of milk. I plopped at the kitchen table, gathering the materials that I'd avoided reading for long enough.

My mother slid a warm sticky bun in front of me, dripping with brown-sugar syrup and pecans. A pregnant daughter made for an excellent taste-tester. I took a huge bite and gave her a thumbs-up as I reached for a napkin. "There's something different."

"Different good or different bad?" she asked genuinely.

"Definitely good. What's the flavor in the syrup?"

"I mixed honey in the brown sugar and added orange blossom. What do you think?"

"Best yet."

"Okay. Adding these to the list, then. How's the reading going?" My mother wasn't one to push, but I knew she was eager to discuss the topic I consistently avoided.

I walked to the sink to wash away my sticky fingers and delay my response.

"Have you made a decision?" she asked.

"I've made some elimination decisions."

My mother sighed. "What does that mean?"

"It means some of these adoption agencies feel kind of self-righteous. They're worse than the women at Grandma's church and I don't want to have anything to do with them."

"That's fair."

"But there are good ones too," I said quietly. "I'm reading through those now. The sooner I make a choice, the better."

"You don't have to rush this decision, Tess," my mother said gently.

I shook my head. "If I sign with an agency and select a family, they cover all the medical expenses. We don't have health insurance. I need to make a choice."

"We already talked about this. We're not going to let money make these decisions." She reached for my hand and stared into my eyes. "*You* make these decisions."

"I like this place," I said, pushing the brochure for an adoption agency in northern Virginia across the table. "It isn't affiliated with a church. The people look nice. No *abortion is murder* propaganda. No *helping the whores* vibes."

My mother's eyes rolled upward as she swatted the air. "Tess, stop. I hate it when you talk like that."

"That's how a lot of these places make me feel."

"Then don't pick those places."

"They also gave me this." I handed my mother a binder. On each page was a picture of a happy couple. It was the same story again and again. They were very in love. They were very good people, with good jobs and good homes. They just needed a baby to make their lives complete.

My mother started flipping through the binder. I wondered what she thought. Could she see something about these people that I couldn't—the couple that was actually on the brink of divorce, the couple that fought so loudly the neighbors called the police, the couple with the controlling husband and the alcoholic wife. Because I knew those couples existed, but I didn't know how to pick a family for my child when all I got to see were the shopping mall photo studio versions.

"It's a big decision," my mother said.

I wanted to scream, "No shit!" but I nodded instead.

My mother closed the binder. "You could keep the baby. It won't be easy. But that is one of the choices too, Tess."

I shook my head. "I know you did it, but I can't. I don't want to. It's not the life I want for the baby—for me."

I didn't mean to hurt my mother with my words, but I could tell I did. Instead of telling me that, she said, "I understand."

I knew I was lucky—to have a mother who understood my desire for more.

My hand rested on my stomach. "I'm going to start showing. It's one thing to be the new girl at school. It's another thing to be the new, pregnant girl."

My mother walked across the room and rifled through a box. She came back to the kitchen table with a photo album and started flipping through it. I pushed away the brochures and the binder and inched my chair closer to my mother's.

She stopped turning pages at a picture of her at about my age. Her hair was teased high, and she had on ridiculous blue eye shadow. She was wearing a plaid shirt and flared jeans.

She pointed to herself and said, "I was seven months pregnant then."

"Really?" My eyes narrowed in on the photo. The shirt was oversized. There was a fullness to her face and her legs looked slightly bigger than normal, but otherwise she looked like a typical teenager.

"Lucky genes," she said. "Grandma was the same way. I didn't really show until the last month, and even then, it wasn't bad."

"So maybe the other kids at school won't know?" I asked.

"Maybe. My guess is a few bulky sweaters and some baggy jeans and you'll be able to cover it up. If you want."

"That makes me feel better. It's stupid to worry about, I know. But it's hard feeling so alone and different."

"You are not alone. I am here."

I leaned my head on my mother's shoulder, grateful for her support, but yearning for Grant's presence. It was almost as if she could read my thoughts.

"Have you heard from him?"

"No. Nothing." I didn't want to cry, but all of a sudden, I was sobbing. I could try blaming it on the pregnancy hormones, but I knew that wasn't the reason.

"You don't want to tell him? Maybe he should know that you kept the baby."

"I'm not keeping the baby," I said between choked sobs. "I'm giving it up for adoption."

"I know. I just meant that you didn't go through with the abortion. Do you think it would change things between the two of you?"

My mother asked the question that ran on repeat through my brain.

"Probably," I answered honestly. "He thought he was right. He couldn't understand my choice. If he knew I changed my mind, maybe he'd love me again. But I'm not sure I want that kind of love."

"What kind of love is that?" my mother asked.

"The kind with conditions."

"All love has conditions," my mother said, wrapping her arms around me. "All love has limits. Not all love gets tested the way yours and Grant's did. Love is not like those books you read."

I'd never seen my mother go on more than a handful of dates. I dismissed her perspective on love and romance readily, not realizing that maybe there was more to her story than what she showed her teenage daughter.

"If he really loves me, he'll come for me," I said naively. But of course he never did.

Twenty-Three

OCTOBER 26, 2021

I tell Grant everything. How I went to the clinic but left pregnant. How I kept the money. I watch as his face pulls in a million directions, the emotions of this long-held secret seeming to break any restraint.

I should have told him, long before today. But at seventeen, I thought our love was stronger than our convictions. Grant proved me wrong. Maybe that's why I lied to Dean for so long. I knew love required hiding your worst parts.

"One phone call, Tess. One letter. It would have changed everything," Grant says.

"Would it?" I ask. "I took the money, Grant. I knew your father was a monster. I left you with him." I take a deep breath as I say the words that I should have said then. "I'm sorry."

"I was going to come for you," Grant says. "Then he told me about the payment. I was so angry that another person I loved could be bought by him. I didn't want his control anymore."

"I thought you wanted to control me. I thought you stopped loving me because I didn't do what you wanted."

"No, Tess. That was never it. I never stopped loving you. I was devastated by you."

I swallow my nerves, unaware that it was possible to feel more guilty.

"Tess, tell me what happened next," Grant pleads. "What happened to the baby?"

"I found a family. A good family," I explain with detachment. "I remember the wife's name was Iris. I thought your mother would like that."

Grant is patient as I continue. "I wanted it to be a closed adoption. I didn't want to have any contact with the family before or after the birth."

"You don't even know their last names?" he asks.

I shake my head. "I got their first names, their jobs, how long they were married, but nothing more. I knew I needed it to be like that. It would be too hard otherwise."

"But now, Tess? Do you still feel that way?"

"I can't answer that, Grant. You have no idea how difficult it was to make these decisions as a kid."

"We have a child somewhere, Tess. There has to be a way to find the family. He's an adult now. Maybe he wants to find us."

"Grant." I whisper his name like a warning.

"I know you had to do this all alone, but you aren't alone now. I want to know my firstborn son."

I shake my head.

"I bet he has your dark eyes," Grant says. "And maybe my light hair. He's probably stubborn because he gets that from both of us. What if he's in medical school? Or maybe he's an architect."

"Stop," I plead.

"I know this was never a real person to you. It was something you could end or give away. But to me, this is my child and I want to know him." Grant doesn't even try to hide the judgment in his voice.

"That is unbelievably unfair, Grant. Fuck you."

"I have a vote in this situation. I want to know my son."

"You think this wasn't a real person to me? You think I'm some kind of monster? He's real to me," I say. "He was real when I was deciding to have the abortion. It was an impossibly difficult decision. I don't know if I made the right choice. But just because I decided against the abortion doesn't mean it was because I had some sudden realization that it was a real person growing inside me. I always knew that. I always knew that he could become a doctor, or have my brown eyes, or infuriate me the way you do. That's what made that choice so hard. Your lack of support made it unbearable."

Grant softens and I wonder if maybe he is beginning to understand. "I know," he says. "There are things I'm sorry about too."

"I grew a baby inside of me for months. I felt it move and I wondered about its life. I made the best choice I could think of at seventeen. That was to give this baby a fresh start somewhere else. Without our selfish bullshit screwing up his life." My voice is full of conviction, absent a single shake.

"We would have been good parents," Grant tries to justify.

"No, we wouldn't," I reply too quickly. "We didn't support each other. That's not love."

"I loved you, Tess." Grant reaches for my hand, trying to connect us amid so much disagreement. But I turn my back to him.

"Stop, Grant. You need to hear the whole story."

"The whole story? What else happened?"

I try to find the words to explain the worst day of my life. I'm quiet for too long, but Grant doesn't make me rush. He waits, patient to hear about this darkness.

"I was almost seven months along," I say. "My mother was managing the bakery by then. She was exhausted all the time. We both were. She'd leave at four in the morning, so when I woke up that day, I was by myself."

I start shaking, the pain of reliving this time taking over my body. I wrap my arms around my waist as my eyes drift across the room.

"I was in so much pain. My body bent in half when I felt this warm sensation. At first, I was embarrassed. I thought I'd peed my pants." I half-laugh as I say, "There are so many disgusting things about pregnancy that no one talks about."

When I start speaking again, all humor is erased. "I remember reaching into my underwear and pulling my hand out. It was covered in sticky, red blood. The cramps got worse and worse, sucking the air out of my lungs with each wave. I stood up and a gush of blood streamed out. My pajamas were soaked."

"I didn't have a car," I explain. "I didn't have a cell phone. The last thing I remember was thinking I'd try to knock on the neighbor's door. I never made it out of our apartment. My mother found me unconscious when she got back from work."

Grant's eyes are focused on mine. I don't know him well enough anymore to decipher the emotions on his face.

I continue. "I remember waking briefly on the way to the hospital. There was so much blood everywhere. They couldn't stop the bleeding."

Grant seems afraid to ask, but he does it anyway. "What happened, Tess?"

"They performed an emergency C-section and took him

away. I was hemorrhaging. The bleeding wouldn't stop." My voice is flat, almost as if I'm relaying a news bulletin instead of the most terrifying day of my life. "I don't remember much. It's like this highlight reel of terror. I went in and out of consciousness. I woke up the next day and my mom was there. But the baby was gone."

"They took him while you were in surgery?" Grant asks, confused.

"No, Grant." My eyes well over with tears as he finally seems to understand. I shake out the painful words anyway. "The baby died."

Grant looks away. He may not have known about the baby before today, but the pain he feels at hearing about his death is evident. Finally, Grant asks, "And you? Were you okay?"

"No," I reply. "I've never been okay. Not since the day I left this room."

"I should have listened to you," Grant says. "I should have at least checked on you. If I had been there, everything would have been different." Grant's arms wrap around my shoulders and I find myself collapsing into his chest.

"Even if you had stayed, he still would have died," I say. "You would have given up everything for nothing. It's better this way. Your life is better."

Grant shakes his head. "I should have been there with you. If I'd been there, maybe he would have lived."

I look away. "I was never meant to be a mother. We were never meant to be a family." I gesture to the space between us and I feel the air pushing us apart. "It's different for you. You wanted to be a father. You get to have a good family now. We would have been a mess."

Grant swallows as he says, "I could be a good father, but I'm not. I spend too much time away from the twins. I rely on Cecilia for too many things. Maybe, with us, it would have been different."

"No," I say, clear in my statement.

"I think you would have been a pretty great mother." Grant says it like a compliment, which makes me slow my words because he clearly doesn't understand my feelings.

"I'm not a lesser person or a lesser woman because I recognize that I don't have the capacity to be a mother. My life is complete without children. I don't need judgment for feeling that way. I don't need your pity."

"I don't pity you," Grant says quickly. "It feels like everything I say is wrong. I hate that you went through so much alone."

"I wasn't alone," I say, softening. "My mother was there. The couple that I never wanted to meet came to visit me at the hospital. They brought flowers, a bouquet of goldenrod in January because on my intake form for the agency I said they were my favorite."

"They were being kind," Grant says.

"I didn't deserve their kindness. I couldn't keep their baby alive," I say, my voice cracking.

"Tess, don't do that to yourself," Grant says softly.

"I've made peace with my life," I say, recovering. "Even the rest of that horrible day."

Grant looks into my eyes and squeezes my hand. "Tess, what else happened?"

"In order to stop the bleeding, the doctors had to perform a hysterectomy." I stumble over the last word but recover with a deep inhale that I hold inside unnaturally long.

I've never spoken publicly about the reason why I don't have children. It's a question I'm asked frequently and my answer is always some variation of the same: "Family planning is a private, personal decision. I'm happy that you don't ask the male candidates about their decisions and I wish you'd extend the same courtesy to me." I usually get an embarrassed laugh and a quick topic change.

Most people assume I'm focused on my career. They don't know that I never had a choice.

I think about how Dean and I talked in circles for years. I told him my career mattered. I told him I didn't want to be a mother. But he kept pushing. He wanted to understand and that only made me more defensive. My beliefs shouldn't require justifications. But really, I didn't want to think about the shame and regret that swirled around so much loss at such a young age—my baby, my uterus, my future. And every time Dean asked about a family, I masked the pain I felt inside with frustration that I needed to explain myself again.

When Dean and I first started sleeping together, he asked about my period. I remember uttering a response about how my periods were always irregular. It was a partial truth, and all the explanation he needed. Because it never came up again. After all our years of marriage, he never once wondered about the absence of tampons in the house or any sex scheduling around cycles. And every time he asked about a baby, I never answered with the truth because I was angry. I let that anger build and it rightfully pushed away the husband I loved.

As my breath releases, I say, "I shouldn't be able to have kids. It's the way it was supposed to work out." Tears stream down my cheeks.

Grant cups my face and wipes them away. "No, Tess. None of this worked out the way it was supposed to. I should have called."

"You should have called," I repeat, nodding.

"Is it too late?" Grant asks.

"Too late for what?"

"To admit I made a mistake?"

I begin to shake my head, but Grant stops me, reaching for my hand and winding his fingers around mine. "We've both made too many mistakes, Grant."

He squeezes my hand. "I shouldn't have left you, Tess. I may not have agreed with your choice, but I should have fought for our relationship. I should have showed you how much I loved you."

"It's too late," I say, refusing to look in his eyes. I wonder if he can tell I'm lying.

"If it's too late, then I won't tell you that being with you feels like home." Grant holds me tighter, words I've waited decades to hear washing over me. "There's never been a place, not this house, or any house I've ever lived in, that feels truer or safer than sitting next to you," he says. "I've spent my life convincing myself that I'm fine without you. I've lied to myself and said what we had wasn't real. No one meets the love of their life at eighteen."

I stare at the floor as I say, "We are such different people, Grant. We've always been different, but those differences have grown since we've been apart."

"At the first debate, you started reciting statistics about juvenile detention centers because you were nervous. You always recite facts to calm your nerves. You did the same thing when you started rambling about sandwiches the first day we met."

I look at Grant and the corners of my mouth rise into a slight smile.

"There might be some differences"—he rakes his hand through his graying hair—"but we are the same people."

Our eyes connect. One of Grant's arms wraps around my waist, pulling our bodies together. His other hand moves upward, eventually cradling the back of my head as his fingers weave into my hair. He says the words I've waited decades to hear. "I love you, Tess. I've always loved you."

He pulls my face toward his. Our lips melt into each other's and all of a sudden, our hands are moving everywhere, searching, frantic to connect with skin. Our hands follow the paths they created so many years ago, the muscle memory of intimacy.

His tongue dives into my mouth and I moan briefly. My arms wrap around his neck and my voice cracks slightly as I say, "Grant, we lost so much."

"We make up for it now," he says.

I lean in to his hard body, feeling our hearts beat against each other. There's an added confidence to his motions that makes me swallow harder. It feels like a dream being with Grant. One I don't want to end. My mind and body are consumed with this man I've loved for so long, making it hard to think of anything else, especially not the people outside these walls who we've destroyed.

I feel his fingers on the zipper of my dress. It would be so easy to let him continue. To let our bodies reconnect after decades apart. But somehow, I pull back and stop.

His hands pause and his eyes flutter closed. When they open, they meet mine and he smiles.

Our faces are inches apart as I say, "I don't want to feel guilt when it comes to you. We've hurt people who loved us, Grant. They deserve better." I take a step back as I say, "One of us is going to be governor next week. We have to slow down."

"Slow? We've waited twenty-five years. No person, no campaign, has ever mattered more than you, Tess."

I'm not sure if I agree, but I nod anyway.

Twenty-Four

OCTOBER 26, 2021

Grant drops me off a few blocks away from my headquarters. He smiles as he leans across the car, opening my door and depositing a kiss on my neck. My body stiffens unconsciously and he senses the change, squeezing my hand reassuringly.

"I could turn the car around. We could start driving and never look back."

I cup his face in my hands. "We always look back. That's our problem."

Grant nods. "There's a lot to talk about, Tess."

"I know. Let's get through this week. It will be tough for me to sneak away tomorrow, but I'll try."

Grant leans forward, reaching around my waist to pull me in for a kiss. I place a hand on his chest, glancing nervously at the people walking down the street, knowing they can't see in the tinted windows of his car but cautious, nonetheless. "We have to be careful."

"Practical Tess," he says, poking my side like he did when we were kids.

"One of us has to be practical."

"Nah, I think we're due for some reckless behavior."

I raise my eyebrows. "Everything about us is reckless, Grant."

His easy smile appears and it affects me the same as always—a calming happiness and a jealous longing.

"I recognize that this is crazy, Tess. But I feel like I can breathe for the first time in years. Having you back in my life changes everything." He kisses my forehead as he says, "Don't overthink this. Don't spiral into panic, Tess. I will see you tomorrow. We will find a way."

I hop out of Grant's car and walk briskly toward my office. I immediately ignore Grant's instructions as my mind starts reeling with the countless ways in which our lives could spiral. I know Grant assumes what will happen next. He's the most self-assured person I've ever met. I fell into his arms this morning and now he thinks that I've fallen back into his life.

But my gut churns in confusion. My seventeen-year-old self was so desperate to be loved by the boy who left her. Desperate to hear his regrets. Maybe it was that desperation that caused me to slip backward. I thought I was stronger. But I was wrong.

Even with so much uncertainty—the election, our marriages, our futures—it is still easy to imagine myself in his life. I saw the house he shares with Cecilia in a magazine feature of his family. If I'd been smarter, I would have ignored the article, but I didn't. Instead, I studied the pictures of Grant and Cecilia Alexander, lounging in their mansion with the cedar shingles and stone columns. It was an effective article, displaying Grant's strength as a master of wealth mixed with pictures of him building wooden train sets with his twin sons, Cecilia smiling lovingly in the background. I couldn't help but wonder what kind of father Grant had become. I studied those pictures, trying to parse out the kernels of truth and the manufactured façade. I've seen so many pictures of Grant and Cecilia together that those shots didn't bother me. It was the one of Cecilia arranging flowers on their kitchen counter while Grant stood behind her. That was the one that made me light-headed. Because it was too easy for me to slip my face over Cecilia's and wonder what could have been.

I open the door to my campaign headquarters and Mara is immediately at my side.

"What's wrong? You have that constipated look on your face," Mara comments. She's wearing a simple black suit with a blue button-down shirt, her short brown hair parted down the middle, swinging above her shoulders. Mara always does the right thing and always looks put together.

"I'm fine. Just nervous about the campaign," I deflect.

I ignore the calls of my name and walk straight into my office. I try to shut myself away, but Mara is too quick. She walks inside and asks, "Everything okay?"

"Close the door, Mara."

She complies as she comments, "You don't look so good." Mara watches me closely, concern growing on her face. "Tess, did everything go okay at the doctor's office? You're as white as a sheet."

"I wasn't at the doctor's office," I say.

"Where were you?"

"I was with Grant Alexander," I confess.

Mara's eyes widen. "I have a million questions, so please start talking," she barks.

That's exactly what I do. I tell Mara everything, something I should have done months ago. Other than Grant, she's the only person who gets the whole story, full of my deepest flaws and darkest regrets.

Mara listens. She doesn't react when I tell her about the pregnancy or the money I took from Richard Alexander. Her face remains flat when I tell her about leaving the abortion clinic and looking for an adoptive family only to lose the baby. It's when I tell her about the hysterectomy that I see a momentary softening in her eyes. But then she's immediately back to business mode.

"I need to know where Dean fits into all of this," Mara asks.

"He found the picture of Grant and me," I say. "He was the anonymous source." I see a flash of anger across Mara's face and explain, "I never told him about Grant or the pregnancy. He found the photo and he found my ultrasound picture. Even when he gave me the chance to confess, I didn't."

"He never knew? About any of this?" Mara asks, not trying to hide her shock.

I shake my head, knowing it was a mistake to hide myself from Dean. I thought if I removed that part of my history, I could be the person I always wanted to become. I didn't want to be the person who could be bought off. I didn't want to be the person who put herself before the people she loved. Because that's what I did. I resented Grant, but I hated myself.

I closed off that part of my life, hoping that I could move forward a better person. But I should have known I could never escape my worst self.

"Where do you and Dean stand now?" Mara asks. "I need to plan for every possible scenario and I need to know if he will be next to you in any of them."

I shake my head again and then force myself to say the words out loud. Because I know I cannot deny reality any longer.

"Dean wants a divorce. He won't say anything before the election. But our marriage is over."

Mara nods but doesn't ask more. Maybe she knows that the inner workings of a marriage are a mystery, sometimes even to their members. I'm not sure whether Dean will ever forgive me. I hope someday. But I know he gave me too many chances to ever trust me as his wife again.

Mara rubs the back of her neck as she stares at the ceiling. Finally, she asks, "What about Grant? Do you see a future with him?"

I hesitate, considering my answer but ultimately going with the truth. "I don't know. He's talking about a future, but I have no idea if that's possible. Or if that's the best thing for either of us."

Mara seems to categorize this information, along with the list of confessions I've dumped on her this afternoon. I know her mind is swirling, but there is one thing I need to make clear. "Mara, I want to be governor. This election is important. What do I need to do? And will you still be the person to do it with me?"

She has every reason to quit. After everything I've hidden, after the political disasters I've opened myself up to, Mara would be crazy to stay. But when I see the flicker of an eye roll, I know she is exactly that crazy.

"For now, you need to focus on this evening's events. I'll work on our crisis plan . . ." Mara is interrupted by a knock on my office door, polite at first and then more frantic.

When Mara swings the door open, there is a pale-faced intern standing in front of us, her voice quivering as she stutters, "The news alerts. Check your phone," she says as she walks away.

Mara hastily rushes over to my desk and reaches for her phone, turning on the ringer she'd silenced at the beginning of our conversation.

By this point, I can hear the televisions in our campaign headquarters and my name is being repeated again and again.

I walk into the room, my entire staff silent as a reporter says, "Virginia candidate for governor Tess Murphy had an abortion at seventeen."

A few muffled gasps escape from embarrassed staffers, but otherwise the room is quiet. Mara is at my side. I know she wants to scream "I told you so" a few dozen times. But instead, we both listen as the reporter provides further details on this "breaking story."

There are several cardinal rules for female political candidates. Purity is number one. It cannot appear as if you've ever had sex, told a lie, or broke a rule, because men may be able to survive those things, but women cannot. Election-eve scandals destroy campaigns, but an abortion is a nuclear bomb for a female candidate's campaign.

The reporter says there are records from the clinic, confirming my ten-week pregnancy and the D&C scheduled for that cool September morning.

I watch the gaping faces of my campaign staff, the frenzy of action, and feel a mix of emotions. But my overwhelming feeling is relief. This is a part of the story I can explain.

I've imagined scenarios where my relationship with Grant surfaces. In every one of those scenarios, I'm unable to share our history. Not how it began and certainly not how it ended. The love and pain and betrayal are swirled into a confusing slush. The way my heart grew and shattered baffles even me. But I can describe what happened to my body.

Mara swings into action, developing taking points and a strategy for responding to the latest reports.

I've never seen my campaign office as tense as it was in those hours following the news report. I know this is happening to me, but it almost feels like I'm watching a movie disaster scene, powerless to stop the events.

I'm quickly pushed through hair and makeup because we all agree that my only chance of salvaging my campaign is to speak directly to voters.

I'm scheduled for all the local news broadcasts and even a cable news segment.

I sit in front of the TV cameras and I criticize the breach of medical privacy, the scrutiny of a woman's private decision. Then I apologize for the lack of candor with my constituents.

I admit I was pregnant. I admit I had an appointment at an abortion clinic. And I admit I changed my mind. With glassy eyes, I tell the world how I lost the baby several months later and had medical complications that prevented me from having future children.

Then I very clearly repeat again and again: this was my body; this was my choice; this choice was not easy, nor without pain. Most of all, I, like every woman, am capable of making this messy, difficult, complicated choice on my own and without the interference of anyone else, most of all my government.

I give the press all the records my mother hid away—hospital bills and adoptions forms, even my school absence report for when I was hospitalized. I don't want there to be any doubt about what actually happened. As I leave the newsroom, I hear the rumblings about press integrity and verifying sources before running with breaking news stories. But I know that won't be the headline. The pregnant teenager is always juicier.

The entire night is a blur. I collapse into the front seat of Mara's car before we can tell whether the press appearances made a difference. The pollsters are scrambling, watching numbers jump up and down. It is impossible to predict what will happen.

Mara insists Grant's camp is responsible for the leak. She claims it's a desperate move on their part to gain traction. I tell her she is wrong.

"This is too tidy, Tess," Mara says as she drops me off at the hotel she booked so that I can avoid the reporters swarming my house. "Grant's campaign carved out part of the scandal that left him clean and destroyed you. Can't you see what he has done?"

Mara and I debate whether I should reveal my past relationship with Grant. I'm adamant that no good can come from sharing that information. I assure Mara the leak didn't come from Grant's campaign. I also tell her that it doesn't matter. It's the pregnant girl that causes the scandal, a boy's responsibility seemingly irrelevant. No reporter even asked about the father.

Mara calls me foolish, unable to understand how I can protect Grant, even now. It's because I know Grant. I know what he is capable of and it isn't this. After all of our betrayals and secrets, I can't believe he would ever hurt me again.

That's why I'm blindsided when I look at my phone before falling asleep.

There's a text message from Grant: **I'm sorry. It was me.**

Twenty-Five

OCTOBER 27, 2021

I pour myself a cup of the hotel's complimentary coffee and take a sip. It is slightly thickened and bitter, left over from when it was made sometime earlier, maybe even the day before.

I glance at the clock. I've had exactly two hours and thirty-nine minutes of sleep. In an ideal world, I'd be sitting down to hair and makeup so that they could craft a perfect look. I need to look like a polished woman, capable of running an entire state. Instead, it will be a miracle if I can avoid being called haggard. Time vaporizes in a crisis, and all I can manage this morning is a quick bun.

As I leave the hotel, I pick up the paper. The headline says "Fall from Grace," and I know the story is about me. I laugh at the irony. Anyone who has ever seen me attempt to run knows I've never had any grace. So much of politics is an image portrayed. My public image is far from reality. And yet, the public will claim they've been deceived because they didn't know about a part of my history from twenty-five years prior. As if that has anything to do with my ability to govern this state. Maybe that's why the public is so disillusioned with politics. They expect perfection and are disappointed to find humanity—regular people, living regular lives with the same amount of messiness as everyone else.

Mara texts me the preliminary numbers and they're bad. A part of me feels like it didn't matter what I said about the pregnancy. This type of information, days before the election, creates too much uncertainty. We'll see what the public decides.

I ignore the other text messages flooding my phone, mostly from Grant. He says he's sorry. He wants to explain. But really there's no point.

I should have known this would happen. I might have hoped for better, but I always knew that if any part of our past came out, Grant would survive. I would be destroyed.

I've battled with Mara. She insists that the only chance I have at winning is revealing Grant's role. Not just that he leaked these lies to the press but that he is the one who got me pregnant. As Mara says, "The public needs to know what a manipulative bastard he is."

But I'd like to win this election without any more betrayal or blame. And maybe swallowing those words, concealing Grant's role in this scandal, is what I need to do to erase my guilt. Because I did take the money. I did leave Grant with his monster of a father. And I did lie to everyone I care about. This is what I deserve.

I walk into my headquarters and look around the room. I may have slept only a few hours, but Mara and the team haven't slept at all. Strained eyes, frazzled nerves, and short tempers fill the space.

As soon as Mara sees my face, she's by my side, handing me an agenda for the day, mostly more meetings with the press.

She's relaying more disturbing polling results when we are interrupted.

"The Alexander campaign is making a statement," an intern says.

"This should be good," Mara comments. We all walk toward the giant screen in the middle of the headquarters. Work seems to stop as Grant Alexander appears on the screen.

His hair is falling across his forehead. As the camera zooms in, the dark circles under his eyes are visible. He looks like shit. It makes me feel better.

He clears his throat and adjusts a microphone. "As I'm sure you are all aware, yesterday news was leaked about my opponent, Tess Murphy," Grant says.

"False reports surfaced that Ms. Murphy had an abortion at seventeen. Ms. Murphy has spoken about her past, providing the public with details about her personal life that she never should have been forced to discuss." Grant's voice is clear and powerful.

"I know the reports about Ms. Murphy's abortion are false because those leaks came from my team."

Neither Mara nor I are surprised by this information, but the rest of my staff is. There are gasps and rumbles throughout the office as Grant continues. "I take full responsibility and the staff member who provided misleading documents to the press has been terminated. I want to personally apologize to Ms. Murphy for the pain this situation has caused. That is all."

Grant walks away despite the frenzy of questions from reporters.

"That's all?" Mara mumbles. "Pretty sure there is a hell of a lot more he could have said."

"Mara, let's go in my office," I say, as Mara is pinged with questions from every staffer in the room.

"Give us a few minutes, team. Keep going with our plan from last night," Mara instructs the room.

Mara closes the door and immediately starts ripping into Grant. "He should have admitted he got you pregnant. And he should have outed what a sleazy, manipulative scumbag he has for a father."

I interrupt. "Then it would have looked like I wasn't honest."

She shakes her head. "No, you protected the identity of the father because you felt it wasn't your place to reveal that information. You took money at seventeen because you were a scared, desperate kid being manipulated by a powerful, grown-ass man."

"You don't need to make excuses, Mara. I know what I did."

"This stops now, Tess." She places her hands on either side of my desk and leans forward. "Stop beating yourself up. Stop second-guessing your choices. At seventeen, you did the best job you could."

My chin quivers. "Thanks," I whisper. I close my eyes, processing Mara's words. I've often wondered what I would have done differently. Knowing what I do now, I imagine a dozen different scenarios where I was a smarter, kinder, better person. But in all of those scenarios, I remember a terrified girl who wanted a chance at the life she'd dreamed about. And maybe it's time I start forgiving that girl's choices. Maybe Mara's right.

Mara takes off her blazer and dumps it on the back of a chair. "By the way, if I ever meet Richard Alexander, I will inflict pain upon him." She rarely shifts out of campaign manager mode, but I know how Richard Alexander can make people act out of character. "He deserves all of our man-bashing on tequila night."

I need this sliver of friendship Mara offers, especially in a moment that feels so fragile. My phone starts buzzing.

I look at the screen and say, "It's him. It's Grant."

She steps forward. "We do not have time for this, Tess."

"I know. But I can't do anything else until I talk to Grant."

I answer the phone, taking a deep breath to clear my ragged emotions.

"Tess, I'm so sorry. Please let me explain." Grant's voice fills my ear as his pleas are repeated. "I need to see you."

"Okay," I meekly reply.

"When? Where? I'll meet you anywhere." Grant's voice seems filled with relief.

I glance at the schedule Mara prepared. "Can you come to Charlottesville? You can pick me up down the street from my headquarters."

"Yes," Grant says, hope lacing his words. "Thank you."

I hang up the phone and look at Mara. "I know you don't understand. But Grant didn't have to make that statement. He could have gotten away with it. He's different than you think."

Mara grabs her blazer, ready to resume full campaign manager duties. "I don't need to understand. I need a candidate who's ready to fight. Don't lose sight of the goal, Tess. No person should ever feel stuck. This campaign is about equal opportunities, no matter the shitty circumstances we're dealt. Do whatever you need to do, then come back ready to work."

I nod, knowing she's right. I have a battle ahead. And for the next two hours, we work. We refine talking points. I'm prepped for afternoon interviews. I finalize another public statement and field a few calls from senior executives at Planned Parenthood.

Then I walk down the street toward Grant's car.

Elections are strange, forcing voters to pick one person over the other, to measure the candidates' value and worth based on promises and plans. When I think about everything that has happened to us, I'm not sure whether I'm more capable than Grant is at keeping promises. But I do know that I'm better at change. And that's what people need, especially when it feels like nothing in the world is working. That's what I want to tell Grant. After decades of living the same life, maybe he's finally starting the change I've been fighting for all along.

"Where do you want to go?" Grant asks as I open the door and climb inside the warm interior.

"You can just drive around." The weather has turned and the heated leather seats of Grant's car feel lush.

"I'm sorry, Tess. I can't say it enough."

I take a deep breath. "Tell me what happened. I heard your statement, but how did this happen?"

"My father," Grant says through a grimace. "My campaign manager worked with some national party operatives on opposition research. I told them not to, but it was largely out of my control. They didn't find much." He smiles, and I wonder what is in the file his campaign pulled together. I don't have to wonder for long because Grant continues, "You drive too fast. You've gotten some pretty impressive speeding tickets over the years."

"It's my vice," I say. "Speeding and . . ." I trail off before I say "you," because Grant Alexander is the most destructive vice I've ever had.

He keeps talking. "My campaign manager, Stuart, reached out to my father. Even though I told him not to. Even though he knew how much I hate that man. But my father is powerful and Stuart knew there was more to our past than I shared."

"So your father gave your campaign the name of the abortion clinic?"

"Yes. All this time, he thought you went through with it."

"Your father didn't care enough to check. I was out of your life and that's what really mattered."

Grant winces, because he knows I'm right, and we both sit silently, clearly thinking about a life that could have been.

"It was a risky move," I say. "I could have revealed you were the father."

Grant nods, then asks, "Why didn't you?"

I stare out the car window. "Because it didn't matter. Not to the reporters or the voters, at least."

"It mattered to me," Grant says.

"I know." I sigh. "You didn't have to make a statement."

"Yes, I did," Grant quickly replies. "It was my fault."

I shake my head and open my mouth to reply when Grant cuts me off. "I've been thinking about everything that happened. I've spent the last two decades convinced that I was right and putting so much energy into hating you and the choices you made."

"And now you don't hate me? Because I made a different choice?"

"No," Grant says. "I don't hate you because I realize there is no right or wrong in a situation like ours. And I'm sorry I made you feel that way. It wasn't what I wanted, but it wasn't worth losing you over."

"Thank you," I whisper.

"You never should have been forced into that position," Grant says. "No one deserved to know that much of your private life, Tess."

"You deserved to know, years ago. So did Dean," I admit.

Grant shifts uncomfortably in his seat as he continues driving. "How is Dean?"

"The same," I say with sadness. "We spoke after the interviews." I tuck a strand of hair behind my ear before continuing. "When Dean and I first met, I told him I didn't want kids. I never told him that I couldn't have kids. He feels like he married a stranger, and he doesn't like the person I really am. I guess I never gave him the chance to know me."

I feel too much responsibility for our marriage ending to feel any anger about Dean's judgment. Maybe I also agree with him. I don't really like the person I am right now either. Dean doesn't give second chances, and I'm someone that needs dozens of opportunities to get things right.

"I'm sorry, Tess," Grant says, squeezing my hand.

"What about Cecilia?" I ask. I want to know, but I also don't want to talk about Dean anymore.

"It's different," Grant says. "Our marriage felt over for a while now. Cece communicates with me through her lawyer."

"And the boys?" I ask.

"I haven't been the father they need," he says, looking away.

"Then change," I state.

Grant nods. "I don't want to be anything like him. I want to love my boys the way they deserve."

"You will," I say, with equal parts hope and confidence.

"What about us?" Grant asks.

The girl inside me wants to fall into his arms and stare into his eyes as we make plans for a life together after so many years apart. I could do it too. I could spend eternity daydreaming with Grant Alexander. We'd catch up on the lost kisses and celebrations and maybe figure out what kind of love the other needs.

But the woman I've become knows that isn't possible.

"We both need to be better people, Grant." The truth of my statement doesn't make it any less painful to utter.

"I've lost you once, Tess. I'm not letting it happen again." Grant swallows and I can see the pain streaked across his face.

"We've hurt each other too much. We've hurt the people around us too much."

"No," he says, his head shaking. He's been driving in circles and pulls the car over a few blocks from my office. Grant pleads, "It might be messy, but we're meant for each other, Tess."

"If we're meant for each other, then we'll know. Maybe someday," I say, trying to hide the crack in my voice.

For the first time in our lives, I look at him and say the words first. "I love you, Grant. I always have. But I think the pain may be bigger than the love."

I kiss his cheek and then turn, getting out of the car before he can respond.

I leave Grant, my heart aching. But I walk into my campaign headquarters and get to work.

Twenty-Six

NOVEMBER 2, 2021
ELECTION DAY

Cautiously optimistic, those have been Mara's words all day. She thinks there's a chance. Grant's admission somewhat balanced the drop from the pregnancy bombshell. Voters seem to want a male candidate who can control his team just as much as they want a female candidate who is perfect.

Results have been trickling in all day, but the real action is now. Downstairs, there is a ballroom full of volunteers and supporters dressed in cocktail attire, nibbling on chicken skewers and sipping gin and tonics, hoping for a win. I'm upstairs in a suite with Mara and a few other key staffers watching the results and trying to distract ourselves from frayed nerves.

The day has been a blur. My throat was hoarse by mid-afternoon, with Mara having me speak at every opportunity she could find. The exit polls have been erratic, creating more uncertainty in an already unpredictable election. The surprising tide has been the number of women voting today. We expected higher numbers, given that I'm the first female candidate for governor, but nothing like this. There's no consistency in the way women vote, a fact that makes me smile. Women have long been an untapped mystery in politics, rarely following the predictions of pundits. Today is no different.

As the ballots are being counted, the after-work voters filling the polls, I wait in an elaborately decorated hotel room. I should be holed up with Dean, stuffing ourselves with cheese pizza. Cheese pizza was our celebration food and our commiseration food. Months earlier, when we daydreamed about this night, Dean had said, "Just make sure whatever dress they make you wear isn't too tight for a pizza feast." Instead, I'll be eating alone.

I look over to the closet in my room and see my dress hanging. It's what I'll wear when I walk onstage to either accept or concede victory.

The consultants wanted a purple pantsuit, but the color made me feel like a cartoon character. Mara wanted white. I vetoed immediately, knowing myself and the high likelihood of visible stains. I need to eat and I'm a notorious dripper.

Ultimately, we agreed on green. Because I like green. It reminds me of days spent in the gardens and it feels like a strong color against my dark hair. I need all the strength possible tonight as I sit in this hotel room alone, wondering what will happen. I slip on the emerald sheath dress and the matching blazer. I have a gold locket that belonged to my grandmother that hangs discreetly in the v of the blazer. Otherwise, the only jewelry I wear is my wedding band, which I haven't stopped twisting all day. I'll take it off tonight, because Dean is filing our divorce papers tomorrow.

I finish dressing when Mara starts shouting. "Get out here, Tess! The results are coming in."

I walk into the living room of the hotel suite and look around at the faces, trying to uncover the answers to my future. But everyone's eyes are glued to the television screen. We've been waiting on the voting districts in northern Virginia. These are the most populated areas of the state, and once those polls close, the election will be over. It's Grant's territory, but it's also a traditionally liberal part of the state.

Mara grabs my hand and squeezes it tightly.

The phones in the room begin erupting in sounds, a symphony of ringtones and buzzing.

"This is it," Mara says. "You ready?"

"Does feeling like vomiting mean I am ready?"

"It does," Mara says.

"Well, answer your phone, then," I instruct.

I close my eyes, hold my breath, try to stop every unnecessary movement as I wait for my life to change.

"They've complied exit polls from Arlington, Alexandria, and Loudoun counties," Mara relays. "Too close to call in Alexandria."

I swallow.

Mara continues, "But they feel comfortable with the numbers elsewhere. NBC is going to announce and is asking for a statement."

"What are they going to announce, Mara?"

I open my eyes, and that's when I see the giant smile across her face. That's when I see the room focused on me. There are tears forming in the corners of my eyes as Mara shouts.

"You won! Tess Murphy is the seventy-fourth governor of Virginia."

The room erupts in applause. Hugs are exchanged. There is a flurry of activity as Mara formulates an official statement and preparations are made for me to make my way downstairs. I smile at all of the hardworking faces surrounding me, trying to mimic their joy.

But really, I've never felt more alone in my life. I've never worked harder for anything. I've never been closer to losing everything. And for the first time I wonder whether it was all worth it.

I feel like I am sleepwalking as I make my way downstairs to the conference room pulsating with celebration. I vaguely recognize that someone is touching up my makeup, tugging my hair, adjusting my suit jacket with the brush of a lint roller.

Mara is whispering instructions in my ear about the prepared speech on the teleprompter as my fist clenches and unclenches.

It shouldn't be empty. My hand should be wrapped around Dean's. We should be walking onstage together, arms raised over our heads. But I'm alone as I begin my speech.

I look out over the sea of cheering faces, a crowded room that has gathered to celebrate a victory I'd only hoped was possible. There are people chanting my name and tossing back drinks as I place my hands on either side of a simple wooden lectern.

"There's something inherently selfish about campaigns," I say, the crowd starting to quiet. "I've spent the last few months meeting as many people as possible, telling them about myself and my ideas. I've stood on stages just like this one, listing why everyone should vote for me instead of someone else. I've been selfish."

The room quiets as I clear my throat.

"Tonight is a fresh start. I'm relieved to stop talking about myself. Because as much as I've been selfish these last few months, I've also been listening. I've been listening to the challenges facing the people of Virginia. I'm ready to put the campaign behind us and get started on the work, tackling those problems and coming up with solutions together."

My eyes survey the room. There are outlines of faces staring in my direction, distorted by the warm lights spotlighting my body.

"There are big and small problems facing every person in this room, myself included. I'm not immune from problems. I'm not perfect and I apologize if I ever gave anyone the impression otherwise."

I look offstage and see Mara shaking her head. I'm not reading from the prepared speech and Mara's eyes are wide in panic.

"I've made many mistakes in my life and I'm grateful for most of them. I believe in learning from mistakes, taking lessons from failure and foolishness, and applying them toward a more informed, more purposeful future."

I sense an uneasiness in the crowd, but I plow ahead.

"But there's one mistake I repeated. I took for granted an important person in my life."

It's obvious I'm on the stage alone. Dean's absence has been stark all evening, but even more so now as I continue speaking. Most will assume I'm skirting around some discussion of Dean, that it's him I took for granted. And although that's true, I've also realized that I took myself for granted, especially when it came to my relationship with Grant. I was a masochist for self-harm, lust, and longing, and maybe a lifetime of insecurity trumping my beliefs.

I take a deep breath before continuing. "We are only as good as our worst moments. We are only as strong as our weakest times. I promise to wake up every morning committed to working hard for every person in this state."

"I may never feel like I deserve this honor. As a girl, I dreamed about ways to make the world a more beautiful, loving place. I tended gardens, helped those in need, and tried to lead with love. I haven't always succeeded, but I've kept trying. I may not deserve the honor of being the governor of Virginia, but I will try every day to be a person worthy of this office."

I walk offstage alone. I go home alone. I fall asleep alone. But I'm ready for a fresh start.

Twenty-Seven

JANUARY 2022
INAUGURATION DAY

"Can I have a few minutes?" I ask Mara.

She gestures toward the desk in the center of the room. "You want to spin in the big chair, don't you?"

"Yes, Mara. That's the first thing I want to do as governor." My voice is sarcastic, but she's not wrong. Spinning around in that giant office chair looks very tempting.

"Take all the time you need," Mara says. "You earned this, Tess. You're going to be a phenomenal leader."

She leaves, and I'm grateful for her words. I'm grateful for so much from Mara. She stood beside me on the stage this morning as I was sworn into a position I'd only dreamed of reaching. She's been by my side as I navigate this new life.

I'm the first. The first woman governor. The first divorced governor. A year ago, when my campaign was ramping up, I imagined a very different ending.

I walk toward the giant picture window framing my new

office, providing a view over the expansive gardens that surround the governor's mansion. Perfectly manicured boxwoods border a brick patio that leads into rows of bare beds, just waiting for an explosion of springtime tulips.

Kay's words echo in my mind. *Maybe someday you'll live in a grand home that you earn yourself.*

I know I didn't become governor on my own. There are countless people who got me here, donating their time and money and faith.

But this isn't a life I was born into, like Kay. And I didn't marry into it either, like my mother hoped.

I earned this, both the good and the bad. I earned the votes that brought me to this office. And I earned an empty home because I never let go of my teenage insecurities.

I walk around the room, its two-hundred-year-old history of male occupants evident through ominous oil paintings and dark wood covering almost every surface. I don't feel like I belong. It's a feeling I'll always have. But I don't mind it much anymore. I finally figured out that everyone feels the same.

Some days I wonder if I'd feel less lonely if Dean were by my side. But in our months of minimal contact, conversations mostly focused on logistics, I've realized that the absence of a person doesn't make you lonely. I hid myself away from Dean. Honesty and acceptance are better companions. I've been working to make sure I never lose them again.

For weeks after the election, I wrote letters to myself, trying to make sense of how I'd strayed so far from the person I wanted to become. I might be governor, but that's in spite of my mistakes. My teenage bravery was replaced with decades of fear. I don't want to spend the second half of my life afraid. I wrote down every memory I had of the summer I met Grant

Alexander, hoping to make sense of the love I felt and the hope I held. I wanted to understand how I fought to have a bigger life but didn't take the time to figure out what that meant to me. I was too busy proving everybody wrong instead of figuring out my feelings on what is right.

It was only after I'd written everything I could remember that I realized how much I hid. Another person deserved to read about that summer. I wanted Grant to hear my story, full of messy truth and without insecure lies.

I didn't expect a response. But I packed up my letters describing the moment I arrived at Madeline Milton's home until the day I lost the baby. I mailed those letters to Grant, knowing they would probably sit unopened in his mother's empty home. But I hoped to feel some relief in finally being honest with someone I loved.

Instead, I got something better.

In December, Grant wrote back. He wrote about his side of that summer. My heart broke and healed reading his letters.

Then we kept on writing. Some of our letters are sharp. We both have decades of unsaid feelings. Some letters are simple, what we ate, an article we read, something that reminds us of the other. Our lives are very different than we imagined, but through our letters, I'm getting to know the man he's become. I'm figuring out the woman I want to be. As teenagers, we sat by a river and shared our dreams. Now we write them down, not any less hopeful, but more aware of the work required.

Grant moved into his mother's home. His sons visit often, filling the house with laughter. It's what Kay would have wanted. Grant left his hedge fund to focus on being a father, a luxury unavailable to most parents, but he seems to know that. He wrote about the day the boys surprised him with breakfast and the number of hours he spent scraping dried egg off his kitchen ceiling. He wrote about the trip to the emergency room after Declan fell off the patio wall and the sleepless nights that followed, Grant hoping that more vigilance would prevent future accidents. He sent a picture of a fort he built with his sons out of fallen limbs and a picture of the boys digging in Kay's garden. She would have loved it and hated it at the same time. Grant hasn't made up for the years he spent too little time with his sons, but he's trying. And that's all kids want.

I take one last look around my office before I walk toward the door to find Mara. But my eyes are drawn toward the table in the corner filled with flower arrangements. Elaborate bouquets from donors and interest groups, former colleagues, and people already in line for favors. I walk over and survey the explosion of color, but my eye is immediately drawn to the center.

Surrounded by symmetrical arrangements of expensive roses and flashy, exotic orchids is a simple wooden vase filled with yellow blooms. I push the other flowers aside as I reach for the goldenrod.

Kay was right, it is a weed. It blooms on the side of highways and in empty fields before it's mowed away. But it has always been my favorite. It's abundant in fall, but in the middle of a cold January, it can't be found. It's not important enough to sell in a flower shop. But someone sent me a bouquet and it means just as much now as it did the last time.

My fingers hover over the card. There are only a handful of people who know about my love of this flower.

I open the small envelope and read the message inside.

Maybe someday, it says in Grant's scrawl.

I clutch his note. Not yet. But I can imagine it. A day when

Grant and I are finally together. When we sit on the back patio and sip a glass of wine as the sun sets over the Blue Ridge Mountains. When the pain has faded and we're strong enough to stay woven together despite the differences that try to crack us apart.

But for now, I have a job to do. And that's my focus.

"Mara," I shout with a smile. "What's next?"

Acknowledgments

I started working on this novel many years ago, but it took time and help from others to craft the story I wanted to tell. My biggest thanks to the incredible team at Zibby Publishing. Zibby Owens has created a special corner of publishing, and I'm unbelievably grateful to be an author in this book family. I'm indebted to Kathleen Harris, whose vision, support, and painstaking work has made this novel so much better than anything I could have achieved alone. Gabriela Capasso is not only a talented editor, but her enthusiasm for this story from the beginning has made the entire experience a joy. Anne Messitte, Jordan Blumetti, Sherri Puzey, Diana Tramontano, Graça Tito, and the entire Zibby Publishing team have helped shape and launch this book beyond my wildest dreams.

Thank you to my agent, Dani Segelbaum, for championing my books and finding them a home.

Many friends, family members, fellow authors, and booksellers have encouraged my work along this journey. Thank you to Jennifer Miller, Maria Fehretdinov, Meagan Fitzsimmons, Sara Colangelo, Julie Gilchrist. Joylyn Hannahs, Cindy Chandler, Sandy Crittenden, Nina Crittenden, Bonnie Volk, Rachel McRady, Neely Tubati-Alexander, Joelle Babula, Leah Fallon at Birch Tree Bookstore, Mary Beth Morell at Middleburg Books, Flannery Buchanan at Bluebird & Co.,

Acknowledgments

Diane Castro and Tija Brown at Sweet Home Books, Sharon Davis at Book Bound Bookstore, and Anderson McKean at Page & Palette.

A special thanks to my sister, Meredith Kimener, who is always my first reader and is never afraid to tell me exactly what she loves and exactly what needs fixing in every draft.

My mother, Pam Laning, has been this book's champion from day one. Her countless refrains of "this is my favorite" fueled my writing and fed my spirit.

My children, Isabel, Henry, and Leo, remain my greatest inspirations and best distractions. I'm honored to be their mother.

Lastly, endless thanks to my husband, Jeff. This novel wouldn't exist without his support. With each draft, he told me to keep going because this is a story worth writing. I love chasing dreams together.

About the Author

Audrey Ingram is the author of *The River Runs South* and *The Group Trip*. She is a graduate of Middlebury College and Georgetown University Law Center, and she practiced law in Washington, D.C., for fifteen years. When not writing, she can be found digging in her garden or hiking the Blue Ridge Mountains. An Alabama native, she currently lives in Virginia with her husband and three children.